SATURDAY LUNCH

And Other Stories

by

RICHARD R. KARLEN

Ironbound Press, Scotch Plains, New Jersey
September, 2003

SATURDAY LUNCH
Published by Ironbound Press
55 Highlander Drive
Scotch Plains, NJ 07076

E-Mail—ironboundp@aol.com
Web site—www.ironboundpress.net

First Paperback Printing

Publisher's Note

This is a work of fiction. Names, characters, places and incidents either are the product of the author's imagination or are used fictitiously, and any resemblance to actual persons, living or dead, events, or locales is entirely coincidental.

Library of Congress Control Number 2003109592
ISBN: 096608313x

Cover painting by Ai Iwano
Photograph by Kim Karlen
Cover design by HM FotoGraf/x

ACKNOWLEDGMENTS

I dedicate this book to my wife, Hiroko and my six children, Michael, Naomi, Andrew, Debbie, Kim and Alex. The hope is that one day their children will read these stories and in doing so will perhaps find out a little about their grandfather.

Not to be forgotten are my brother Bill and my sister-in-law Ikuko, who are always managing to pop up in my books.

Special thanks to Mike Gale and Ellen Diamond for their valuable editorial assistance in helping me prepare this manuscript.

I would also like to thank my good friend, writer Mickey Diamond, for being such an astute listener in between our wolfing egg-white omelets at the Windsor diner.

The collage on the front cover was done by my mother-in-law, Ai Iwano, a first rate artist and one of the kindest women that I've ever known.

September 26, 2003

Books by Richard R. Karlen

Devil's Dance, a novel

Looking for Bernie, a novel

Answer Man, a novel

Murder at the Sexi, a novel

Saturday Lunch and other stories, short stories

TABLE OF CONTENTS

"A confessional passage has probably never been written that didn't stink a little bit of the writer's pride in having given up his pride."

J.D. Salinger, *"Raise High the Roof Beam, Carpenters; and Seymour: an Introduction"*

Pedophiles come in all different sizes and shapes. They are for the most part miserable, unhappy people, who usually wind up either institutionalized or in jail. But like many things in life, you have to be careful when you generalize on those perversions that are most abhorrent to us and the effects the perpetrators have on their victims.

This is a story about a pedophile that I knew almost sixty years ago. Except for an occasional stretching of the truth, what went on between us is pretty much the way I remembered it.

SONATA FACILE

"That's him, that's Moe, the homo," Ziggy Berlow whispered to me in his cracking, adolescent voice.

"Why are you whispering?" I asked. "He's a hundred yards away."

Ziggy always whispered when he had something unbelievable to tell, even if there wasn't anyone within miles. His sense of the dramatic could get on your nerves, but, after a while, you sort of got used to it.

Ziggy was my best friend at Camp Klatzman-on-the-Hudson in the summer of 1943, and we remained good friends until he got his head blown off by a North Korean hand grenade near Pusan in 1950. They awarded him a medal posthumously. Who'd ever figure a smart guy like Ziggy doing some dumb thing like going to Korea and then getting his head blown off?

Ziggy and I were standing on a narrow porch, a sturdy, unpainted, wooden extension of Cabin No. 11, our eyes fixed on a large, round man striding slowly across the infield grass of the ball field.

"I thought Moe wasn't coming 'till tomorrow," I said.

"That's what The Ripper told me."

The Ripper referred to Jack Horowitz, our senior bunk counselor, the nickname having been tagged onto him by the collective mentality of Ziggy, myself, and the other five thirteen-year-old campers of our cabin, the *paratroopers,* because his first name was "Jack."

Yesterday at lunch, the founder and owner of the camp, Herman Klatzman also had informed us that Captain Morris Schwartz would be visiting the camp and during his two-week stay would live in our cabin. He explained to us in that gruff, booming voice that could reduce you to the size of an earthworm, how before the war Captain Schwartz had been a counselor for many years at Klatzman-on-the-Hudson, and had always been in charge of Cabin 11, the *Paratroopers.* Now that he was a distinguished officer in the United States Army serving our country in this terrible war against Fascism, we were all obliged to make sure that he enjoyed a super vacation during his leave.

Ziggy, who had groaned at Klatzman's pronouncement, shrank into his seat when the camp owner had lifted his bushy eyebrows and focused his terrible dark eyes on him.

"And what's eating you, Mr. Berlow?" Herman Klatzman had roared.

"Nothing, Chiefy, nothing at all. A little food got stuck in my throat."

Believe it or not, the printed brochure that the camp sent before the season opened stated that the owner Herman Klatzman was to be called *Chiefy* by the campers. As it turned out even the counselors had to call him *Chiefy,* if they wanted to keep their jobs. I swear I'm not making it up.

At the first period after lunch, while we were playing around with clay in Arts and Crafts, making ashtrays so we would have something to show to our parents on visiting day, Ziggy gave me the lowdown on Captain Morris Schwartz. Last year Ziggy had been a *Marine* in Cabin 10, when Moe had made his annual visit to the camp and then, as now, had stayed with the *Paratroopers* in Cabin 11. What went on in Cabin 11 had been no secret to Ziggy, whose reason for existence was to be a master spy.

"He likes kids," Ziggy whispered.

"So what?"

"What do you mean, so what? He likes boys. Don't you get it, lunkhead?"

"Yeah, sure." I didn't have the faintest notion what he was talking about, but I'd be damned if I was going to look like some sort of moron to Ziggy Berlow.

Ziggy saw right through me. "He's queer," he said.

"How's he queer?"

"He's a homo, for chrissakes."

I knew from a general science course I had taken in Eighth that human beings were "Homo Sapiens," but to be perfectly honest I had no idea what Ziggy was talking about.

"Great," I said. "Now what do you say we sneak over to Archery? We can finish these stupid ashtrays tomorrow."

But Ziggy wasn't about to end what he considered one of the most important discussions of our lives. I was his best friend and I had to be warned. "Don't believe anything he tells you," he said. "One false move and he's all over you like a boa constrictor. For the next two weeks, we stick together like glue."

You'd have thought that by age thirteen I would have had some idea of what a 'homo' was. Today, it's a

3

different world. Even my six-year old grandson knows about gays and lesbians, gay liberation, gays in the military, AIDS. On TV and in the movies, stories about homosexuality are commonplace. Not so in 1943.

In 1943, what mattered when you were thirteen was collecting baseball cards and reading the latest comic books. I was so dumb that I didn't even know what a hardon was. A month before camp, at a grammar school graduation party, Jennifer Sperling sat on my lap during a game of Spin the Bottle, and sucked my lips like a hungry guppie. In bed that night I kept thinking about Jennifer's warm mouth pressing against mine, until I discovered that my skinny, limp organ had swollen and become stiff as a rock. It wasn't until I concentrated on Snuffy Stirnweiss stealing home against the Red Sox that the damn thing went back to being normal again and I was able to relax.

Ziggy's final warning was: "At night, don't let him slip a hand under the covers. And always wear a jock strap."

"What for?"

"Protection, stupid."

"Yeah, I getcha." Of course, I didn't get him at all, but when he talked about wearing a jock strap, even a moron like me could begin to figure out what part of my anatomy needed protection from Moe.

So there we were on this hot, steamy day in August, standing on the cabin porch awaiting Captain Morris Schwartz, who had dropped his suitcases and was standing on second base wiping his forehead. With one broad sweep he seemed to take in all the cabins that circled the perimeter of the ball field, until he spotted Ziggy and me. Joyously, he waved to us, then picked up his luggage and with a quickened step started toward the bunk.

Ziggy put the palms of his hands together as if in prayer and looked to the heavens. "Lord help us, here he comes," he whispered desperately. "Let's get out of here."

But it was too late. We were *The Welcoming Committee!* And there was Moe, dressed in army tans, open collar, service hat tucked inside his belt, double silver bars pinned to his shoulders, standing in front of us, a huge smile plastered across his round, amiable face. He was even bigger than Ziggy had described him, but not big in a menacing way, sort of like a good-natured, grizzly bear. He had soft, brown hair, thinning a little on the top, and nice eyes, large ones, round and blue, eyes that could look you over in a glance and didn't make you feel as if you were an insignificant kid, which is the way most adults looked at you.

Then Moe did the most extraordinary thing. He saluted us! Just snapped to attention and whipped up his right hand to his forehead like he was reporting for duty, and we might have been Eisenhower and Patton. He wouldn't give up on the salute until we saluted him back, and then he tossed his suitcases onto the porch and vaulted the railing with surprising ease for such a beefy man. He then proceeded to embrace poor Ziggy in a powerful hug.

After releasing Ziggy, who looked as if he were going to collapse, Moe turned to me and stretched out a big, fat hand. "Moe Schwartz," he said.

"Lowell Franklin," I said. Moe did most of the shaking, my hand totally swallowed up within his.

"Hey, where's everybody?" Moe asked.

"Swimming," I replied.

We led Moe inside the cabin and showed him the bunk bed that The Ripper had given him, which turned out to be the lower half of the double-decker that I slept in. The Ripper had asked me to move to the upper half of the double-decker, normally Ziggy's bed, after Ziggy had volunteered to move to an empty cot on the far end of the cabin.

"How come you guys aren't swimming?" Moe asked, as he sat at the edge of his bed.

I pointed to a bandage just above my left elbow. "Infected mosquito bite," I said. "Nurse doesn't want me to swim for a few days. Ziggy's been keeping me company."

Moe reached over and tousled Ziggy's hair. "Why don't you go ahead and take your swim now?" he said to Ziggy. "I'll keep Lowell company."

"Great," said Ziggy. So much for loyalty to friends. I couldn't believe the way that turd had caved in so easily after all the bull he had been handing me about how we had to stick together while Moe was around.

Ziggy gone, I sat on the bunk bed next to ours and watched Moe unpack his things into an empty cubby-hole. Moe didn't look especially dangerous as he unloaded his belongings, and I began to wonder whether Ziggy wasn't off his rocker with all his talk about Moe.

While he went about his business, Moe began to ask me questions, stuff like how long I'd been coming to camp, did I like it here, where did I live, the usual junk.

Then he told me a little bit about himself, like he also lived in Newark where he had taught English at one of the high schools. What was more interesting was the stuff he told me about how after Pearl Harbor he had been drafted into the army and because of his Master's degree he had wound up as an officer working at the Pentagon.

"It's probably where I belong," he said. He laughed self-consciously. "As much as I hate the Nazis and the

Japs, I don't see myself leading troops into battle. I guess you might say I'm basically a pacifist."

"What's a pacifist?"

He sat down on his bunk, the weight of his big frame causing the mattress to sag a notch. "A pacifist, Lowell, is someone who believes in trying to solve problems peacefully, who tries everything possible to avoid violence."

I looked at Moe's thick wrists and huge arms and thought that when you're built like a grizzly bear it's easy to be a pacifist. Who would ever want to mess with Moe?

"How about you, Lowell?"

I shrugged. "If I'm in the war, I'm going to kill as many Nazis as I can. I guess I'm no pacifist."

Moe laughed. "A good thing, too. If everybody was like me, how would we ever win this damn war?"

He stood up and continued unpacking his belongings, which included a bunch of books and a chess set and board. He placed them neatly on the shelf behind his bunk, and then turned to me.

"You play chess?" he asked.

"Don't know how."

"Would you like to learn?"

"I guess so."

You could see how much the idea that I might want to learn to play chess pleased him and right off the bat began to explain the game to me. The guy had a real schoolteacher mentality.

"Chess is like war," he began. "The objective is to capture the king. It doesn't matter how many pieces you lose in the process. You capture the king and you win. That's the way generals think. It doesn't matter how many men are sacrificed as long as you win the war."

I didn't really know what Moe was talking about with his bull about chess and war and everything. But to tell you truth, right off the bat I liked the way he talked to you like you weren't some dumb kid without a brain in your head.

"I know how to play checkers," I said.

"How about tonight after dinner we'll set up the chess pieces and I'll teach you a few basics."

The time after dinner was usually a free hour before evening activities. Sometimes Ziggy and I would go down to the lake and catch frogs, or play one on one basketball. I mean, we'd do just about any damn thing we pleased. Playing chess with Moe would not be in my top ten list of things to do after supper, nevertheless, I said, "Yeah, sure. Sounds like fun." Why I said that I don't know, except maybe it was because Moe had this sort of expectant, trusting look on his face, and you didn't want to be the one to change it by disappointing him.

"I think I'll take a little swim before it gets too late," Moe said, after he had finished putting away all his belongings. "Want to go with me?"

On the walk down the long, dirt path leading to the lake, Moe continued to ask me questions about myself and my family, this time a little more personal. I hate it when people want to know everything about you when they don't even really know you. I think Moe was the sort of adult who liked to ask questions because he felt uncomfortable with a kid if he wasn't saying something to him. Anyway, rather than be impolite, I gave him a bunch of short answers, which seemed to be okay with him.

When we finally got to the lake, I made a beeline to Ziggy, who was standing on the dock ready to dive in, while Moe began to talk to one of the swimming counselors.

"I thought we were supposed to stick together," I said to Ziggy. "How come you walked out on me?"

"What did he do?" Ziggy asked in his frenetic way that made you want to scratch.

I shrugged. "Not much."

"He didn't try anything funny, did he?"

"What're you talking about?"

"You know."

"All he did was unpack his bags, and now he wants to play chess with me tonight after dinner."

Ziggy looked disappointed. "That's it?"

"What the hell did you expect?"

"He's clowning around, throwing you off guard. When you least expect it, he's going to make his move."

While we were talking, Moe had disrobed and put on goggles and a swimming cap. He went over to the edge of the dock and seemed poised to dive into the lake. The campers swimming in the deep area between the dock and the raft were instructed by the head waterfront counselor to return to the dock. Once the area had been cleared, Moe inhaled mightily and dove into the water. The dock was crowded with campers and counselors watching what turned out to be a world's record for Camp Klatzman-on-the-Hudson. Moe swam three times back and forth to the raft—*underwater*. With the final lap, he had broken his own record, one he had set last year. Even Ziggy was impressed.

"The guy is a human hippo," he said.

Campers and counselors were crowding around Moe, congratulating him, patting him on the back. Then, to my surprise, he brushed everyone aside and walked over to Ziggy and me.

"I was thinking of going for one more lap," he said to us, "but I wasn't sure if I could make it."

"Yeah, that would have been great," I said.

I have to admit that I felt a little special because Moe had singled us out to speak to immediately after breaking the world's underwater swimming record. Dressed only in a bathing suit, he looked even bigger than he did with regular clothes on. He had a huge barrel chest and a pair of shoulders as wide as some of those wrestlers we'd watch on Seymour Bass's eight-inch TV back home in Newark. You definitely did not want to be around Moe if he lost his temper.

What he did next, however, I didn't appreciate. Without warning, he mussed up my hair and then patted me on the back. "Let's go shower up," he said.

I turned to Ziggy. "You coming?" I asked him.

"No," the skinny, redheaded bastard said without a blink. "I think I'll swim a little more. See you later."

At the bunk, Moe showered while I lay on my bed and pretended to read the latest Captain Marvel Comics, wondering when Moe was going to make his move. I couldn't imagine exactly what that move would be, but whatever it was, I had to be ready. As it turned out, the only move Moe made, after coming out of the shower, was to play a 78 inch record on his RCA turntable before lying down.

The music, some classical thing, was really annoying, and when Moe asked me how I liked the record, I said not to be rude. "It's okay." I mean the guy was really ecstatic about the piece.

"You've got to develop a taste for Bach," he said, and then quickly added, "like good champagne."

I wondered why he'd figure that I'd enjoy this composer? Actually the music was the most unpleasant noise I had ever heard, bordering on sheer torture with its repetitive, busy, grating sounds. The worst part about it was that there was no singing. Hell, how could you sing to music when there wasn't any melody? Actually, my father liked classical music, but a different sort, opera stuff and big loud symphonies, especially the one where Fate is knocking on the door.

My mother's taste was Bing Crosby and Rudy Valley. Sometimes she'd tune in to *The Kate Smith Hour*, but only when my father wasn't around. I remember him saying once that if he had to listen to Kate Smith sing "God Bless America" one more time, he'd throw the radio out the window. Personally, I liked Frank Sinatra and old muscle-throat, Vaughn Monroe, the best. In a million years I didn't think I'd ever enjoy this Bach guy.

That evening after supper, sure enough I got stuck with Moe, who trotted out the chessboard and with terrific patience went about teaching me the fundamentals of the game. I was pretty upset at missing out on a pick-up softball game between the *Paratroopers* and the junior counselors until I began to get the hang of the different moves of the chess pieces.

In fact, I started to look forward to our nightly chess games, and after a week, I was beginning to move the pieces like I had some idea of what I was doing. I liked the way Moe wouldn't let me beat him, though he'd spot me a queen and a rook, which he said was all the advantage he was going to give me.

"During the winter join a chess club," he advised me. "You could be good. You'll see, next year we'll be playing even up."

While we played chess, Moe liked to talk about all sorts of books he had read.

"Reading books can open up a whole new world for you, Lowell. A person writes a book, and if that book is honest you find out about a complete stranger's life, the way he looks at the world, the things he loves and hates. Maybe the way he sees things is different than yours and then you become a little smarter than you were, a little richer as a human being."

Moe's favorite book was *Moby Dick* by an author named Herman Melville. "Yeah," I said ecstatically. "I read that." What I meant, of course, was that I had read the Classics Comics version of *Moby Dick.*

"So what did you think?" asked Moe.

"It was pretty good. I liked the ending when the whale, all harpooned and mad, charged the boat and sunk it. Captain Ahab was really a nut case. To tell you the truth, the rest of it didn't make much sense."

"For Melville, Moby Dick was more than a whale. He was a symbol of the power of nature. Man can never change nature, and if he tries he's doomed."

Moe liked to talk about books that way, always trying to give you the inside dope on what the book really meant, not what it seemed to mean. When he talked about books, it was with a lot of enthusiasm, as if it was a truly important part of his life. I guess you had to respect that but since I hadn't read these books myself, other than the ones I knew about from Classic Comics, sometimes I'd get a little bored when he'd start up with *another one of his favorite books* stuff.

One night, maybe about eight or nine days after Moe had been living in our bunk, I think it was the day when I had almost beaten him with the queen and rook spot and he had said that starting tomorrow he was taking back the rook, Moe kissed me. I mean it wasn't any big deal, just a little good night peck on the cheek while I was lying in bed.

Taps had sounded and I was thinking about how damn close I had come to checkmating Moe in our game that night, when there he was, this huge shadow, standing next to the double-decker and without warning planting his lips on my cheek. I really didn't mind that as much as the alien hand on my back that began to deliver this funny little massage, a sort of herky-jerky rubbing of my skin. Was this the boa constrictor Ziggy had talked about that was getting ready to strike? I held my breath. After a few long seconds the hand abruptly withdrew from my back and without a word, Moe walked away.

The next day at Archery I told Ziggy about the kiss and the massage. He got all upset. "That's it," he said. "He's making his move. What're you going to do about it?"

I shrugged. "I don't know. What am I supposed to do? I mean, what's the big deal?"

"Everybody's been noticing how much time you've been spending with Moe."

"So what? The guy's fighting the Japs and the Nazis. The least we can do is be nice to him on his vacation. They might ship him out tomorrow and he could get his head blown off. How would you feel about that, smart ass?"

"Last night his hand was on your back."

"So what? All he did was rub it a little."

"Before you know it that hand will be on your ass."

"How do you know?"

"'Cause that's the way a homo operates. First he rubs your back a little, and then he squeezes your ass, and before you know it, he's got your dick in his mouth."

"That's disgusting."

"You'll see."

That night after we finished our chess game, Moe asked me if I'd like to take a walk. I was feeling pretty damn good since even with only a queen spot, I had given him a tough match and I said okay, why not. We went down to the lake and sat down on the grass. There was a pretty neat sunset, a lot of purple and orange in the sky that looked like a giant version of a painting I saw last year when our class took a trip to the Museum of Modern Art in New York. Like always, Moe asked me a lot of questions about myself.

As I got to know Moe, I found that it was really easy to talk to him about stuff that bothered you and that you didn't want to talk to your parents about. I liked the way he always seemed to be listening to you when you spouted off on just about any subject, never interrupting, never trying to pawn off some adult crap about how when you get older you'll understand better all those little things that bother you when you're thirteen. On our way back, we stopped at the rec room and Moe sat down at the piano, an old console that always sounded a little out of tune. I couldn't take my eyes off those hands that had massaged me last night as they flew across the keyboard turning that beat-up old piano into a great music-making machine.

I asked him what he was playing.

"Mozart. The Sonata in C major. You must have heard it before. It's sometimes called the *Sonata Facile*. *Facile* in Italian means easy, but the music isn't easy at all. That's Mozart's trick. The beauty is in its extraordinary simplicity."

He started the piece again, but played very slowly. "You gotta love Mozart," he said without looking up. "His music touches the soul."

I didn't know what he was talking about, but I had to admit that I liked this better than the other music I had heard on his record player. I mentioned that to him.

Moe smiled. "Comparing Mozart to Bach is like comparing Joe DiMaggio to Ted Williams. It's just a matter of choice. They're both pretty good." And then he asked me, "Do you play at all?"

"I can play the top part on *Heart and Soul*."

"Let's do it."

It was a bit of a tight squeeze on the bench. Moe being such a big man, our hips butted up against each other. I began to plunk away the melody with one finger, while Moe did a great improvisation on the bass part. Afterwards, we laughed, and then Moe reached over and squeezed my knee affectionately. The thing is he didn't take the hand off the knee right away, which sort of made me feel uncomfortable. Finally, I stood up, though if it wasn't for that lousy hand, I would liked to have played the piano with him some more. He didn't say anything, and we walked back to the bunk.

That Sunday was Parents' Day. I went out boating with my Dad, while Moe spent a lot of time talking with my Mom. After dinner, I walked my parents back to their car. Mom couldn't stop talking about Moe.

"He's such a gentleman," Mom said. "And he seems to like you so much, Lowell."

"You should see him swim underwater," I said.

"He invited all of us down to Washington for a weekend," she said. "He wants to show us around the city. Isn't that nice?"

Moe only kissed me a couple more times before his vacation was up and he had to report back to duty. On the day he left, he was standing in front of the bunk, his bags at his side, a huge smile plastered all over his big, round face. All the campers were instructed to be on the porch to say farewell.

"Thanks for a great two weeks," Moe said, then proceeded to shake everyone's hand. After shaking my hand, he reached across the railing and gave me a big hug, which was embarrassing as hell.

Sonata Facile

After Moe left, Ziggy approached me. He was all upset. "Last night, Moe even gave me a kiss," he said. "The guy is really a sicko."

"He invited my parents and me to visit him in Washington."

"Are you going to do it?"

"Mom seemed to think it might be fun."

"Are you going to tell them?"

"Moe's a goddamn Captain in the United States Army."

"You better tell them or you're an even bigger *schmuck* than I thought you were."

Mom and I went to visit Moe in Washington on the first weekend in November. Dad's colitis was acting up, and he insisted that we go without him.

Moe shared an apartment with another officer in the Georgetown section of Washington. The apartment consisted of a small kitchen, a decent sized living room, one bathroom and two bedrooms. The sleeping arrangements were as follows: Moe's roommate occupied his own bedroom, Moe offered his bedroom to my mother, and Moe and I would have to share a sofa bed in the living room. My heart sank.

Moe was a terrific host. On the first day he gave us the grand tour: the top of the Washington Monument, the Lincoln Memorial, the White House, Congress, all the stuff you're supposed to see in Washington. Tomorrow he was going to take us into the Pentagon. But as much fun as I supposed to be having, all I could think about was sharing that sofa bed with Moe later that evening.

But I was prepared. Under my pajamas I put on two jock straps and over the jock straps underwear briefs. We weren't in bed five minutes before Moe began to whisper to me some sort of crap about how I needed to relax, and then his big hand started in the massage routine on my back. I squirmed about like an earthworm, but there was no getting rid of that hand.

"I want to go to sleep, Moe," I kept repeating over and over, and he kept repeating "Relax, relax." His breathing seemed to have quickened, and I kept remembering Ziggy's warning: *"First he rubs your back a little, then he squeezes your ass, and before you know it, he's got your dick in his mouth."*

The two jock straps provided a small measure of comfort, but how were they going to stop Moe's hand from squeezing my ass? Finally, I said, "Moe, if you don't let me go to sleep, I'm going to tell my mother." I must have spoken in an unfamiliar voice because immediately Moe quit the hand massage and the heavy breathing and, like a giant panda, rolled away from me. Within minutes he was sound asleep, heavy gasping noises emanating from that great barrel chest, probably the only chest in the world large enough to hold enough oxygen for a full three minutes to enable a person to break underwater swimming records.

The *"I'm going to tell my mother"* threat really turned the trick. The next night, after spending the day at the Pentagon, the FBI building, and the Mint, Moe merely registered a quick kiss on my cheek before rolling over onto his side of the bed.

All in all, you'd have to say that the weekend was a big success. My mother had a great time, and Moe never got to suck my dick.

Two months later, Ziggy's father called my father. The shit had hit the fan because that asshole Ziggy had spilled the beans about Moe.

After the conversation with Ziggy's father, Mom and Dad cornered me in the sunparlor. "Did you know about this man?" Dad asked in his infamous *watch what you say* voice.

"He only kissed me a couple of times," I said.

Mom got all flushed and began to fan herself with the palm of her hand. "He seemed like such a nice man," she half-gasped.

"Where did he kiss you?" Dad shouted. He began to breath so hard I got scared that he was going to have a heart attack.

I pointed to my cheek. "No big deal."

Dad turned to Mom. "The man is a pedophile and you let him sleep in the same bed with Lowell?" Poor Mom, I thought she was going to faint.

A couple of days later, I overheard Mom talking to her sister, Sydell. "To tell you the truth, Sydell, the one I thought he was interested in was me."

Ziggy's father wrote a letter to Moe warning him that if he ever went back to Camp Klatzman-on-the-Hudson or tried to make contact with any of the campers, especially Ziggy or myself, that he'd write to Moe's superior officer and have him court-martialled. A week later, Moe wrote back to Ziggy's father: "I will comply." The note was scribbled on a torn piece of paper. He signed it with his initials MS.

The next year Moe failed to return to Klatzman-on-the Hudson for his annual vacation. We all assumed he must have been in Europe fighting the Nazis since no one had heard from him or had any notion of what had happened to him.

About ten years later, I bumped into The Ripper at a Yankee ball game and asked him about Moe. Klatzman had told him that several years ago he had read an article in the *Central Jewish News* that Moe had been killed in an automobile accident in Germany. He had called up Moe's sister to offer his condolences. She told him that the information that had been released by the army was inaccurate. Moe was dead all right, but there had been no accident. Moe had shot himself with his service revolver.

Last month my wife and I went to a concert at the Performing Arts Center in Newark. The pianist played the Brahms Second Piano Concerto. After he had finished, the applause was so enthusiastic that he graciously played an encore—the first movement of the Mozart Sonata in C Major, the *Sonata Facile*.

The soloist received a standing ovation. While we were applauding, my wife glanced at me. "Lowell, you're crying," she said.

"Dammit, I can cry if I feel like it." I ran a hand across my eyes. "Concerts over, let's go home," I said, the *Sonata Facile* still playing in my mind.

There are some things in life that you can never explain. Maybe Ziggy would have understood. Of course, Ziggy never got to play chess or *Heart and Soul* with Moe on that crappy out-of-tune console in the rec room, but he did watch Moe break the world's underwater swimming record, not a bad achievement for a fat, out-of-shape, lonely English teacher.

This is the story of friendships that existed between three Jewish professional men for seventy years. The love they felt for each other seemed almost lost amidst the petty bickering and teasing that to them was normal behavior. But then, most life-long friendships are addictions of a sort and the reasons for their existence are often forgotten long before they end, either by separation or death.

SATURDAY LUNCH

In 1960 I was discharged from the Air Force and went into the practice of dentistry with my father in the Iron-bound section of Newark. At the time my father was sixty-two years old, a short heavy-set man with a quick temper and thick wrists, who could extract a first molar from a heavy-boned mandible with remarkable ease. Though we battled constantly, we somehow managed to share the same office for fifteen years, until his retirement in 1975.

The first Saturday after I entered the practice, we went out to lunch with Will Goldstein and Oscar Lunin, two old friends of my father's, both local physicians. Traveling in Oscar's Caddy, we drove to Peterman's on Clinton Avenue, where instead of the usual tuna or egg salad, which was the best the deli across the street from our office could offer, one could get a decent pot roast or corned beef sandwich.

At the restaurant Will was all smiles as he asked me about the Air Force and my new Japanese wife.

"It-it's good to see you back, Rich," he said.

Will had stuttered as long as I had known him, which was from the earliest moments of my life. The first syllable of every thought he tried to express was torturous for him, but once uttered he would then speak quickly, almost as if he were afraid to get locked into another stutter.

He was a neat man of medium height and built who smiled easily and exuded confidence as a physician despite his handicap. When I was four, he treated me for whooping cough. At six, he removed my tonsils. Over the years he treated me for mononucleosis, chicken pox, torn muscles, a broken toe. In those days, doctors made house calls and when you needed Will Goldstein, he was always there for you.

Will never complained about his health, though he was a diabetic and daily injected himself with insulin. Lunch at twelve was more than a noonday break for Will. During the next fourteen years I witnessed him slip into hypoglycemic convulsions on several occasions because a busy waitress was slow bringing him his split pea soup. My father and I would hold him while Oscar poured orange juice down his throat.

After Will would come around, we'd finish our lunch as if nothing had happened. My father and Oscar were especially careful not to say anything that would further humiliate Will, rare moments of consideration between these old friends.

"Lucky boy," Oscar said to me. "A practice set up for you on a silver platter. Do you appreciate what a deal you got, kiddo?"

"I do." What else was there to say?

Oscar Lunin, nicknamed by my father, "The Mad Russian," after the character played by Bert Gordon on the Eddie Cantor radio show of the thirties, had a large head set upon a thin, scrawny neck. Within deep, bony sockets, his eyes circulated like those of an irate rooster. He enjoyed speaking with his mouth open, the food churning between yellow plastic teeth, splattering along the sides of the denture bases and clinging to his lips, until finally, to everyone's relief, he'd swish them clean with his tongue. When he wasn't talking, he was often grimacing, a sort of mocking smile that slowly spread across his great triangular face.

"What kind of a dumb question is that?" Will asked Oscar. "Of course, he appreciates going into practice with his father. I wish my son had become a doctor."

I had known Oscar almost as long as Will, though he was as much name as person to me until Saturday lunch.

At the turn of the century, the three men, Will Goldstein, Oscar Lunin, and my father, Max Kanowitz, had grown up in the Ironbound, that part of Newark that had been a melting pot for Irish, Italian, Polish, and Jewish immigrants. Together they had attended the Anne Street grammar school and East Side High School. After college and professional schools, all three returned to the Ironbound to practice their professions. About twenty years ago, Oscar gave up his practice to become the company doctor for Ballantine's, the huge brewery that had slowly spread across their old neighborhood.

"Don't worry," my father said to Will and Oscar while we were waiting for our sandwiches, "I'm not going to make it so easy for him."

"Remember what it used to be like?" Oscar said. "You worked fourteen hours a day for peanuts. Kids today have it made." He clicked his dentures together as the food arrived. After he took his first bite, he turned to my father and announced, "These dentures aren't worth a plug nickel. I could die trying to get a decent bite out of them."

When my father would become annoyed, his eyebrows seemed to bend toward the center of his face. "Stop in and I'll adjust them," he said to Oscar.

Later, I discovered that now and then Oscar would send to Will and my father workman's compensation cases, for which he demanded kickbacks from Will, and new dentures from my father every two years.

"That's what you did last time," Oscar said, "but they still hurt. Here, see." Before anyone could stop him, Oscar had flipped out his lower denture and was rubbing a finger along his gums. Pieces of food were stuck to the denture base lying in the palm of his hand.

"Oscar, for Chrissake, put the denture back in your mouth!" my father growled. "They fit you perfectly. Don't be a goddamn pain in the ass."

"Must you carry on at lunch?" Will said to Oscar.

Without the denture in his mouth, Oscar's cheeks caved in. He looked ninety years old. "It hurts me even when I sleep," he said gumming his words.

"Don't sleep with them," my father shot back. My father wasn't about to cave in to Oscar Lunin. "It's like going to bed with your shoes on."

"You ever go to bed with a woman without teeth?" Oscar asked.

Oscar replaced the denture in his mouth, pushing against it with his tongue until it felt secure. "I'll come in on Monday," he said.

"Nine sharp. I've got a busy day."

"I can't make it before eleven."

"You think you're my only patient?"

"Before I die, I'd like to eat a solid meal without crying from pain," said Oscar between chomps on his corned beef and pastrami sandwich.

"Can we talk about something else?" said Will.

After Oscar dropped us off, I asked my father if I was expected to lunch with him and his friends next Saturday.

"You didn't like Peterman's pot roast?" he asked. He looked me over as if I hadn't taken a shower in a month. "For thirty-five years, Oscar, Will, and I have been lunching on Saturdays. It's a free world. Do anything you like." Once again the eyebrows bent. It was time to run and hide.

During the week, I thought: you make a commitment, you might as well go all the way, and there I was with the three of them at the next Saturday lunch.

Except for vacations and illnesses, the four of us met for lunch for the next six years, until Oscar and my father once again got into it over Oscar's latest dentures. It was the second pair my father had made for him within the year, and Oscar had stalled on paying the lab bill. The quarrel continued during the week and on Friday, I heard shouting over the telephone.

My father stormed into my operatory. "For sixty years I've put up with Oscar Lunin. The man's a miser and an ingrate. Even when we were kids he'd try and cheat you out of a nickel every chance he got."

For the next five Saturdays, Will and I lunched alone, neither Oscar nor my father willing to risk a confrontation in which one of them might have to make a concession to the other. Then, out of nowhere, Oscar referred a juicy compensation case to our office; a brewery worker had two front teeth knocked out when a defective wrench had slipped.

The following Saturday Oscar called at nine sharp and informed our receptionist that he'd be picking us up for lunch at twelve. We should be sure to be waiting downstairs since he didn't want his motor to overheat.

As soon as we stepped into the car, he handed my father a check for the lab bill. Later, he picked up the lunch tab.

My father never said a word, not even a simple "thanks," and on the ride back to the office, he poked me in the ribs, a triumphant grin sprawled across his face.

Four more years passed. There was a fight between Oscar and Will over a compensation kickback. Will failed to show up for Saturday lunch and during the meal Oscar began to attack Will until my father told him to eat and keep his big mouth shut.

Oscar's lower denture almost slid out of his mouth. He called my father a shoemaker, and then turned to me and said, "Richard, I ask you in all fairness, if I send a man twenty-five thousand dollars business a year, does he have the right to insult me and swindle me out of a few measly bucks?" He was referring to Will, but I caught his sideways glance at my father.

"Why don't you send the work to another man?" I asked in all innocence.

Oscar's eyes bulged. "What are you talking about?"

My father put down his fork and said to me, "Who asked for your opinion?"

Two weeks later a compromise was reached between Oscar and Will and once again the four of us went back to our Saturday lunches. The subject of the compensation kickback was never brought up.

In 1972, Oscar's wife, Hannah, died. She was fifty-two, twenty years younger than Oscar. They had been married eighteen years and had no children. Hannah, a nurse, had worked in Oscar's office for more than ten years, and the rumor was that when they had finally married he had made an honest woman of her.

We didn't see Oscar for a month after the funeral. At the first Saturday lunch after he rejoined us, he shed tears into his potato soup. "I'm the one who's supposed to die," he moaned.

My father looked around at the crowded restaurant and whispered, "For God's sake, Oscar, everyone's staring at us. We all feel sorry for what's happened, but you're behaving like an infant."

Oscar wiped his eyes with a great monogrammed handkerchief, and then blew his nose. "I heard a grunt and woke up," he said. "She was gasping for air. Then she went out on me, just like that." He snapped his fingers and sat back in his chair. "I married too late in life. No children, only a crazy niece who lives in Seattle. I'm alone for the rest of my life."

Later, as Oscar drove us back to the office, he asked my father if he could stop in and have his new dentures checked. They hurt even more than the old pair.

Less than a year later Oscar had his first heart attack. Two months later Will followed suit. Both were back at work within three months. Oscar walked slowly, his shoulders were rounded, his back slightly bent. He paid more attention to his diet, cut his working hours. Will, however, pretended that nothing had happened to him, working, eating and drinking with his usual abandon, which made Oscar furious.

"You should take better care of yourself," he said to Will at Saturday lunch. "The way you push yourself is suicidal."

The worse Will looked, the angrier Oscar became. A month later Will told us that for the past five years his ascending aorta had become almost entirely calcified, that he was living on borrowed time. Then he smiled and ate an extra piece of apple pie.

"You mock Death," Oscar warned him with an almost biblical ring in his voice.

"I never get excited about things I have no control over," said Will.

Oscar was so upset he left Peterman's before coffee.

Six months later, Will died. I went to the funeral without my father, who was recovering from gall bladder surgery. During the ceremony I sat next to Oscar, who seemed more interested in the mosaic windows than the Rabbi's prayers. Afterwards, he grabbed hold of my arm like a blind man as we walked toward his car.

"Are you okay?" I asked.

"My arthritis is killing me. I've been taking gold injections and they make me bloated and unsteady." He stopped to rest in front of the hearse. "Will Goldstein was a goddamn fool." He turned away, I think not wanting me to see his tears.

Without Will, Saturday lunch became a long-running show without one of the stars. Oscar complained continuously about the pain in his gums. My father exercised surprising patience toward him, until finally at one lunch he blurted out, "Oscar, I'm fed up with your bellyaching.

Oscar's eyes lit up in anticipation of a good fight. "My gums feel like spoiled Jello," he said. "I could starve to death before you did anything." His voice lacked the old crackle and zip, but the intent never wavered.

My father rose to the challenge. "I've got my own problems," he said. "A hip that doesn't give me a moment's peace. I eat aspirin like candy."

"I should have your hip," Oscar countered. "My joints are like balloons. And what about my eyes? Did you know that I'm developing cataracts?"

"Cataracts? What about the pressure in my eyes? Any day I might go blind," my father roared back.

Later that year the brewery retired Oscar. He was seventy-four. He talked about opening up an office, doing insurance work, simple compensation cases. With his contacts he could make a fortune.

The new office never materialized, but we continued having Saturday lunch, though Oscar had to drive in from South Orange. He had lost weight and his face seemed almost skeletal. His clothes hung on him like old paper bags.

My father badgered him over coffee. "Why don't you buy yourself some decent clothes? You look like a street bum."

"If my gums didn't hurt so much, I'd be able to chew food other than mush, and then maybe I'd gain some weight and my clothes would begin to fit."

About six months later, Oscar had his second heart attack. It was touch and go, but he made it. After recuperating for three months, he called the office. My father had retired and no longer worked Saturdays. Peterman's had moved to the suburbs. Still, Oscar wanted to pick me up at twelve. He knew a place uptown—better deli than Peterman's.

He looked awful. His jowls hung like an old bull-dog's, his eyes were watery, his skin was slightly jaundiced. He clung to my arm as we crept across the street from the parking lot. Once inside the restaurant he pepped up and managed one of his primordial, twisted smiles.

"How's your old man these days?" he asked.

"He complains, but he's feeling pretty good," I said.

"The man is a hypochondriac. He'll live to be a hundred and ten."

"And how are you feeling?" I asked to be polite.

He immediately pepped up, as I knew he would. "Everything hurts. I have a hernia and I need an operation, but I don't want to take a chance. These days I'm afraid to move. I sit in the apartment and stare at the walls. I can't see well enough to read. I don't like television. I listen to the radio and hear stupid people talk about homosexuality and drugs." His voice fell to a whisper. "Richard, if you promise not to tell your father, I'd like you to make me a new set of dentures."

The following week, I took snap impressions for Oscar's new dentures. My father, like a monarch in exile, still marched in and out of the office when it suited him. By chance, he spotted the plaster models for Oscar's base trays on a shelf in the lab and immediately confronted me.

"What's the big idea?" he said. "There's nothing the matter with the dentures he's wearing."

"It's my time. Don't interfere."

"He's got no business bothering you." It was now my office and I was supposed to be the boss, a supposition my father never accepted.

Without another word, he stared at me angrily, and then stormed out of the office, bad hip and all.

The following Saturday, Oscar arrived before lunch, and I took the final impressions for the dentures. "Make them fast," he directed me.

At lunch Oscar was uncharacteristically quiet. It was an effort for him to chew his sandwich, though he had ordered white bread instead of his usual pumpernickel. His eyes were half-closed. "Richard, call the waitress," he said. "The corned beef is too fatty." I started to raise a finger. "Never mind, I don't feel like eating anyway."

That night Oscar died. In the morning, the cleaning woman found him lying in bed, fully clothed, his dentures settled at the bottom of a small jar of water.

He was buried next to Hannah on an overcast, chilly Tuesday morning. The only mourners were several neighbors, his lawyer, a second cousin, my father and myself. As my father and I walked back to the car after the rabbi's final prayers, my father said, "I guess that makes me the last of the Mohicans."

The next Saturday I called my father in the morning and asked him if he'd like to come down at noon for lunch. I was treating.

"I should drive all the way into Newark for lunch?" He seemed almost offended.

"It's only twenty minutes," I said. "How about if I pick you up?"

Saturday Lunch

There was a brief silence. "I didn't sleep well last night," he said. There was another pause, and then he added, "Some other time, Richard."

I worked straight through. After my last patient, I hung around the office filling out insurance forms, catching up on some paper work, hoping that my father might change his mind and call, but he never did.

I went home and had a late lunch with my wife, who was surprised to see me so early on a Saturday afternoon.

Twenty-five years ago, I treated a patient with MS. He was a middle-aged man who had been ill for more than fifteen years. He was no longer ambulatory and an ambulance service brought him to my office.

The man was suffering from considerable dental pain and asked me if I could relieve him of his distress and construct fixed bridges to replace those teeth that he knew would have to be extracted. He was deathly afraid that if I replaced the missing teeth with removable dentures, he might choke to death, since he was barely able to raise his arms.

I devised a treatment plan and we scheduled a series of appointments. He was a proud man and insisted on paying me. I said I'd charge him my costs.

The next day, his wife came storming into the office. She insisted that I do nothing but extract his bad teeth. He would have to make do with whatever teeth he had left. She wasn't about to squander whatever little resources they still possessed when he wasn't going to live much longer anyway.

The conflict was resolved when I said that I'd return directly to her the money her husband had agreed to pay me, but I asked that she not tell him. I knew I was violating the patient-doctor relationship, but there are times in life when you can't always worry about legalities.

After successfully completing the husband's dental work, I never saw or heard from either one of them again.

THE ARRANGEMENT

Katz wakes up wet. He doesn't mind the odor as much as the clammy feeling. Stretching sore neck muscles, he turns his head and observes Rose snoring on every third breath like clockwork. From the morning light that seeps under the window shade, he judges the time to be around six. She'll awaken in another thirty minutes, but he doesn't think he can wait that long.

He daydreams that he's sitting on a beach of white sand on a Caribbean island. The sea is a pure blue-green, glistening like emeralds sparkling in the distance. A young black man brings him a glass of ice tea. He sips the drink and watches young people snorkeling by the reefs. He feels the tropical sun beating down on him, warming his flesh, making him feel that his life isn't over, that there's still a reason for him to go on living.

A mosquito ruins the fantasy, circling above him, whining as it zeroes in on him. Futilely, Katz blows at it, but it lands on his right cheek and bites him. He slowly raises his good left arm, but before he can swat at the insect, it flies off.

"Rose, wake up," he says, no longer willing to wait the thirty minutes when she would be normally arising. When she fails to stir, he raises his voice, "Wake up!"

Rose opens her eyes, peers suspiciously about. "What is it, Phil?" Her voice is thick. She's still half asleep.

"You can't smell it? I'm wet again."

"Damn! Did you take your medication yesterday?"

"You gave it to me yourself."

"I'll call Schneiderman. Maybe we should increase the dose."

Rose slides out from under the blankets and sits up on the edge of the bed. She glances at the alarm clock. "It's only ten to six," she says. "Couldn't you wait a few more minutes before waking me?"

"You're not the one who's wet."

"And you don't have to stand on your feet twelve hours a day."

It saddens him to realize how waitressing at the diner had taken its toll on Rose. Her once-beautiful legs are knotted with hideous varicosities.

When they were first married, she had wanted to go back to school and get her teacher's degree. Soon, however, she became pregnant with Janet. Now that Janet is old enough to take care of herself and she could still go back to school, she is forced to work all sorts of hours at the diner because his monthly social security disability check isn't enough for them to live on.

"It's the first time it's happened in months," he says. "Maybe it'll pass."

Next month she'll be forty-two years old, four years younger than he. When she combs out her long fine hair, dabs a little rouge on her pale cheeks, paints her lips, she is still gorgeous, but now, sitting before him, vapid, washed-out, dejected, she looks ready for the scrap heap. His disease has taken its toll on her, no less than if she, too, had been stricken.

"And if you call Schneiderman, what's he going to do?" he asks.

"He said he wanted to see you again if you got worse."

"I'm sick of him poking at me, telling me to be patient. 'New research, Phil, new research. It's on the way, buddy. Keep the faith. One day MS will be a disease of the past, like smallpox or polio.'" For fifteen years Schneiderman has been voicing a mindless optimism, while Katz has slowly, inexorably continued to deteriorate.

Rose starts for the door. "I'll get some fresh bedding," she says in a resigned, stoic voice.

He calls after her. "Later I want to talk about something." But she has already left the room.

He tries to stretch his legs, but the effort quickly tires him. Within the last three years, he has lost the use of both legs and one arm. He no longer has any lateral vision, and periodically he becomes incontinent. Schneiderman tells him that he ought to be grateful that his mind still works.

Fifteen years ago, on Janet's first birthday, he had been cutting the cake when his hand froze and he dropped the knife. Later that same evening a knee buckled while carrying the baby to her crib. The following morning the knee buckled again on the way to the bus stop. He made an appointment to see Schneiderman.

Schneiderman told him he was working too hard. He advised him to take a vacation. In those days he only charged twenty-five dollars for his opinions. If you pay a man good money, you better take his advice. So they left Janet with Rose's mother, closed the dress shop, and took their first vacation since the honeymoon three years before. On their way to Newark Airport, Katz ran the car into a side rail on the Turnpike. He claimed momentary blindness. So much for Paradise Island.

Schneiderman checked him into Beth Israel Hospital, where the doctors ran him through more tests than his insurance covered. After reviewing the results of the tests, the neurologist charged him two hundred dollars for a fifteen minute examination and confirmed Schneiderman's suspicions that Katz had Multiple Sclerosis.

"There's no cure, but it doesn't kill you so fast." Schneiderman is a physician who prides himself on never kidding his patients. At the same time he doesn't like you to look at him like he's some sort of assassin.

Rose returns with the bedding and pajamas. Janet trails after her.

"I don't want Janet here," Katz says.

"I need her to help," Rose says.

"It's okay, Dad." Janet rubs her eyes. She's still in her pajamas.

Katz looks away from his teenage daughter. "Please, Rose," he begs. His skin is blotched from healed bed sores, his once powerful limbs are atrophied from disuse.

"I'd like to help," Janet says.

Rose says to her. "I guess I can manage it alone."

After Janet leaves, Rose lays the new sheets at the foot of the bed. She pushes against Katz's right shoulder in an attempt to turn him on his side. He tries to help, but he is barely able to raise his hips. She tugs at the bottom sheet, finally managing to slip it out from under him, and then removes the rubber pad, also. His pajama pants slide off easily, but removing his tops demands a painful twist of his torso. She goes into the bathroom and returns with soap and a basin of warm water. She washes him, wipes him with a towel, and then pats baby powder around the genital area.

"You want me to wash your back?" she asks.

"It's not worth the turning."

"Schneiderman warned us that if you don't move around, you'll keep getting bed sores."

"Schneiderman once told me to take a vacation."

She closes the top of the baby powder can and places it down on the night table to the right of the bed, next to half a dozen different medications and a radio. A phone with memory rests on the night table to Katz's left. With his good left arm, Katz can call the police, the diner and Janet's school, by pushing buttons.

"I'll wash your back tonight," she says.

She slides a new pad and a clean sheet beneath his body, rolling him back and forth until she has it right. Then she dresses him in fresh pajamas, putting the paralyzed right hand into the sleeve first. When the left hand degenerates, he wonders how she'll manage to get a shirt on him. The pajama bottoms barely cover his pubic area, but she's too tired to pull anymore. She sits at the edge of the bed and rests. She is breathing heavily.

"Can we talk now?" he asks.

The radio-alarm sounds. She shuts it off, and stands up. "I've got to get these wet things into the machine before I go to work."

"So you'll be a little late."

"I was late twice last week. They do a big breakfast business, and Jack isn't happy when I come waltzing in whenever I feel like it."

"Who's giving me breakfast today?" he asks.

"I told you yesterday. I've made a new arrangement with Hilda."

"What happens if I wet again?"

"You'll call the diner. I'm home in fifteen minutes."

"What about Schneiderman?"

"I'll call him this morning."

"Never mind."

"Make up your mind, Phil."

"Let's wait and see what happens. Maybe last night was an isolated incident. I'll cut down on my water."

"Schneiderman said that wasn't good for your kidneys, and that you needed to drink water because you're constipated."

"Great. If I don't drink enough water, I won't be able to shit and if I drink too much, I'll be pissing all night."

"This discussion is not doing my nerves any good."

The new dry sheets and pajamas are a pleasure and after Rose leaves, he tries going back to sleep, but after fifteen minutes of tossing about, he gives up. He needs a Valium, but has no way of taking one, since the pills are out of his reach on the table to his right, Schneiderman's idea after he over-medicated himself last year.

He picks up the remote control placed on the night table to his left, his good side. At this hour the shows he likes best are the cartoons. He loves the old Popeye ones. A can of spinach and Popeye sends Bluto skyrocketing to the moon. Ah, thinks Katz, if only one more time in his life he could feel his muscles charging up, the blood surging through his arteries.

Janet enters the room. She's dressed in jeans and an oversized long sleeve shirt. Her school bag is strapped on her back. "I'm on my way," she says.

"Did you eat breakfast?" he asks her.

"Sure."

"I'll bet. You're too skinny. Do you want to wind up an old maid?"

"Then I can take care of you."

"That's not funny." In two months Janet will be sixteen, almost a woman. He worries about her. She is too shy, too introverted. She doesn't seem to have friends. "You won't forget about the library," he reminds her.

"Why do you want to know about the West Indies?"

"Just bring me the books."

"Don't worry. I'll stop off on my way home." She lingers in front of the door. "You want me to brush your teeth?"

"I haven't eaten yet. Go before you're late."

He hears her bouncing down the front stairs of the two-family house. If they lived on the first floor, it would be a lot easier for him to get out. Janet could wheel him to the park where he could watch the boys run up and down the basketball court. Tomorrow he'd ask Rose to begin looking again for an apartment on the first floor. He dozes off during a *Tom and Jerry* cartoon.

Hilda Kaplan wakes him up. She shuts off the TV and sits down next to him. "I didn't have to use the key," she says. "The front door was left unlocked."

"Janet must have forgotten to push the button."

The Arrangement

"A burglar could come in, push a pillow over your face, and ransack the house."

"He'd be doing me a favor," Katz says. "In the meantime, I'm starving."

"You're getting fat as a horse, Phil."

"Eating is my only pleasure."

"It's not healthy for you to put on too much weight."

"Tomorrow I'll run a mile before breakfast."

He watches her walk out of the room, carefully observing the swing of her hefty rear. She returns in ten minutes with a tray of food. "Scrambled eggs and toast," she says. "We won't worry about your cholesterol today."

"Your eggs are always a treat." His mouth is already watering.

"I made the toast nice and crispy. A little butter, a little strawberry jam. Not too much. Just the way you like it."

She hands him a piece and he takes a healthy bite. She waits for him to swallow the bread before she begins to feed him the eggs.

"Rose said she had made a new arrangement with you," he says between mouthfuls.

"She offered me an extra twenty a week to feed you breakfast as well as lunch."

"Good. I know you could use the money."

Hilda's husband died of a heart attack three years ago. There was a little insurance money and a small pension. Other than a part-time job selling children's clothes at a nearby mall, she has no other income.

"I would have done it for nothing, but Rose insisted."

"She needs you. I need you. It's like God sent you to be our neighbor."

"Thanks, Phil." He notices a sore in the corner of her mouth, and wonders if he ought to mention it to her. "Did you like the eggs?" she asks.

"Delicious."

"How're you feeling today?" She wipes his mouth with a paper napkin. "You look a bit pale."

"I had an accident last night." He tells her about his wetting the bed. Except for Rose and Schneiderman, she is the only one he can talk to without embarrassment.

"That's lousy," she says. "Drink your coffee, it'll get cold."

"Help me hold the cup."

After breakfast she washes his face, shaves him, brushes his teeth and combs his hair. "Now you're handsome," she says. She reaches under the covers and fondles his penis.

"No dice," he says. "It doesn't want to work anymore."

"You want me to give it a try?"

"Maybe tomorrow." He gives her a wink. "You're some card, Hilda. I wish I could put my arms around you and give you a hug."

"You're arms aren't big enough." She laughs at herself. "I've put on a little weight myself lately, or haven't you noticed."

"You're still a knockout."

She grows serious. "I wish I could do something big for you, Phil."

At different points in their lives they had both needed each other. "We had some good times together, didn't we, Hilda?" Katz said.

"What a tiger!" she makes a growling sound, then stands up. "I have to clean my house and go marketing. Can I get you anything?"

"A pack of Trojans."

"Smart-alec. I'll bring you back a nice pizza for lunch." She kisses him on the mouth and leaves.

The Arrangement

After the Regis and Mary Lou show, he watches an old Errol Flynn swashbuckler. Flashing swords, lots of action. Faces are not much more than ghosts on the twenty-five inch Sony screen. He's grateful that at least his hearing is normal. Rose walks in during the eleven o'clock commercial.

"Things were quiet and Jack let me go until lunch," she says.

He switches off the TV. "I've seen this movie four times this month. Don't they ever change their schedules?"

"Watch another channel."

"I like the old movies. They're less complicated than the ones they make today. You're never disappointed."

"I called Schneiderman," Rose says. "He said he might be able to fit you in tomorrow."

"What about the ambulance service?"

"First I have to get the appointment."

"What good is the appointment if you can't work it out with the ambulance service?"

"Don't worry, I'll arrange it."

"If there's a problem, cancel the appointment."

She gives him her exasperated look, and then she asks, "Are you hungry?"

"Hilda made me eggs." Rose makes a sour face. "That's what we hired her for, wasn't it?" he says.

"I suppose the kitchen's now a mess."

"She makes delicious eggs." Fair is fair.

"I'll bet." Rose sits down and kicks off her shoes. "Sam Kaplan always looked like he hadn't eaten in a week."

"He was on a Pritikin diet. He thought every breath was going to be his last, and that a salt free diet might save him." When he realizes that she isn't paying attention, he says, "I've got something important to tell you."

She lifts her head. "Can't it wait? I've got a splitting headache." She stands up, shoes in hand. "Right now I want to clean my kitchen before I go back." She moves toward the door.

"Always later!" Katz clenches his teeth in anger, and a molar cusp, undermined by decay, fractures. "Christ!" he roars from a pain that feels like a raw nerve has been electrified.

Rose rushes back to the bed. "What is it?"

"Toothache." He holds his breath.

"I'll call Schneiderman."

"What does Schneiderman know about teeth?" he whispers between groans.

"I'll call Goldstein."

Last year Goldstein, with his manicured fingers and Listerine breath, hovered over him like a vulture and informed him that the teeth under his old bridgework were rotting out. To save the teeth and make new bridges would cost about ten thousand bucks. The alternative was to pull them all out and make dentures. But suppose a denture became loose. He could choke to death before anyone would be able to help him. He decided to live with the occasional toothache, and the rancid odor in his mouth.

"Don't call Goldstein," he says. "The pain is starting to go away." He sucks on the offending tooth, gently bathing it in his saliva, the sharp pulsations gradually fading into a dull ache.

"I've got to get going. I guess the kitchen will have to wait. Will you be all right?"

"Give me a pill," he says.

She hands him a Valium, then carefully screws the top back on the bottle. "You're running out. When you see Schneiderman, ask him for another prescription."

She bends down and puts on her shoes. "By the way," she says, "your disability check came in. I'm going to cash this one. Janet could use a new winter coat, and so could I. Whatever's left over will help pay some old bills."

"Deposit the leftover," Katz says. "I need the money."

"You need the money? What for?"

"I have an idea that would make life easier for you."

"Don't talk anymore—that would be a start."

He tries to raise his good left arm in protest. "I've been thinking about this for months. I want you to listen to me. It's important."

She folds her arms across her chest. "Make it fast, Phil. I don't want to be late."

"I want to live on an island in the West Indies."

She stares at him for a moment, and then begins to laugh. "You've cured my headache." She sits down at the edge of the bed.

"Go ahead and laugh," Katz says angrily. "And when you're finished, maybe you'll listen to me. Maybe you'll realize that I'm still a human being with feelings." She turns her head away from him, looks towards the door. "I don't want to die without ever breathing or smelling fresh air again."

She jumps to her feet. "You want to smell the air!" She marches to the window and forces it open as far as it will go. "Okay, now smell."

"I'm not dead yet, Rose," he shouts at her. "I still can—" He wants to tell her that no matter how sick a person is, if his brain still works, he can still find some pleasure in life. But he is interrupted by Janet, who is carrying half a dozen books in her arms.

"I've got to go right back," Janet says, laying the books on the bureau.

"Wait a second," Rose says to her. "Come listen to your father. He wants to take a cruise."

"I don't need much," Katz says "My disability check would be enough. There are places to live where a man could rent a room and someone to take care of him for a song and a dance." Katz is drifting into a familiar reverie. "I could be outside, see the ocean—"

"—smell the air," says Rose.

"Yes," he says defiantly. "Would you deny me that little bit of pleasure?"

Janet steps closer to the bed. She picks up one of the books she has brought from the library. "It's a great idea," she says. "Which island are we going to live on?" She begins to thumb through the book.

"Two nuts in the family," Rose says. She looks toward Janet. "Go back to school. I want to talk to your father."

"Why don't we go to Guadeloupe?" Janet says. "French is my best subject."

"You'd better go," Katz says to Janet. "We'll look over those books later."

After Janet has left, Rose says, "Enough is enough, Phil."

"Schneiderman once told me that MS patients do better in warm climates," Katz says. "Anyway, if I leave, you can divorce me. You're a free woman, Rose. How much longer do I live?" Schneiderman said that he could live for years this way, but Katz knew better.

"You stay here until you die," Rose says. "That's the way it is."

"Why won't you try and understand?" Katz pleads.

"Understand what? That you want to run away from your family, abandon your wife and child?" She throws her arms above her head, clenches her fists. "You have responsibilities," she cries.

"I know what's eating you. It's my disability check. For a lousy four hundred and twenty bucks a month, you'd let me rot here until I became a vegetable."

"Ha! I wonder if Hilda Kaplan thinks you're a vegetable," Rose says.

"What's Hilda got to do with this?"

"You think I don't know what's been going on around here?"

"I don't know what you're talking about."

"Don't lie to me, Phil. I've put up with it for years because I've needed her. But don't think you two have ever fooled me."

Katz sucks on his sore tooth nervously. "It's not what you imagine," he says "Anyway, how could it make any difference to you now, Rose?"

She moves around the side of the bed, until she is standing almost on top of him. Her face is flushed. "Nineteen years we've been married," she says, "and I'm not supposed to care?"

"You're jealous?" He had never blamed her when she had turned away from him. It isn't fair that she blames him now for accepting the occasional pleasure that Hilda would offer him, more out of friendship than desire. "Let me go," he begs her. He can see the hate in her eyes. "It is the money, isn't it?"

"Bastard!" she cries. She raises a fist to strike him, and then runs out of the room crying.

A few minutes later Janet sneaks back into the room. She sits down on a chair by the bed. "I thought you went back to school," he says.

"I was in the kitchen." She picks up one of the books off the night table. "Should I read to you?"

"You'll be late for school."

"I'll tell them I got sick."

"Don't bother reading. If your mother won't let me go, then the deal is off."

"She's pretty upset."

"Yeah, well I'm the one with MS."

"Maybe she still loves you."

He stares into his only child's large, brown eyes. After her acne clears up, and she puts on a few pounds, she'll be beautiful. "Go back to school, sweetheart. You'll read to me later." When she doesn't move, he adds, "Please."

"Okay," she says reluctantly, then kisses him on the forehead and leaves.

The tooth begins to hammer away again, but he makes no attempt to will away the pain. Suddenly, he feels himself urinating. Call Schneiderman! Call Goldstein! He closes his eyes and bites his lips before shouting Rose's name into an empty room.

The relationship between the dentist and the dental technician is more often than not a stormy, love-hate partnership. While each is equally interdependent on the other's skills to ensure the best possible treatment for the patient, one would never guess that to be the case if either dentist or dental technician were to be questioned. The dentist considers himself the dominant partner. He is "the doctor", the one who feels ultimately responsible to the patient for the success or failure of the crowns or dentures that are fabricated by the technician. Rare is a dentist who will concede that he had ever sent an inaccurate impression to a technician. When there is a failure, it is always because the technician doesn't know what he's doing.

Technicians nominally kow-tow to the dentist, but not necessarily. Over the years I have known a few cracker-jack lab men who would rather lose the business of a mediocre dentist than admit that it was their fault that a crown or a denture didn't fit. This story is about one such technician, a man whom I worked with for more than fifteen years, and who taught me not only how to become a decent crown and bridge man, but that dentistry is more than just collecting a fee from a trusting patient.

THE MAN WHO WROTE THE BOOK

"Don't let Harry Berlow push you around," my father said to me. "Just remember: you're the dentist and he's working for you."

"I thought dentists and dental technicians worked to-gether as a team." I really believed what I was saying.

My father gave me his special look, the one that questioned how he had managed to sire such a stupid human being. "Harry Berlow thinks he wrote the book," he said.

"What book?" I asked.

"*The book,*" my father said. Then he waved his hand, another one of his favorite gestures, which meant that if I didn't get it, I needed electric shock therapy.

My father and I were having lunch in the small deli across the street from the building in which my father had practiced dentistry for the past forty years. On the ground · floor of the building was a dress shop. Above the shop, on the second floor was my father's office—five small rooms, usually crammed with patients.

"What were you and Harry fighting about before lunch?" I asked.

Above the whine of the dental drill, my father had been on the phone roaring at Harry. The expression, "In a pig's eye," had been repeated at least half a dozen times.

"Harriet Koningsfeld's crown wasn't even close. The man had the nerve to tell me that I gave him a distorted impression."

"How can you distort an impression?"

It was an honest question. In three years as an Air Force dentist, I had never taken a copper band impression of a tooth since I had never made a crown. Who made crowns in the Air Force? This was 1960 and the dentists at the clinic where I was stationed spent twenty-five percent of their time plugging amalgams and extracting teeth and the other seventy-five percent sitting in the lounge smoking, drinking coffee and reading Playboy magazines.

At the time of this conversation, it had only been three weeks since I had returned to New Jersey from Japan and had gone into practice with my father. I think it was my father's almost maniacal desire for me to enter the practice with him that helped in his acceptance of my marriage to a Japanese woman.

The old man couldn't wait to get his hands on me, to instill into my deficient brain a smattering of his forty years experience as a dentist. He had good cause to be concerned about my professional skills. I had almost flunked out of dental school. In the Air Force my patients had been young men who could do little by way of protest if the dental treatment they received was not to their liking. On the other hand, my father's patients were real people, who paid real money for his services. Initially, I was so terrified of maltreating a patient, that to my father's chagrin, all I was willing to do was what I had done successfully in the Air Force: plug amalgams and pull teeth.

"I was taking copper band impressions before you were born," my father said. "You think I don't know when an impression is distorted? Harry Berlow is an egomaniac—"

"—who thinks he wrote *the book*," I interrupted.

"Don't be a smart ass."

"So why don't you get yourself another technician?" I asked, not realizing that the question would throw him into a frenzy.

"Are you crazy?" he shouted. "Why would I want to do that?"

Harry Berlow came to the office one Saturday morning about two weeks later to assist my father with a patient who had complained about the color of four anterior crowns that Harry had made for her.

A slightly stooped, broad-shouldered man, Harry towered over my father, who at five-two resembled a little bulldog. With broad features and a nose that was bent as if it had been broken several times, Harry looked more like an old club fighter than a dental technician.

He extended a huge paw after we were introduced. "Glad to meet you, Richard," he said, shaking my hand enthusiastically. "I've heard a lot about you." I wondered how such thick fingers could carve wax patterns and polish crowns with any degree of precision. "If you're going to be working for the old man, you'd better be good."

"I'll be doing my best." What else could one say.

Then he whispered, "Do what your father tells you, but don't tell him I said so. He thinks he knows everything, which he doesn't, but then, who does? But I tell you confidentially, he's one of the top ten in the state." Then he said rather unexpectedly, "I understand you're married to a Korean woman."

"Japanese," I corrected him.

"My son was in Japan after the war. He said you could buy a steak for a buck and a woman for five."

"Where is he now?" I asked to be polite.

"In Eastern Oregon. He married an Irish girl from the Bronx, who wears long skirts and has hair that falls down her back to her waist. They live on a commune and eat carrots and soy beans and believe that working for money is a sin against humanity. He should have stayed in Japan."

The unhappy patient finally showed up. Harry talked to her for ten minutes until she conceded that the caps were works of art.

"One hundred and five percent," Harry said to her.

The woman paid her bill, and after she left the office, Harry gave me a big wink. Personally, I thought that the veneer facings were a little on the dark side and in my ignorance mentioned it to Harry and my father, who were standing side by side, Mutt and Jeff, discussing another case. Neither bothered to acknowledge my existence, let alone give my opinion a serious thought.

Three weeks later I took the plunge and made my first crowns, gold veneers on two broken down centrals.

"They're too large and the color looks like someone rolled them in mud," said the patient, Mrs. Hortense Brown, my Aunt Edith's maid.

Since Hortense was only paying half of our usual fee, my father had decided to give me the case. She accepted the arrangement without a fuss, apparently accustomed to that sort of professional discrimination. What she wasn't willing to accept, however, was a lousy job, no matter who did it.

I decided to consult my father. He brought Hortense into his chair and carefully examined her, then took me aside in the laboratory. "Have you been drinking?" he asked me. "She looks like a beaver."

I called Harry and detailed the patient's reaction and my father's comments.

"What do we do?" I asked.

"Make them over," Harry said without hesitation.

My heart sank. No matter how much Novocain I had injected into Hortense Brown's gums, she had bounced around in the chair as if she were being electrocuted while I was drilling her teeth. I would have preferred being publicly lashed with a cat-of-nine-tails then to try and reprep Hortense's centrals and take new impressions.

"They're only in temporarily. Couldn't we just fix them up?" I pleaded.

"Did the patient pay for a patch job?" Harry asked.

In a voice sweeter than honey, I explained to Hortense that I had to agree with her that the crowns weren't quite what we would like them to be. Then, with my heart banging away, I blamed Harry for the rotten job. "The technician must have been drunk," I said, borrowing a phrase from my father. "But don't you worry. He's not going to get away with it. We're going to make him do it over again, and this time I'll make sure he does it right." I couldn't believe I had made that little speech. I was my father's son, all right. The realization was almost a religious experience. Suddenly, I was brimming with confidence.

"I ain't paying anything extra," Hortense said. Then she leaned back against the headrest and closed her eyes. "Let's get it over with," she said solemnly, as she awaited the needle.

After I had repreped the teeth and took the new impressions, Hortense said, "You get it right this time?"

"I guarantee it," I said, trying to disguise my inner panic by using a voice that exuded sureness and faith in oneself.

Two weeks later I tried in the new crowns and handed the patient a mirror. "Aren't they beautiful?" I felt like an artist showing off his latest painting.

"They're okay," Hortense said.

"You don't think they're better than the old ones?" I would have preferred a blow to the solar plexus than her blasé, nonchalant attitude.

"Anything is better than those other dogs."

After she left, I ran to the phone and called Harry. "She liked them," I cried exuberantly.

"Who cares what she liked. Did you like them?" Harry asked.

"Sure. They looked great."

"One hundred and five percent?"

"I guess so."

"Even the lingual margin on the right central?"

"What's the matter with the lingual margin on the right central?"

"The impression dragged. I had to guess the finishing line. Did you check it?"

I had been so delighted with the way the crowns looked that I had never bothered to check the margins. Was Harry actually going to suggest that I remove one of the cemented caps and do it over because of a possible minor imperfection on a lingual margin?

"I'm sure it's okay," I said.

"And if it isn't, and five years from now the tooth rots out because of an open margin?"

I told my father about my conversation with Harry. "When you tried in the castings, didn't you check the margins?" He and Harry sounded like the same broken record.

Perhaps my father noted the stricken look on my face, for he suddenly changed his tone, reacting to my anguish, perhaps, with the unexpected compassion of a parent rather than the exacting professional that I knew him to be. "Was the patient satisfied?" he asked.

I nodded affirmatively.

"Then forget about it," he said.

But I couldn't. I felt as if Harry Berlow had dropped a crawling insect down the back of my shirt. A week later I called Hortense Brown.

"I thought I was all done," she said.

"I like to check my crowns after a job is finished, make sure they're okay. It'll only take five minutes."

"What's this going to cost me?"

"No charge. Part of the job."

After two cancellations, she finally showed up. Sure enough you could slip the tip of the explorer under the lingual margin of the crown on the right central. Food could get trapped between the crown and the tooth and pathogenic bacteria would invade the dentin. Over the years the tooth would slowly decay, and one day Hortense Brown would be mopping my Aunt Edith's kitchen and she'd straighten up and howl in pain.

I called up Harry and told him what I had discovered.

"It doesn't matter how a crown looks. If the margin is open, the crown is no good," he said. Then he hung up. He had no time to waste on fools and incompetents.

"Mrs. Brown," I said, "we're going to have to do one crown over."

Before she could object, once again I anesthetized the tooth, removed the crown, and took a new copper band impression. Two weeks later, I cemented in the crown for the third time. The color didn't quite match the one already in place, but Hortense Brown said she'd live with it and growled that she'd rather drown in the lake at Weequahic Park than let me go near her mouth again. She left without a goodbye.

"You've won the battle, but lost the war," my father said when he found out what was going on.

Once again I called up Harry. "The crown fit," I said.

"One hundred and five percent?" he asked.

"One hundred and five percent," I replied grimly.

Fourteen years later, at the age of seventy-five, my father had his first heart attack. Time to retire. After he recovered, he spent good portions of the day at the JCC swimming and playing bridge. Once a week he'd come down to the office to go over the books and check on what I was doing. He could never quite get used to the idea that I could run the practice without him, but I had to admit that if something bothered him, he usually managed to keep it to himself.

The tenant in the adjacent apartment retired and left the state. I signed a new lease with the landlord, and then brought in a Portuguese construction company that in two weeks knocked down the walls and built an office three times its original size. I bought new units and mechanized chairs for each operatory, decent furniture for the waiting room, a large mahogany desk in the business office for my father to enjoy, and, to make the office complete, there was a good sized lab, fully equipped with a sandblaster, a model trimmer, and an electronic casting machine.

To go with our new lab, I hired a dental technician, a young man from Grenada, to do the partial and full denture work. I would still be sending the more complicated, more expensive crown and bridge cases to Harry's lab.

Harry volunteered to come to the office on Saturdays to help train Andrew, my technician.

"You're doing the right thing," Harry said, "providing we can teach this dumb *shvartsa* a few tricks."

"Harry," I said, "this is 1975. Andrew is a black man, not a *shvartsa*."

The rough, old Jew smiled and said, "Richard, do me a favor and write a letter to the editor."

Within six months, Andrew was finishing and balancing dentures Harry Berlow's way.

"Ninety-five percent," Harry said as we were standing around in the lab one Saturday morning.

"Oh, Lordy," sing-songed Andrew in the lilting Island accent he would sometimes use on Harry, "how 'dat man do like to punish his fellow human bein'."

Later at lunch Harry announced that he was thinking of quitting the business. Forty years ago he had purchased a thousand acre ranch in Arizona for "peanuts." Today it was worth a million. At age seventy-two he could retire in style if he wished. "I'm going to ride horses and watch TV," he said, "but first, I'm going to make a crackerjack gold man out of that dumb—'colored' man."

For the next six months Harry continued to work with Andrew on Saturdays. Like a miracle, Andrew's posterior full cast crowns began to fit.

One Saturday my father dropped in. He took me aside. "What's Harry Berlow doing here?" he asked.

"He comes every Saturday," I said.

"What for?"

"He's training Andrew."

"For nothing?"

"I give him fifty bucks."

My father was astounded. "Every Saturday?"

"Sometimes I give him a little more."

"What for? He doesn't need the money."

"He's worth it."

"He's a disruptive force."

There was a level of truth in my father's accusation. Harry, with his bossy, controlling attitude, created serious tensions among the office personnel, though, personally, I enjoyed having the old technician around. For the past fourteen years, we had made hundreds of crowns together. Harry Berlow had taught me to be a first rate crown and bridge man.

"He's still the greatest," I reminded my father.

"He should stay in his own lab. Why is he spending so much time here?"

"Don't you understand—he's training Andrew?"

"I don't get it. What's in it for him?"

"Maybe he's doing it for me."

"You watch out for Harry Berlow," my father said. Even at age seventy-five, my father needed to have the final word.

A month later my wife's parents flew in from Japan for a three-week visit. My mother-in-law was having problems with her teeth and the Japanese dentist wanted to do multiple extractions and make her partial dentures. After I examined her, I called Harry.

"We can save everything," I said. "But she's going to need an upper eight unit bridge and a lower four units. The problem is that she's only going to be here for three weeks. Can we do it?"

"Get to work," Harry said.

With Harry picking up and delivering personally on an almost daily basis, all the metal work for both bridges was completed in two weeks. There remained only to bake the porcelain onto the metal, grind the case in, and then the final glaze. We were going to finish twelve units of fixed bridgework that normally would take up to three months to complete and beat my mother-in-law's return reservation by two days.

The morning of the try-in, Harry never showed up. I called the lab. He wasn't there. He had never called in. Even worse, nobody at the lab knew where the work was. I tried Harry's apartment; no one picked up.

All day and into the evening I alternately called the lab and his apartment. At ten P.M., his wife, Estelle, answered the phone. "Harry's had a heart attack," she said. "He's at the Beth Israel. My life is over if that man dies."

I called the hospital and spoke to the ICU resident-in-charge, who turned out to be a man I had played against last year in an interclub tennis match. He remembered me. "As heart attacks go, this one's not too bad," the resident said. "He seems to be out of the woods, but you've always got to worry about the second one. Is he a personal friend?"

"Like a father," I said.

"He said he had been out riding a horse and the horse began to give him a hard time, so he reached around and punched him."

"He punched a horse?"

"That's what he said."

"Is he conscious?" I asked.

"On and off. He's under heavy sedation and sleeps a lot."

The next morning, using the resident's name, I slipped into the intensive care unit and found Harry's room.

Standing in front of his bed, I stared down at the big man, who, in spite of the life support system hooked into him, remained an imposing figure. He appeared to be sleeping. I sat down on a chair opposite the bed and waited. After a while, he opened his eyes and saw me. With his one free hand he pointed toward the oxygen mask. I went to the bed and lifted it off his face.

"Your mother-in-law's case is in the trunk of the car," he whispered. "Estelle has the keys."

I reset the mask and stood up. "You had to fight with a horse?" I said.

He made a fist, and then waved me away before closing his eyes.

That afternoon Andrew and I ground in the unglazed porcelain bridges, correcting the bite, and then Andrew drove the work over to Harry's lab for the final glaze. The case was cemented in the day before my mother-in-law returned to Japan.

On the way back from the airport, I stopped in at the hospital. Harry was sitting up, reading the Wall Street Journal. This time he removed the oxygen mask himself.

"How'd it go?" he asked.

"One hundred and five percent," I said.

He smiled. "I wish I could have seen it."

"She'll be back in a couple of years."

"Good. Then I'll see it."

A month after leaving the hospital, Harry retired and moved out to Arizona to live on his ranch. Other than a New Year's card on *Rosh Hashannah*, I didn't hear from him for almost a year. Then one day he walked into the office, as if he had never left, though his large frame seemed slightly more bent than I had remembered, and his iron gray hair had turned almost entirely white.

"Retirement is not for me, Richard," he said. "Some men need to work, or they die of boredom."

"Are you going back to Essex Dental?" I asked.

"Never. I thought I might come to work for you. Pay me three-fifty a week and I'll make you a million. Think about it. I've got plenty of time."

But there was nothing to think about. I knew that my entire office staff, including my associate, an earnest young man who had been working for me since my father's retirement, would rebel at working with Harry. And what would happen to faithful, hard-working Andrew? If Harry took over the lab, he would relegate Andrew to pouring up impressions and making dies.

I waited several days before I called Harry at his home.

"The problem is: what am I supposed to do with Andrew?" I said. "Our lab isn't big enough to accommodate two men, even if there was enough work for both of you, which there isn't."

"That's okay, Richard," he said. I winced as I envisioned the sardonic little smile that would creep across his ancient, rough face whenever he was confronted by an unpleasant truth. "I was just hoping—" His voice trailed off. He had too much pride to beg.

"It's not that I don't want to—"

He cut me off. "Now and then I'll stop in and we'll have lunch and talk."

But he never did. I had broken his heart.

Six months later, I was invited to play tennis in Westfield and, while walking off the tennis court, I bumped into the same resident who had treated Harry at the time of his heart attack. He asked me if I knew that Harry was back in the hospital. He had an inoperable lung cancer.

I called Harry's wife, Estelle. She was cold and uninformative after she realized who I was. "Harry doesn't want any visitors," she said before hanging up.

I waited a week, and then went over to the hospital anyway, but Harry was no longer there. The next day my father called to tell me that he had just read Harry's obit in the *Ledger*.

"I'll go to the funeral with you," I said.

"You can't. I called the house. It's one of those funerals where you've got to be a relative or a close friend to get invited," he said. "I thought he was still in Arizona."

"He's been back for a while."

"They got a nerve not letting you go to a man's funeral. I knew him all my life," my father said.

A month later I received a letter from Estelle. "For fifteen years Harry thought of you as a son," she said. "Where were you when he needed you?" My heart sank. I read on: "The least you can do is to give a twenty-five dollar contribution to *Hadassah* in his name." Enclosed was a stamped envelope with the *Hadassah* address.

I thought about writing Estelle a long letter in which I would tell her how much Harry had meant to me and how anguished I was when I discovered he was sick, but then I changed my mind. I decided that Harry and I had something special together for more than fifteen years and what happened at the end wasn't something I needed to explain to someone who could never understand.

That afternoon I made out a two hundred dollar check to *Hadassah* and mailed it in the stamped envelope, but no amount of money can appease a bad conscience.

The next morning I was examining an old patient. I checked an anterior bridge, which had been made about ten years ago. I noted the good aesthetics. More important, the margins were still perfect. The bridge would last forever.

"Everything okay, doctor?" the patient asked me.

"One hundred and five percent," I said.

"Thank God," she said, and Harry's crowns smiled

The Man Who Wrote The Book

into my face.

Dental school at NYU was my own personal night-mare. To this day, almost fifty years later, when I think of the anxiety I experienced as a student, I break into a cold sweat.

Included in our Physiology and Pharmacology courses were experiments performed on animals. I can still recall the mournful looks of the dogs as we led them out of their cages and prepped them for the day's experiment, almost as if they understood what was going to happen to them. The poor pigeons didn't have a clue as to the fate that awaited them.

I wrote Anatole and the Pigeon not because I have any special axes to grind on the subject of vivisection. I told the truth, just the way it happened.

ANATOLE AND THE PIGEON

1954

We spend Friday afternoons in the Physiology lab. The lab, located in the old science building, has a seedy late Nineteenth Century look with its rows of wooden operating tables and plastered walls covered with colored charts and diagrams. Upon entering the room you are immediately greeted by an unpleasant, amorphous odor of animal feces, alcohol, and ammonia.

In the back rooms are the dogs, monkeys, and pigeons. It is depressing to observe the sad-eyed canines as they lie cramped in their tiny cages, struggling to stretch their limbs. Some bark as you approach them, some whimper, most lie quietly and stare at you. The monkeys, on the other hand, screech and snarl, ill-tempered primates who would bite off your finger if given half a chance. The pigeons perch on ledges in the back of their cages, cooing contentedly, oblivious to their fate.

After lunch, we wander into the lab wearing our soiled white lab coats, not as cocky as we were a year and a half ago as entering freshman, and before we discovered that the janitor in the basement was treated with greater civility by the faculty than the students.

Gathering into groups of four, we go to our assigned tables and begin to prepare for the afternoon's experiment.

Jack Kahn brings our pigeon in from a back room. Her feet and beak are taped securely. She squirms trying to escape Kahn's thin, strong fingers clamped around her neck.

"You don't have to strangle her," Anatole tells him.

"What's the difference?" Kahn says. "She'll be soup in a couple of hours." He laughs. Kahn considers himself to be the class wit.

Anatole doesn't laugh. He shakes his head philosophically. At one time or another Kahn will manage to rub just about anyone the wrong way. Kahn's father is a Park Avenue oral surgeon, a member of the Alumni Board, a fact that some believe explained why Kahn wasn't booted from school last year when he was caught red-handed cheating on the Anatomy final. Only Anatole appears to tolerate him, but then Anatole is the sort of man who goes through life looking the other way.

Another member of our team, Eddie Schwartz, brings the surgical equipment and lays it on the table. He spots our pigeon.

"Give it here, Kahn," he says.

Schwartz is determined to try and secure a commission in the US Navy after graduating dental school. To achieve his goal he must obtain quality grades and decent recommendations from the faculty, which makes him all business and a good man to work with in any group experiment.

Kahn hands the pigeon to Schwartz, who carefully places her on the table. I begin to lay out the equipment that we'll be using, while Anatole studies the lab manual.

"Look at him." Kahn points a bony finger at Anatole. "You'd think he was prepping to do a pre-frontal on some catatonic."

"Can't you ever shut up," I say to Kahn. Personally I have little patience for his big mouth. I regret now that I didn't tell him to take a walk at the time he begged to join us in this experiment when no other group wanted him.

"Be useful, get the ether," Anatole says to Kahn.

Kahn mutters to himself on his way to the supply room. He slaps Myrna Kay's bony rear end as he passes her table. Myrna whirls around and gives him a middle finger.

"You shouldn't let him get under your skin," Anatole says to me.

"The guy's a creep," I say.

Anatole lays down the manual and picks up the pigeon in one of his huge hands. "She's a beautiful bird," he says.

"Yeah, she's a beaut," I say. "It seems a shame, doesn't it?"

Our pigeon *is* a prize. Her back is colored a deep blue and streaked with silver-gray lines, while her chest is pure snow. She stops squirming, her small round head bobbing slowly, almost as if she's resigned to her fate.

I ask Anatole if he's ready. He nods. It's Anatole's turn to be surgeon; I'm to assist, Kahn is the anesthetist, and Schwartz will read from the manual. The experiment: removal of one side of the cerebral cortex, then following recovery from spinal shock, observation of the pigeon's reflexes. Our conclusions will be drawn from the pigeon's post-op reactions as compared to her normal reflex pattern as described in the manual.

Anatole continues to study the pigeon in his hand. "Do you know that homing pigeons can fly a thousand miles right to the mark?" he says.

"Where'd you read that?" I ask him.

"I'm into birds," he says.

Anatole Mazorkias is the class mystery man. He goes about the business of being a dental student with a silent constancy and resolve, neither expressing approval nor disapproval toward any of the faculty, or his classmates. He's a tall, strongly built, black-haired Greek with dark brown eyes, full lips, and a nose with a slight bend that gives him his Mediterranean look. He's five or six years older than the rest of us, but no one has any idea what he was doing before he was accepted into dental school. This past year his basement locker was located next to mine. Other than that he lived by himself in the East Village and owned a canary, I could extract no more information from him than anyone else in the school.

On his broad back there's a thick, ugly scar that twists diagonally from a shoulder blade almost to his waist. Many times, as we changed our clothes, I found myself gaping at the scar, wondering what kind of terrible accident he had been in to produce such a ghastly memento.

About a month ago, he surprised me and said, "I was wounded in Korea. A piece of shrapnel got me in the back."

"I'm sorry, I didn't mean to stare," I said.

He nodded, and then resumed dressing. I thought the conversation was over when he began speaking again. "Actually it was a land mine. Two men in the patrol were killed, a third had a leg blown off. I was the lucky one: a month in a hospital, but the end of the war for me."

It was the first time he had ever talked to me about anything but his canary. Even more surprising was that he invited me to join him for a cup of coffee in the cafeteria. It had been as if my knowledge of the wound had created a special bond between us.

In the cafeteria, as we sipped our coffee, I asked him how he had managed to be so lucky as to wind up in Korea.

"I volunteered," he said.

"Who volunteers for Korea?"

One of the reasons I had been pre-dental in college was to avoid being drafted. Lots of guys were getting killed in a war that made little sense to me.

"My parents were immigrants," he said. "They worked in my uncle's restaurant until they could buy their own. For them America was the Garden of Eden. They hated the Communists, and when I volunteered, they were filled with pride. After I was discharged, my father wanted me to work at the restaurant with him, but I decided to go to college."

"Did you ever kill anybody?" It was a question I had always wanted to ask someone who had fought in a war.

"Only one for sure. The rest—I don't know. You never saw the people you were shooting at."

"What did it feel like?" I felt compelled to ask. "I mean when you killed the man."

He shrugged. "I shot him before he shot me. I wish it had never happened."

"If you had never been there, it never would have happened."

I think I must have sounded a little like my father, who blamed all wars on politicians and generals. According to my father, politicians created wars to make themselves popular and generals liked to try out new weapons.

"There are things you can't take back," Anatole said. "It's a waste of time to brood about them."

"Some species of pigeons mate for life," Anatole says. He hands the pigeon back to Schwartz and begins checking the equipment I've laid out.

"And this one?" I ask.

"Order Columbiformes, common domestic variety. Some do, some don't."

"Maybe this one's mate is still in the back room."

"Or on one of the other tables."

Kahn returns with the ether. He seems out of breath. Kahn is always restless, always on the run. "Let's finish fast," he says. "Pinochle game in the lounge starts in an hour."

I remind Kahn that the manual says it takes an hour for the bird to come out of spinal shock.

"We cut fast, make it look good," Kahn says. "Later we can check another table's results."

Schwartz, who is also a pinochle player, nods his head. "Jack's plan is not without some merit," he says. "On the other hand, there's risk. I heard Dr. Maxwell express an angry sentiment about guys not finishing their experiments legitimately."

"I can't leave if you guys don't." Kahn is annoyed. He knows that, unless we all leave together, his absence will be conspicuous.

"Come on, Jack," Anatole says. "Bad enough we're going to butcher this animal. At least it ought to be for a reason."

"Yeah, what?" asks Kahn.

"Let's get on with it," I say.

Schwartz hands the pigeon back to Anatole while Kahn sops up the ether in a big wad of absorbent cotton, then squashes the cotton against the pigeon's face.

The pungent aroma of ether fills the air. "Take it easy with that stuff," warns Anatole.

The pigeon reacts violently, twisting her body convulsively. Anatole holds her tightly. His hands are large and strong, and she is helpless in his grasp. Finally, she goes under, and we are ready to operate.

Carefully, Anatole slices through a small portion of the crown on the right side, and with his periosteal elevator meticulously peels back the skin to expose the tiny bald dome.

Impatiently, Kahns says, "Not tomorrow, but today, Mazorkias."

"Get lost," I say to Kahn. One day I swear I will punch him out.

"Wake me up when you're finished," says Kahn.

Anatole, without looking up, says, "Jack, concentrate on your job. Make sure she doesn't come out too soon." Kahn, unaccustomed to the rough edge in Anatole's voice, backs off.

Getting through the skull proves more difficult than laying the flap, and Schwartz is dispatched to obtain the special bone forceps. Another group is using it, and we're forced to wait, which further irritates Kahn. "Jesus, they're almost finished at table four," he says.

"Be patient, Jack," says Anatole. "We'll get it done."

"What's the point of this whole goddamn experiment anyway?" Kahn says. "You can read the manual and find out what's going to happen."

Anatole studies the pigeon, her tiny skull now half-stripped of its skin, her broad white chest heaving slowly, an almost anguished respiratory movement. "I don't know what the point is," Anatole says to Kahn. "But sometimes you've got to do what you're told to do without question, and hope that it's the right thing."

"Great philosophy," says Kahn. "I hope you live to be thirty."

Schwartz arrives with the forceps and Anatole chisels his way through the bone. It's a slow, tedious job—too much pressure and he'll drive the chisel through the brain and kill the bird, ruining the experiment. Beads of sweat form on Anatole's broad forehead, and I offer to take over for a while. He declines. He doesn't trust anyone else to work on his pigeon.

As the last bit of bone is removed, a large blood vessel is torn. Quickly, a dark red pool of blood accumulates. I sop up the blood with cotton, while Anatole gropes to clamp off the torn vessel. Kahn leans over the table, partially obstructing Anatole's view of the surgical field.

"I think I see it," says Kahn. "Let me do it."

Anatole gives Kahn a savage look and I worry that Anatole will finally annihilate Kahn, when suddenly the pigeon begins to stir. "She's coming out of it," Anatole says excitedly.

"More ether," cries Schwartz.

Kahn hastily pours the ether into another blob of cotton and pushes it into the pigeon's face. The air is over-saturated with toxic fumes, and I fear we'll all be asphyxiated. Once again the pigeon lapses into unconsciousness, and Anatole continues to try to stop the bleeding. The table is cluttered with bloody cotton blobs, and I am about to advise Anatole to pack it in, when he isolates the bleeding vessel and clamps it off. He pauses to wipe his forehead. He is breathing heavily.

"Calm down," I say to him. "It's only a pigeon."

"What's that got to do with anything?" Anatole says.

"Give me a break, for chrissake," says Kahn.

With his periosteal elevator Anatole begins to scrape off the exposed cortical layer of cerebrum, the next phase of the experiment.

"Easy now," I remind him. Too much pressure and he will kill the pigeon.

The cortical tissue, endowed with a rich vascularity, bleeds profusely as Anatole picks at it. Neuroblasts, fibroblasts, lipoid cells, congealed protoplasm, alive and vital, dangle under his probe. He seems to pick at each cell as if it has a special meaning, a unique function.

"That looks clean," I say, as I swab the area.

"Sew the damn thing up already," Kahn says, a lit cigarette already dangling from his thin lips.

An instructor appears alongside our table. "That's an open bottle of ether, doctor," he says to Kahn. "Put out the cigarette."

Kahn is annoyed with the instructor, a graduate student working for his fellowship in the department. He packs little weight, and Kahn stomps out the butt with a murmur of protest. The instructor examines our bird, and says to Anatole, "Your patient isn't breathing, doctor." He then walks on to the next table.

"Artificial respiration!" cries Schwartz.

Placing a hand under the pigeon's wings, Anatole applies a firm, interspersed pumping action on her smooth, white chest. He maintains it for several minutes, until suddenly the chest swells and, miraculously, our pigeon begins to breath again. I lay a thin strip of gauze saturated with coagulant over the exposed brain, and then Anatole slowly sutures the skin together. When he's finished, he lays the pigeon on the clean end of the table.

"Finally!" Kahn says triumphantly. "I'll be back later."

There's another cigarette in his mouth just before he disappears through the side doorway.

Anatole and the Pigeon

Schwartz and I clean up the table while Anatole washes the blood from the pigeon's chest and beak. After Schwartz and I finish, Schwartz says he's going for coffee. Anatole tells me to go, too, that he'll watch the pigeon, but I decide to hang around, and Schwartz goes off by himself.

Anatole and I sit facing each other on opposite sides of the table. The pigeon, suffering from spinal shock, lies between us.

"In an hour," I say, "she'll be hopping around as if nothing has happened."

"Except that half her brain is missing," he says.

We lapse into a curious silence, both of us staring at the unconscious pigeon, as if we are mutually bonded to it. Then Anatole says, "Maybe Kahn's right? I mean, what is the point?"

"Don't you think it's better that we practice surgery on a pigeon before we try doing it on a human being?"

"I suppose so—unless you're a pigeon."

Without warning, the pigeon stops breathing again. We both see it at the same time. Anatole snatches her up and once again begins to compress her chest. The pigeon lies limp in his hands, an inert mass of feathered flesh. He refuses to give up and keeps squeezing for another fifteen minutes. But she doesn't respond.

"She's dead, Anatole," I pronounce solemnly.

"A little bit more. Maybe she'll come around."

Once again he's sweating. I want to grab the pigeon from his hands, but I become drawn to what has now become his obsession, keeping the pigeon alive. I watch silently as he continues to apply pressure to the pigeon's chest.

Schwartz returns, and a few moments later, Kahn appears. They observe Anatole and the pigeon.

"What's with him?" asks Kahn pointing a bony index finger towards Anatole.

"The pigeon's dead," I say. "Anatole thinks he can bring her back to life."

"God at work." Kahn doesn't bother waiting for a response. "I'm off," he says. "See you at lecture. Don't forget to copy another table's results." On his way, he stops at Myrna Kay's table and whispers in her ear. She laughs, and then pushes him away, but not too hard. Kahn has made a conquest. It would appear that there's no accounting for taste.

Schwartz finds a table where a decorticated pigeon has emerged from shock and is on its feet, groggy, but quite alive. I stay with Anatole as he continues to try to resuscitate life back into his pigeon. He mutters angrily, "Breathe, you bastard bird, breathe!"

Finally I leave him and join Schwartz at the other table. Their pigeon is now hopping about crazily, a mass of disorganized reflexes, completely paralyzed on one side of her body. We study the bird's reactions to different stimuli, and then carefully record our observations. After everyone has finished poking at the bird, she is held down and exposed to a lethal dose of ether.

I look back at our table. Anatole is still sitting there, silently observing the pigeon's limp form as it lies in his large hands. I walk over to the table and stand next to him. "Come on, Anatole, lecture starts in a few minutes."

He stares at me. For a moment I think he doesn't recognize me, then his lips part faintly, but he doesn't speak.

"Come on," I say again.

"You go on." He rises to his full height and takes a deep breath. "Get going or you'll be late," he says. "I'll take care of the pigeon."

"What're you going to do that's so important that you're willing to cut a pathology lecture?" I ask him. Anatole never cuts a lecture.

With care he lays the pigeon down on the table, pokes it very gently as if he is trying for the last time to get it to respond. "I think I'll take a walk," he says.

"Lately, they've been taking attendance," I remind him.

He wraps up the pigeon in a plastic bag and dumps her in the designated box, and we go downstairs to our lockers, and change. "I guess that's that," he says.

"Aren't you going to the lecture?" he asks me.

"Tomorrow I'll copy Schwartz's notes during lunch-break. I thought I'd walk with you, if you don't mind?"

"Glad for the company."

At the corner grocery store, Anatole buys a box of popcorn and two apples. He flips one apple to me and chomps on the other. Then we head for Union Square, where we sit on a bench and finish eating our apples.

"What made you want to be a dentist?" he asks me.

"My father's a dentist. My brother's a physician. I guess you might say that it's in the genes."

"Not my genes." Anatole flings a handful of popcorn onto the ground and a score of pigeons rush over and begin pecking at the food. "I don't think I'm really cut out for it," he says.

"Because of today?" I asked him.

"Did you know that before I went to Korea, people would tell me that my mousaka was unbelievable? And my spanikita." He throws a kiss into the sky. He becomes alive. His eyes are filled with a warm glow. "My mother would say that at age eighteen I was already a better chef than my father, though he would never admit it."

One of the smaller pigeons in front of us is unable to compete with the larger, more aggressive ones for the popcorn, and stands back on the fringe of the crowd.

"Your turn," Anatole says to the smaller pigeon, and tosses a few kernels directly in front of her. She snatches them up, and looks to him for more. He reaches into the box, and smiles; unafraid, the pigeon wobbles over to him and feeds from his fingers.

In 1972 my wife had a partial hysterectomy. The first evening after surgery, I sat in her room, not trusting the floor nurses in the event of an emergency. Unable to sleep, I did what writers do, I let my imagination run amok and began to write a story.

Years later when I finally got around to finishing this little fantasy of mine, I discovered that the main protagonist in the story was no longer the same person as I had originally conceived. I have no idea how this happened, and since a writer shouldn't always be trying to figure out why certain ideas spring up out of nowhere from his unconscious, I will simply let the story tell itself and see if the reader can figure out what I am talking about.

MATCHMAKERS

After school, Lowell cut across the ball field and headed toward the stretch of woods between the school grounds and the row of split-level houses on the hill. He didn't realize he was being pursued until he came to the path at the wood's edge.

"Hey, hold it a second." Brian's chubby legs struggled to catch up.

Lowell stopped and waited for his friend. "Hurry up," he said. "I've got to get home."

Brian puffed heavily when he came alongside of Lowell. "What's the big rush?" he asked.

Lowell resumed walking again. "My mother's in the hospital."

"So?"

"So, I'm going home to find out how she is."

"Why don't you stop at my house first? It's on the way."

Once again Lowell slowed down. "Don't you get it dimwit, she's in the hospital." Though they were both ten, Lowell was a head taller than Brian. One of Lowell's strides equaled two of Brian's.

"You can still come over for a while. She isn't going anyplace, is she?" Brian had a way of nagging you like a worm chomping on a leaf.

During morning math, Lowell envisioned a masked surgeon operating on his mother. Lowell knew exactly what was happening, for hadn't he seen it on *M*A*S*H* a zillion times. Beads of sweat formed on the surgeon's forehead, the nurse constantly wiping them off. In the background bleeps from the oscilloscope were monitoring his mother's vital signs. During the surgery, all of them, the surgeon, his assistant, the scrub nurses, the anesthesia-ologist, were engaged in a lively conversation about movies and places in the world to visit and stuff like that.

"She was operated on this morning," Lowell explained.

Brian became more interested. "No kidding. What for?"

"They didn't tell me exactly." Lowell sat down on a rock, and Brian was grateful for the rest. Then Lowell added, "My father said it wasn't serious." He tapped his stomach. "Something inside her had to be fixed."

"Maybe she's going to have a baby."

"Don't you think I'd know if she were going to have a baby?"

"How can you be so sure?"

Lowell stood up. He kicked at the rock. "Anyone would know if their mother was going to have a baby."

"Okay, so why is she in the hospital?"

Lowell started hiking up the hill. Brian ran after him and yelled, "They don't always tell you the truth." He caught up to Lowell again and grabbed him by the sleeve. "Watch out, they lie!"

Lowell yanked himself free from his grasp. "What do you know about it?"

"They lied to me about my father, didn't they?" Brian blurted out angrily. "

Last year Brian had called Lowell after school and told him that he wouldn't be able to come over and shoot baskets because his father was in the hospital. He had been in an automobile accident but he was going to be okay. Brian didn't show up at school for the next three days. At his father's funeral, Brian told him that his father had a heart attack while he was driving, and the car had crashed into a telephone pole.

Then Brian said, "Your father doesn't want to tell you how sick your mother is because you're too young and he thinks you're going to have a nervous breakdown."

"What's a nervous breakdown?"

Lowell became more interested in Brian's conversation. Most of the time Brian was a jerk, but now and then he would talk about things that Lowell didn't understand, and you had to respect him for that.

"It's when you get all crazy. My mother had a nervous breakdown after the accident."

"How do you know that?"

"You couldn't get her to cook a decent meal. She'd just sit by herself in the kitchen drinking coffee and crying. My aunt told me she was having a nervous breakdown because she missed Dad."

"Did she ever get rid of it? I mean the nervous breakdown."

"One day, she called me into the kitchen and said that I didn't have to worry about her anymore, that she was finished crying. After that, once in a while I'd hear her in her bedroom late at night, but most of the time she was okay."

A light rain began to fall from the overcast, gray sky as they broke through the woods. Lowell's cheeks quickly became damp. "We'd better hurry up," he said.

By the time they came to Brian's house, a white colonial with Doric columns on both sides of the front door, the rain had intensified. "Come on in 'til it stops," Brian said.

"My Grandma's waiting for me," Lowell said, but it was still another two blocks to his house and he was already pretty wet.

The two boys raced across the thick, green lawn and around to the back, where Brian located the key hidden inside the outdoor grill and opened the kitchen door. Brian went into a bathroom and brought out a couple of towels. Then they settled down with a box of chocolate chip cookies hidden in the cabinet where the cereals were stored.

"Where's your mom?" asked Lowell.

"She's got a new job," Brian said. "She'll be home in an hour."

An eight-year girl carrying a third grade reader and sucking a lollipop came into the kitchen through the back door. She was dripping wet, but didn't seem to care. She looked at the empty box of cookies on the table in front of the two boys.

"You ate all the cookies," she cried.

"There was only a couple left," said Brian.

"Mom said we weren't allowed to eat them 'til after supper."

"Go dry yourself, then do me a favor and drop dead."

Lowell wanted to tell Brian to shut up. Bad enough they had eaten the cookies, but he didn't have to get on

Phyllis so hard. She was only a little kid, and Lowell sort of liked the way she'd smile at him when they'd pass each other in the hallway at school. She probably missed her father a lot. Who wouldn't miss your father if you were only eight, and he just up and died on you?"

"The dentist told Mom that you're not supposed to eat candy and cookies," Phyllis said.

"Get lost, jerkoff," said Brian.

"That's a curse," Phyllis snapped back. "I'm gonna tell Mom about that, too." A triumphant smile crossed her face. She backed out of the kitchen and ran upstairs.

"She's weird," Brian apologized to Lowell. "Whenever Mom's not around, she gets even weirder. Sometimes there's not much you can do but kick her butt."

Lowell had no brothers or sisters. He had always wanted a younger brother, someone he could play with when he had no friends around. He could see that a kid sister really might not be good for much, and could cause you a lot of trouble, ratting on you for every little crime you committed around the house. Still, he didn't think he'd be as much of a bully as Brian if he had a sister.

Lowell telephoned home. While the phone was ringing, he watched Brian pick the cookie crumbs from the bottom of the cookie box, and then like an anteater tongue them from his fingertips one by one. One day Brian was going to look like an orangutan he saw last year at the Bronx Zoo. The big ape sat around eating apples and bananas all day and was so fat he could hardly stand.

"Grandma, I'm at Brian's," Lowell said. "I'll come home as soon as it stops raining." Brian poured himself a large Coke, and then took a piece of white bread and smeared peanut butter and jam on it. "How's Mom?" Lowell asked.

"She just came out of surgery. Your Dad said she was doing fine. He's on his way home now while she's in recovery."

Grandma's voice sounded cracked, unnatural. She had moved into the house yesterday, after Mom went to the hospital. He didn't think he needed any special taking care of, but she had moved in anyway, and now he was going to have to put up with her constant nagging for him to clean his room.

"What's the matter with Mom?" Lowell asked her.

"She had a partial hysterectomy," Grandma said.

"What's that?"

"They remove your uterus, but leave in your ovaries."

Grandma had this annoying way of being very medical because once upon a time she had taught biology in high school. "What are they?" Lowell asked.

"It's the part of a woman's insides that makes babies."

"She can't have a baby anymore?" Lowell asked. A moment of disappointment since Lowell still harbored the notion that one day he might have a brother.

"That's right."

"So why did they have to take them out?"

"I'll explain it better when you come home."

"Is she going to be all right?"

"She's going to be fine."

After he hung up, Lowell opened the back door. The rain was still pelting down hard, and he stepped back into the kitchen and sat down. There was a magenta ring smeared around Brian's lips from the jam sandwich he had been eating while Lowell was on the phone.

"My mom's going to be okay," said Lowell.

"How do you know?" Brian asked.

"My grandma just told me." He tossed Brian a paper napkin lying on the table. "Wipe your face. You're such a slob."

"How does she know?"

"Because she knows."

"They lie, you know. They lie all the time."

"My grandma wouldn't lie to me," Lowell said.

"When they lie to you, they think they're doing you a favor. It's the way parents are with kids." After finishing off the sandwich, Brian gulped down the rest of his Coke, and then pounded the glass on the table.

"What're you getting mad about?" Lowell asked.

"They're all such liars."

Brian found a couple of overripe peaches in the fruit bowl on the dining room table and brought them back into the kitchen. He chomped into one, and then offered the other to Lowell. He suddenly became elated. "I've got a great idea," he said. "If your mother dies, your father could marry my mother."

Lowell felt like bouncing the peach off Brian's head and rolled it around in his hand like a baseball pitcher rubbing off the gloss on the ball before he'd throw it.

"Why not?" Brian asked. "Then we could all live together."

"My mother's not going to die," Lowell said.

"But suppose she does. It's possible, you know. When they start cutting you up, anything is possible." The juice from the peach ran down the sides of Brian's chin. He was too excited with his idea to wipe it away. "That would be great, wouldn't it?"

"That's too dumb to even think about."

"My mother doesn't have a husband; your father wouldn't have a wife. It'd be perfect."

"Maybe they wouldn't want to marry each other," said Lowell, momentarily caught up in Brian's fantasy.

"Why not? They like each other well enough."

"That doesn't mean anything." Lowell bit into his peach. It was too mushy and he tossed it in the garbage.

Once again Brian went back into the refrigerator, this time emerging with leftover hamburgers. He offered one to Lowell who said that he didn't like them cold. Undeterred, Brian unwrapped one and sat back down at the table. Lowell couldn't believe that Brian was going to eat that disgusting, cold, leftover hamburger without even bothering to heat it up.

With a mouthful of food, Brian said, "My mother likes your father. Just the other day I heard her say something nice about him. It'd work out fine, you'd see."

Lowell wondered how any human being could talk with so much food in his mouth, let alone think that anyone would be able to understand him.

This morning, before going to school, his grandma promised that she was going to cook a pot roast for supper. Last winter when he and his parents were visiting his grandma in Florida, she made them a pot roast that was so delicious he ate the leftovers for days. That was a couple weeks after Brian's father had died in the car crash. He remembered his mother telling him to be especially nice to Brian, which he thought was a sort of stupid thing to tell him. When your best friend's father gets killed, you don't have to be told to be nice to him. Why do parents always have to hand out advice, no matter what, like that's their job and if they don't do it right, they don't get paid?

Then Brian said, "Maybe she wouldn't die. Maybe this one time they weren't lying to you."

"Grandma said she had a hyster-something or other. They took out part of her insides."

"I heard my mother once say that people are like cars. They get old, the parts run down, and you've got to replace them."

"People aren't cars, stupid." Lowell said with certainty. "Cars get old and you junk them. You don't do that with people."

"Why are you getting mad? It's just something my mother once said."

Lowell noticed that the rain had let up. He picked up his bag and headed for the door. "I'll call you later," he said. Brian was stuffing the other cold hamburger in his mouth as he left.

His father's car was parked in the driveway, and Lowell went into the house through the garage. In the kitchen his father was talking to his grandmother. When his father saw him, he cut short whatever he was saying to her. Adults had their secret little world, and it was one of those things that kids couldn't do very much about.

"You're soaked," his grandmother said. "Go upstairs and change."

"How's Mom?" Lowell asked his father.

"It was a tough operation, but she's doing fine."

"Can I visit her?"

"Maybe tomorrow when she's feeling better."

"Why can't I see her tonight?"

"Tomorrow. Now do what Grandma tells you."

Upstairs Lowell called Brian. "They won't let me visit her," he said to Brian.

"That doesn't sound good." Brian said.

Brian's skepticism irritated Lowell, and he was immediately sorry he had called him. Nevertheless, he continued to listen to Brian with interest.

"Watch out," Brian went on ominously. "Remember, they lie."

After hanging up, Lowell changed his clothes, and then stole downstairs past the kitchen where he could hear his father whispering to his grandmother. He went into the den, turned on the TV, and flopped down on the sofa. Suddenly his heart began to beat rapidly, and he felt an inexplicable rage toward Brian sitting around eating cold hamburgers and dreaming that his mother would marry Lowell's father.

Someone needed to tell Brian to stop eating before his insides busted open.

I never met a miser who wasn't convinced that his way of doing things wasn't normal and reasonable.

Years ago, I was involved in an automobile accident: college students driving from Chicago to New York, an unexpected snow storm, a treacherous road.

How intriguing would it be, I thought, to pull my college students out of that car and replace them with a miser and his wife, and see what happens.

THE ACCIDENT

March 1975

Charlie Grant pushed the old Thunderbird along the county highway well above the speed limit. Icy gusts of wind swept dead leaves and twigs across the road. In the morning when they had started out, the sky was almost cloudless. Now Tomiko could barely make out the distant hills against a darkening horizon. Within the last two hours, the temperature had dropped precipitously, and a light rain had turned into snow. She wanted to tell Charlie to stop at the first motel, but was afraid to start an argument.

Tomiko leaned back against the car seat and closed her eyes. She might as well try and relax, since there was nothing she could do about the weather, or Charlie. The radio was playing country music. She favored music from the forties and fifties, especially when Frank Sinatra and Nat "King" Cole were singing, but the radio worked only on AM and most good music came over FM. The last time she complained about the radio, Charlie said that he'd take it to the car radio shop first chance he got and get it fixed. That was two years ago.

The Accident

The music stopped. She opened her eyes and asked Charlie why he had shut off the radio. "I can't concentrate with that damn music on," he said.

"Why don't we pull over until it stops snowing?" she said.

"Where? On the grass? You want some crazy farmer to shoot us? Once we're out of these hills and on the Turnpike, we'll have clear sailing home."

She was tempted to remind him that because he had wanted to save a couple of dollars on tolls they had taken the county highway about a hundred miles back instead of the Ohio Turnpike. But what would be the point? He'd get hot under the collar and refuse to speak to her for the rest of the trip. Of course, in fairness to Charlie, who could have predicted this unexpected drop in temperature, and then the rain and now the snow. It was, after all, March 21, the first day of Spring.

To pass the time, Tomiko daydreamed about Japan, a habit that had become more frequent in recent years. When the war ended, jobs were scarce until the Americans took over the air base at Tachikawa. Only after her father had begun to work on the base had he been able to earn enough money to rent a small house and feed his family properly. Life was hard, but not unpleasant for herself and her brother and sister and parents. She especially liked to remember those holiday times when her aunts and uncles and cousins would get together and there'd be lots of good food and laughing and story telling. Five years later she married Charlie, who had been stationed at the air base, and came to the States after he was discharged not long after.

Both her parents had died within the last three years. Now, with her sister Masako gone, there remained only her brother Jiro, who lived in Fuchu with his family. Would she ever see him again? Charlie made it clear that he wasn't interested in traveling back to Japan anymore. Air fares had doubled in twenty years, and he wasn't a millionaire.

After Masako's funeral, Charlie had announced his intention of driving straight through to New Jersey from Chicago. Every day he was away from the shoe store was costing him a bundle, not to mention the extra costs of motels and eating on the road. Tomiko warned him that driving the sixteen hours in a day might be too exhausting for one driver. She was wasting her breath. Once Charlie had made up his mind about anything, it was pointless to try and change it.

"You look very tired," she said to him.

"I'm okay. Stop worrying so much."

"Excuse me for saying this, but if you had ever bothered to teach me how to drive, then at times, like now, I'd be able to help you out."

They had been married about a year when she had first asked him to teach her. "Sure," he had said. "Maybe next month when I've got nothing else to do."

The next month would come and she'd ask him again, and he'd repeat himself. Nineteen years later, she still didn't have a driver's license.

"When we get home, I want you to promise me that you'll give me driving lessons," Tomiko said.

"What's that?"

"I said when we get home, I want you to give me driving lessons."

"I thought you liked to ride the buses." He glanced at her. Did he catch the look of annoyance on her face? "Okay," he went on with little enthusiasm. "Next month we'll work on it. First, I have to finish up this month's inventory."

The Accident

"I'm sorry, but whenever I ask you about this, you always say you have something more important to do first."

"You don't think inventory is more important than your learning how to drive a car? All right. Next month. I promise. Now stop bothering me. I'm having a hard enough time keeping this car on the road."

She knew that when the time came, he would find another reason to break his promise. Still, she mustn't give up hope.

How wonderful, she thought, to be able to drive yourself around any time you felt like it. She could drive into the City, go to a museum, or a show, or even just browse around on Fifth Avenue. Sundays, while Charlie sat like a Buddha in front of the TV watching the Giants play football, she might drive out to the countryside with her daughter, Hiroko. They could walk through the woods, enjoy nature—the beautiful flowers, the lofty trees, their branches hanging a hundred feet above the mossy floor of the forest, the birds chirping away.

"Do you mind putting on the heat? It's getting cold."

"It's on all the way," he said. "I think the thermostat is on the bum. Don't worry, when we get home, I'll take care of it."

"Why didn't you have it fixed before we left for Chicago?"

"Because I didn't know it was broken, that's why."

The Thunderbird was more than ten years old. Jack, the mechanic at the Shell station on the corner, complained that it was harder and harder finding parts to repair the old car, and advised Charlie that he'd be better off buying a new one. Instead, Charlie began to use a Spanish mechanic in Newark, who fixed the Thunderbird at half the price that Jack charged him, using old parts from junkyards off the highway.

Tomiko pulled the ends of her coat closer together. Last year she had written a letter to her sister Masako complaining about Charley. Masako wrote her back and reminded her that though Charlie might worry about money too much, he was also faithful and reliable, and had been a good father to Hiroko, who wasn't his natural child.

Poor Masako. Who could have foreseen that she would die from breast cancer before her fortieth birthday? Standing in front of the coffin, Tomiko remembered Masako as a young school girl in her black uniform, her pigtails hanging down almost to her waist, her round cheeks a healthy pink, swinging her sneakers carelessly from side to side, as she walked to school with Jiro and herself. At the funeral, Leonard, her husband, stood silently, his two teen-age sons flanking him, as the minister read the Twenty-third Psalm. He looked so lost, so utterly depressed.

Charlie missed most of the service. After he had dropped her off in front of the funeral parlor, he couldn't find a parking place near the funeral house because they had arrived late. Since he refused to pay fifty cents in the lot across the street from the funeral parlor, he wound up parking behind a movie theater about ten blocks away. When she criticized his bad manners, he threatened to go back to the motel instead of to the cemetery.

The snow intensified, and the wipers, which only operated on low speed, couldn't clean off the snow as fast as it accumulated. They began to climb a steep hill. Charlie gunned the accelerator, but the old car chugged along as if it were suffering from a serious malaise. Charlie's nose was almost bent against the steering wheel as he struggled to see the road more clearly through his thick lenses.

"Can I please listen to the music?" Tomiko asked. "I don't want to think about what's happening to us."

The Accident

"Nothing's happening. Once we get over this hill, I guarantee that we'll be on the Pennsy Turnpike."

Charlie was so confident. Well, he was a lot of bluster and talk, but Masako had been right about one thing: he had always provided for her and Hiroko.

"Music soothes my nerves," she said.

All music was noise to Charlie. She wondered if there wasn't a cure for tone deafness. One missed out on a great deal of pleasure passing through life without being able to enjoy any sort of music.

The Thunderbird swerved from a sharp gust of wind. Charlie switched on the headlights and in the glare of the parallel beams the snowflakes seemed to hurtle themselves against the rush of the giant machine like raging insects. The inside windshield started to fog up.

"Damn defroster," he muttered, and with the back of his hand, he tried to clean the glass.

The snow began to stick on the road. As the car approached the crest of each hill, Tomiko searched for the lights of the Turnpike that Charlie had assured her would be there. There were no motels or restaurants in sight, only farmhouses set back hundreds of yards from the road, barely visible in the enveloping darkness. The car skidded as it descended a steep hill, but Charlie quickly righted it, while whispering something about the front tires being bald.

The snow continued to accumulate, piling up on the windshield faster than the wipers could remove it. Charlie slowed the car to a crawl. He opened the window and reached around with his left hand to try and wipe away the snow sticking to the wiper blade.

"Maybe you ought to pull over and clean it up properly," Tomiko suggested.

She took out her handkerchief and began to wipe the inside windshield as it clouded up, but Charlie waved her off. "You're only making it worse," he said. He switched on the radio. "Listen to the music and relax. Before you know it, we'll be on the Turnpike."

Johnny Cash was singing. Next to Frank Sinatra and Nate "King" Cole, she liked him best. She leaned back against the seat and closed her eyes and listened to "A Boy Named Sue," a song that always made her smile. "Wake me if you need me," she said. Within minutes she was sound asleep.

She thought she was dreaming when she heard Charlie's voice crying, "Jump!" The next moment she felt her body flying forward, her head banging against the windshield. The car had come to a halt, though the motor was still running. She fell back against the seat, dazed, a sharp pain shooting from her forehead. When she looked into the car mirror, she saw a gash on her forehead just above her right eye. Blood was dripping across the eye and down the right side of her face. She took out her handkerchief and wiped the blood away, then pressed the handkerchief against the wound.

"What's happened, Charlie?" she cried out.

The driver's door was open, and then she realized that Charlie wasn't in the car. She peered through the windshield, searching for him, but could only see the two headlight beams cutting like yellow lasers straight into the darkness.

Then she saw him. He was standing directly in front of the car, spotlighted by the high beams. He appeared to be cloaked in white, like some sort of ghostly apparition. His body was bent, his left arm dangling as if it had been dislocated from its socket. He leaned on the hood and stared at her through cracked lenses. She threw open the door on her side and went to him.

He was barely able to support himself. His face was bruised and dirty; his hands were bleeding; the jacket sleeve on his left arm was torn and hanging down. Twigs and grass were mixed with snow over his clothes as well as his face and hair.

"I'm alive." Charlie laughed almost maniacally. "I thought I was dead, but I'm alive."

The car was angled halfway on the shoulder, the back wheels still on the road, the front bumper pressed against a large tree stump. Tomiko concluded that the car must have skidded off the road and hit the tree stump, which had stopped it from going over the embankment. She glanced down the embankment, a gradual ten-foot drop covered with small bushes and pine trees. She was confused. Charlie must have rolled down the hill. How could that have happened?

"Let me help you," she said. Snow was down her neck. She could feel it beginning to melt.

"Don't touch my left arm," Charlie cried. "I think it's broken."

She guided him back behind the wheel, and then went around to the passenger seat. He flopped his head against the steering wheel, his breathing irregular and heavy. Finally he sat up. "You're bleeding," he said.

"I hit my head against the windshield."

In the excitement, she had forgotten about her own injury. Once reminded, she began to feel a throb in her head, and again wiped the blood off the side of her face.

"What happened?" she asked.

"The car went out of control. It was going over the embankment. I tried to wake you, but there wasn't any time."

"I don't understand."

"What else was I supposed to do? There wasn't any time." He stared at her strangely. She didn't know how to respond, and remained silent. Then he said: "The next thing I knew I was lying at the bottom of the hill waiting for the car to come crashing down on me. I thought I was a goner." To her surprise, Charlie began to whimper like an injured puppy.

She wanted to shake him, this man who had been the rock she had leaned on for more than nineteen years, give him back his confidence, even his arrogance if need be.

After a few moments, he calmed down. He shut off the ignition and handed her the keys. "Go in the trunk," he said. "My spare glasses are in the brown suitcase."

She found the glasses and several towels, and returned to the car. Charlie clutched the wheel with his one good hand, while staring ahead through the partially snow-covered windshield. Then to her relief, he took a deep breath and said, "Here we go," and started up the motor. He threw the car into reverse and cautiously inched it back on the road "Thank God, the old boy is still working."

She was encouraged by a bravado that seemed to return to his voice. "Can you drive?" she asked him.

"We'll freeze to death if we stay here."

Once back on the highway, Charlie pulled over on the shoulder and went outside to clean off the windshield with his one good arm. Miraculously, the snow began to abate and visibility improved. She was relieved that Charlie, while grimacing from the pain in his injured arm, still managed to keep the car on the road.

The lights of the Turnpike entrance were at the bottom of the next hill. "There it is," Charlie cried out. "Just like I told you."

Charlie informed the toll booth operator that they had been in an accident and needed a doctor. The man looked at Charlie, then at Tomiko. Within minutes, two uniformed attendants escorted Charlie and Tomiko into the Turnpike building.

The Accident

While they were waiting for the ambulance, Charlie announced to Tomiko that as soon as his arm was better, he'd give her driving lessons.

Charlie waited almost three months after the cast on his left arm was removed before he started to teach Tomiko how to drive. His constant warnings about the dangers of driving drove her a little crazy. "If you get into an accident, our insurance rates skyrocket," was his favorite admonition. "And remember," he would never fail to add, "it doesn't matter whose fault it is."

While practicing parallel curbside parking in the lot behind the County Vocational School, Tomiko threw the automatic transmission into DRIVE instead of REVERSE. Charlie, who had been standing in front of the car, guiding her into a parking spot, was flattened instantly as she pushed down on the accelerator and ran him over. His neck was broken in two places, and he was dead as a mackerel before the ambulance arrived.

During the inquest, Tomiko's lawyer pointed out to the court that the shift indicator on the old car was broken, and Tomiko, who was a beginning driver, had become confused. Jack, the Shell mechanic, testified that he had wanted to replace the indicator on several occasions, but Charlie had always refused, arguing that he knew perfectly well in what gear the transmission was, so what was the point in pulling apart the steering wheel and dashboard. The lawyer also pointed out to the court that Tomiko and Charlie had been married for nineteen years without a hint of discord before this unfortunate accident had occurred. Where was Tomiko's motive for killing Charlie?

The court ruled that Charlie's death was accidental and the prosecuting attorney dismissed the case.

The Prudential Insurance Company paid Tomiko a one hundred and fifty thousand dollar death benefit. In addition, she inherited seventy-five thousand dollars, which, unbeknown to her, Charlie had stashed in a Savings Account, not to mention ten thousand dollars that turned up in a second checking account.

After the estate was settled, Tomiko sold the shoe store, the car, the house and furniture. Afterwards, she and Hiroko returned to Japan to live with Jiro and his family.

She bought Jiro a bigger house, and herself a new Toyota. She went to driver's school and obtained a driver's license, and then she and Hiroko traveled around Japan, something she had always wanted to do while married to Charlie and they were living in Tachikawa.

"I've seen enough of Japan," Charlie would always say to her whenever she talked about visiting places like Kyoto and Nara. His enough of Japan had been a reference to their twenty mile trip into Tokyo once to watch a special performance at the Takarazuka Dance Theatre.

She was very happy now that she was back in Japan, though once in a while she'd get lonely for the USA and would even miss Charlie a little when he'd be lying around the house, a beer in his hand, so contented and relaxed while watching a football game on the TV.

During those moments of restlessness, she'd listen to Frank Sinatra sing That Ole Black Magic, or I Get A Kick Out Of You, on her new Sony quadraphonic music system, and before she knew it, the lonely feeling would pass on as if it had never existed.

Okay, I admit it. My wife and I are health nuts. When our children were small, we would forever lecture them on the importance of eating well. Eating the right foods was like putting high-grade gasoline into the tank to make the car run better. (We actually said things like that.)

The results aren't in, but I wouldn't be surprised if one day our six adult children barbecue both of us on a spit, and after thoroughly digesting our organs, throw our bones to the hyenas.

A TASTE OF CHOCOLATE

While the adult world was being enraptured by the boob tube, Lowell slid down from the sofa and vaporized, moments later to recrystallize in front of *The Great Tempter*. Beckoning him like a *Playboy* cover girl, the refrigerator door yielded easily to his practiced touch, and then it was revealed, monumental in its deliciousness, more appetizing than he had remembered. A trembling index finger tantalized the soft creamy icing before plunging like a burning arrow into its *devil's* flesh, scooping the very life from its already decimated body.

"Lowell!" The world collapsed. "Get away from there!"

A woman called *Mom* slammed shut the refrigerator door, Lowell's innocent finger narrowly escaping amputation. Did she care?

"I wasn't doing anything," Lowell said.

"But I saw you."

She had coal embers for eyeballs and a deadly index finger of her own that pointed straight to one's heart. The blood drained from his face.

"Just looking," he said. In a flash he puckered his lips and slurped the evidence off the short, stubby length of the guilty finger.

"You were after the chocolate cake," she said. "Now don't deny it."

There was no lying to that Supreme Being. "I got hungry," he admitted sheepishly. Inexplicably, he felt like sucking his thumb, a habit he had been forced to shed four years ago if he were going to survive the first grade.

"You're not hungry," she proclaimed.

"How do you know if I'm hungry or not?" he asked. Enough was enough. Ok, so she knew him pretty well, but that didn't include knowing what the inside of his stomach felt like.

"Because we finished supper less than an hour ago."

Lowell glanced up at the clock hanging above the sink. Another piece of damning evidence piling up against him. It had seemed a lot longer than a mere sixty minutes since dinner.

"I can't help it if I'm hungry," he said. Though his protest lacked conviction, the possibility that an injustice of sorts was being inflicted upon him lurked in the back of his mind.

"Did you or did you not have a nice of piece of cake for dessert?"

"It was smaller than anyone else's piece," he declared self-righteously.

That lousy brat of a sister, Lenore, had a piece as big as her head.

"You know why. It's for your own good."

Go ahead and say it. *You're too fat!* "It's not fair," he protested.

"You know the rules."

When she started spouting rules and regulations, he knew the game was up and he might as well surrender and accept his fate. "It's not fair," he repeated in a voice not much louder than a whisper.

Nothing left to do but escape. He turned his back on his mother and ran upstairs to his room where he threw himself on the bed and closed his eyes. When he opened them, he discovered Supreme Being Number Two, his father, standing in the doorway.

"How come?" his father asked him.

Lowell studied the motionless, poised figure. Nothing fat about him. Whenever the bathroom scale indicated that his father had gained half a pound, he would go on a grapefruit juice diet for a week.

"I was hungry," said Lowell.

"Wasn't it only two days ago that we talked about that?"

Lowell scratched his head. "Two days ago?"

There was this continuing struggle to grab hold of the dimension of time, which the adult world managed to throw at you whenever they wished to trap you into confessing a serious crime you were supposed to have committed.

"Your nine years old, almost ten. Not a baby anymore. Am I right?"

"Sure you're right." Always right. Not only slimmer than anyone else's father, but smarter, too.

"Don't be fresh, mister!"

"I'm not fresh."

A menacing step forward. "I mean it."

The relenting, humiliating, "Yessir."

Another step forward. "And don't get fresh with your mother."

Total subjugation. Another, "Yessir." There was in fact never any point in arguing with that big voice.

"You must learn to develop good eating habits."

"I know."

"If you know, then why do you give your mother such a hard time?"

Silence. Lowell's gaze drifted to the wall behind his father. A pennant of the New York Yankees hung obliquely over a painting of his own. Personally, he didn't think much of the painting, a weird mess of assorted watercolors he had scrambled together one boring, rainy afternoon. Everyone made a big deal of it, how talented he was and all, so he let it hang.

The pennant had been obtained during an afternoon ball game his grandfather had taken him to, made memorable by an acute stomach upset suffered after the consumption of his fifth hot dog. He didn't think it was very nice the way his father had yelled at Grandpa after they had returned home. You weren't supposed to yell at your father that way.

"Well, what's it going to be?" asked his father.

"What's what going to be?"

"We were talking about your eating habits."

"I guess it's going to be all right."

His father paused, then he said softly, "It's your life, you know."

Lowell hated that voice, the one that tried to sneak into your brain and trap you into revealing something that was your own personal business. It was a voice almost as bad as the big, loud one that shut up anything you might say to defend yourself.

"Do you mean it?" asked Lowell.

"Of course, I mean it. Every man has to choose for himself."

"Even me?"

"Especially you."

Light from a passing car flashed into the room beneath the Venetian blind. Lowell sat up. "If it's my life, then why can't I be fat?"

"Do you want to be fat?"

"You said it was my life."

His father ran a hand across the top of his head as if checking to see if his bald spot was still there. At the same time, his eyes were shooting upward, which meant that Lowell wasn't worth looking at. When he went through those little gestures, you could generally predict that some sort of tricky talk was on its way and you had to be on your guard if you wanted to come out of the conversation without being totally wiped out.

"Do you want to be the slowest runner on the block?" his father asked.

"But I'm the fastest." A small lie, which the All-Seeing, All-Knowing King of the Hill would soon make him aware of.

"What about Buzzy Schwartz?" Just as he suspected, the man knew everything.

"Okay," he admitted. "Maybe Buzzy's a little faster."

"Don't you want to be as fast as Buzzy?"

"I guess so."

"You could be."

Lowell shrugged. "Not a chance. But I'm faster than Mark, Andy and Howy Jordan." He wasn't sure about Cynthia Margolies. He thought he could beat Cynthia, but he wasn't going to take a chance of getting caught in another lie.

"But you're not faster than Buzzy."

His father sat down at the foot of the bed. Lowell liked it better when he sat down. He appeared less ominous when you could see that big blotch of naked skin on the top of his skull that looked like a bulls-eye surrounded by tufts of dry hay. His glasses slid down a notch as he lowered his head.

"To be the fastest," his father continued, "you must first learn to curb your appetite."

Lowell pondered the relationship between appetite and speed. He had the feeling his father was leaving out some important detail that should be considered. You couldn't always trust him when he went into one of his "it's for your own good" routines.

"What do you mean by 'curb'?" asked Lowell. Words he didn't understand were another one of his father's crafty devices that he liked to use to win arguments.

"Limit it, restrict it. Stop eating so goddamn much!"

Cursing! Well, it was all right to curse if you were mad. But why was *he* mad? He was the guy who last summer had won this gigantic bronze trophy that stood in all its bigness over the mantelpiece to remind one and all how slim and trim and fast a man with a bald spot can be. Was anyone else's father the singles champ of the Nether-hood Tennis Club?

A silent beat. "I'm waiting for an answer."

"I'll restrict my curb," Lowell said with little enthusiasm.

"You 'curb' your eating."

"That's what I meant."

The inevitable. "It's for your own good."

And the only possible response. "I know it."

Lowell touched his gut. It was true that when he was sitting you could grab a handful of skin from his middle. Still, he could do three chin-ups on the crossbar his father had recently installed in the basement exercise room, and that wasn't bad. When Buzzy had tried it, he did only four, maybe five. Lenore couldn't even do one, and she had been allowed to eat a piece of cake the size of the Empire State Building.

"It's settled then," his father said. "No food between meals without permission. And that especially goes for chocolate cake."

Lowell nodded. He was about to totally cave in when the Empress Of Her Domain entered.

"I'm tired of telling him to stay away from that refrigerator," she said to his father.

"Everything's under control, Gert." His father called his mother "Gert" only when he was annoyed with her. Most of the time he addressed her as "Hon." When he'd get lovey-dovey, he'd call her "Pete".

She looked at Lowell. "Before supper we talked about the cake, didn't we?"

"Gertrude, it's all been settled," his father said irritably.

Getrude! That was worse that *Gert*. Seconds after the last time his father had called his mother "Gertrude," she had thrown a spoon halfway across the kitchen that had bounced off his forehead. For the next month he had referred to her as "The Great Mrs. Spoonthrower" whenever they talked.

Were they going to have another big fight, this time over him? He hated it when they quarreled and wished he could do something to stop it before it got started, but he knew that once his mother got a head of steam under her it was like trying to stop a runaway locomotive.

"I've told him a million times," she said. "Stay away from the fattening foods. He doesn't listen."

"I listen," Lowell said in a futile effort to calm her down.

"You say you listen, but you don't hear," she said.

"How can anyone listen and not hear?" asked Lowell, totally bewildered by this adult double-talk.

She looked up and whistled. "It's like talking to the wall," she said.

"Okay, Gert, enough already," his father said. At least he was back to "Gert," instead of "Gertrude," which meant she would be less likely to start throwing spoons anytime soon. "Lowell has agreed to try and be more cooperative in the future," he quickly added.

"I hope so."

His mother was a small, wiry woman, who, when she wasn't subbing at his grammar school, was exercising at a woman's gym on Route 22. He thought she looked stupid in those tight workout suits with her skinny legs and scrawny neck. These days it seemed that he hardly ever saw her, not like when he was little, and once in a while she'd give him a hug just for nothing.

But who wanted to hug a fat kid who never listened?

"I'm not so fat." The words rumbled out of Lowell's mouth like the tenuous sounds of distant thunder.

"What's that?" his father asked.

"He said that he wasn't fat," his mother said as if interpreting for an immigrant who couldn't speak the English language.

"Well, I'm not." Lowell didn't know why tears had begun to well up in his eyes. He felt stupid.

"Okay, you're not fat," his mother said. "But you're not skinny either, and you don't want to be fat, now do you?"

"What kind of a dumb question is that?" his father said, with a new anger creeping into his voice. "Nobody wants to be fat."

"Don't call me dumb," his mother retorted, her tone becoming nasal, a warning to one and all to watch out.

"You're not dumb, the question is dumb," said his father, and then quickly added, "Anyway, why didn't you hide the cake?"

"I shouldn't have to hide food," his mother replied brusquely. "Lowell is old enough to understand the difference between right and wrong."

"Don't get philosophical," said his father. "You hide the cake, you eliminate the problem. It's as simple as that."

Lowell whispered, "I can run as fast as anyone." He quickly wiped away his tears with the back of his hand, hoping that nobody would notice what a pansy he was.

His father stood up and scratched the top of his head. "I think I'll watch TV." He turned to Lowell. "Discussion over. Everything agreed." And he was gone.

It didn't matter if he agreed with his father or not. If his father said it, then that was it, and there wasn't any point in disputing whatever they had been disagreeing over, because his father never changed his mind. "I guess so," Lowell said to himself. "But I'm not fat," he said loud enough for his mother to hear.

"Nobody said you were fat," she said. "You're just a little husky and we don't want you to get fat." The inevitable final word.

After she left, he finished wiping his tears. He was disgusted with himself. Crying was for the birds. Lenore cried every time you gave her a cross-eyed look. But that was okay. She was only six. How did a nine-year old boy stop himself from crying? How did he stop himself from eating? "If you don't eat, you die" was a quote he heard on some boring TV program where a girl who was all skin and bones had stopped eating entirely.

If only he could get his mitts on just a sliver of that chocolate cake. Four layers of solid icing, creamy rich, brimming with a sweetness that made you willing to jump over Niagara Falls to get at. All he had wanted was just another little taste. A lousy, crummy taste.

A Taste Of Chocolate

"I'm a little husky," he said to himself as he viewed his physique from every angle in the mirror on the closet door. "I'm definitely not fat." He sucked in his gut like he sometimes saw his father do when he shaved in the morning and stared into the mirror. When he was older, Lowell decided, and had plenty of money of his own, he'd buy himself thirty-seven hundred million, seven layer, chocolate cakes and eat until he looked like a Good Year Blimp.

He stared at the stupid watercolor he had painted, and then pulled his desk chair over and stood on it. With a vengeance, he yanked the painting off the wall. The next time it rained in the afternoon he wasn't going to waste his time painting stupid pictures. No way. He was going to sit in front of the TV and watch some cartoon that his parents thought was too violent, and stuff his face with a box of saltine crackers, the same kind that his mother liked to nibble on when she was riding her exercise bicycle.

Then he tore up the painting and tossed the pieces into the wastepaper basket. "Eat that," he told them both, and laughed until his ribs hurt.

Last week I read in the Ledger *that in a parking lot of a large suburban mall, there was a dispute over a parking spot, which ended when one of the parties stepped from his car and shot the other person in the heart.*

The man was indicted for murder. On the CBS Six O'clock News, a psychiatrist was at a loss to explain what could have prompted such rage in a person who had never before been involved in any crime, juvenile or adult.

Carl Jung would probably have analyzed the man's action as a reflection of his collective unconscious. If Jung is right, then we are all in trouble.

A MATTER OF PRINCIPLE

At an hour when he would have preferred to have been in bed, Dr. Reginald Fairchild, Chief of Orthopedic Surgery at Outlander Hospital, wheeled his metallic green SL 500 Mercedes roadster through the narrow driveway leading into the parking lot behind the condo complex. He quickly discovered that someone had parked a car in his assigned spot.

Dr. Fairchild drove around hoping he might be able to squeeze between two cars, but soon gave up. The lot was completely full.

"Rats!" he muttered to himself. He was going to have to park on the street at least several blocks from the entrance to his condo building.

Before leaving, he wrote down the license plate number of the car that was illegally parked. Tomorrow he'd file a formal protest to the condo's executive committee. Not that it would do any good. The guilty party was probably someone's guest and legally there was little the committee would be able to do beyond having the car towed away in the unlikely event that it would still be there by the time the committee called the police to have the car removed. He could hear his thirteen-year old son, Alex, telling him to let the air out of the illegally parked car's tires. Not bad advice, Alex. True justice demands revenge. *"An eye for an eye."*

As Dr. Fairchild entered the neck of the driveway leading out of the lot, an old Thunderbird swerved in from the street. On seeing the Mercedes, the other driver braked his vehicle. Since there wasn't room to pass by the Thunderbird, Dr. Fairchild hit his horn, the blast echoing loudly into the fall night. To Dr. Fairchild's surprise, the driver of the Thunderbird honked back, and then shut off his motor and headlights.

"Well," said Dr. Fairchild, "two can play that game."

Without hesitation, he followed suit—off went his own motor and headlights. The driveway was now in near total darkness. The two vehicles remained transfixed, indisputably blocking each other.

By any standards the situation was too absurd, and after a few minutes Dr. Fairchild decided to back up and allow the Thunderbird to pass into the parking lot. He restarted his engine and switched on his headlights. As he was shifting the transmission into REVERSE, he caught a glimpse of the other driver. The man was sitting in a stiff upright position, arms crossed, has face a mask of unyielding arrogance. Dr. Fairchild remembered the uncompromising swiftness in which this man had precipitated the present crisis. An inner voice exhorted him not to capitulate, and like a saint who has heard the *word*, he once again shut off his motor and lights.

A brilliant half-moon slipped from behind a dark cloud and illuminated the driveway with a faint glow. The two vehicles remained facing each other: immobile, bloodless machines. Dr. Fairchild yawned. His flesh ached for sleep, the natural consequence of a long day crammed with exhaustive professional duties. Dressed for the more moderate daytime temperatures, Dr. Fairchild pulled in his coat closer to his body. His thoughts drifted to his warm comfortable condo, less than fifty yards away.

Surrender, he thought. Back up and allow this fool to enter the parking lot, which would do him no good anyway since it was full up. He, himself, would then drive out onto the street and park.

Of course, sacrifice for a cause gave depth to the cause. The doctor saw himself as an aging warrior, chilled and tired, but holding fast in the dead of night against the enemy. No matter what his initial motivation, he was now moved by the principle involved.

Another ten minutes passed. Dr. Fairchild's eyelids became leaden, but he was unwilling to capitulate to the Thunderbird. Then he had a flash of insight. Suppose his antagonist also saw himself as a man of principle. A show of strength and determination was sound strategy when dealing with blind aggression or animal stupidity. But suppose this wasn't the case here. Shouldn't reasonable men be able to find ways to compromise their differences?

Opening the door, he walked to the front of his car and looked straight ahead. The driver of the Thunderbird appeared to ignore him. As the doctor was about to return to his Mercedes, the man's head shot out of his window. The lips on the head moved almost indiscernibly. "Hey, Mac," the lips said.

"Well, well," said Dr. Fairchild, elated at finally making contact with his adversary.

"How 'bout movin' your fuckin' car out of the alley-way?" The hissing sound of the man's voice was more reptilian than human.

"First of all, my name isn't Mac. It's Dr. Reginald Fairchild, and I don't appreciate your obscenity. Do you mind telling me your name?"

"Hilary Clinton."

"Very funny. Perhaps you'd prefer telling your name to the Chief of Police, who happens to be a close friend of mine." A bluff. His relationship with the Chief went back several years when he had been called in to examine the Chief's nephew, who had suffered a simple fracture of his wrist. He had actually spent less than a minute talking to the man.

"Big deal. Okay, the handle is Horace Smith. So now move your fuckin' car."

"Why don't you get out of your car, Mr. Smith, and then we can talk *mano à mano* and attempt to resolve our differences rationally?"

"All right, Mr. *mano à mano*." Smith walked to the front of his own car. "Here I am."

Five yards separated the men. As a member of a professssion that specializes in sizing up people at a glance, the doctor couldn't help but regard Smith as a weird anomaly. Smith's face, with its long flat nose, paper-thin lips, and pointed chin, seem blunted of any human sensitivity.

The doctor proceeded cautiously. "I assume you're as eager to park your car and go home as I am."

"Wrong. I just love sitting around all night playing with myself," Smith sing-songed.

"Don't you think that we ought to try and reach an understanding? After all, the solution to the problem is really quite simple—"

"—Right you are, Mac. You backs up your car, then I drives in. Then you goes ahead and drives out into the street, or any fuckin' place you want."

"I'm older than you, Mr. Smith, and I can tell you that nothing is ever gained by an uncompromising attitude such as yours."

"Yeah, just what my old lady tells me after I belt her around a little."

"You belt your wife around?"

"Every Sunday. It keeps her in check for the week."

Dr. Fairchild coughed uneasily. "Your relationship with your wife is none of my business." Dealing with Smith was not going to be a simple task. Still, as one who championed the settling of differences of opinion with intelligence and reason, the doctor was determined to give this ridiculous entanglement his best shot.

"Can you appreciate the fact, Mr. Smith, that it was I who have made this first move toward settling our dispute? I did this in the spirit of compromise and good will. But I must warn you, that I can be extremely obstinate when provoked. Being dogmatic can only make a bad situation intolerable."

Smith slowly clapped his hands. "Okay, Mac, you win the debating contest. Now move your goddamn car already."

"I am not *Mac*, and I will not move my car. You're the one who has to move. Is that clear, Mr. Smith?" The man's obstinacy was intolerable.

"Yeah, sure, babe. And how do you figure why I should be the one to move?"

"Decency demands it." Dr. Fairchild paused to collect his jangled thoughts. "Remember, Mr. Smith, the right of way belonged to me."

"The right of way don' belong to nobody in an alleyway, for chrissake."

"It's a driveway, Mr. Smith, not an alleyway, and I was approaching the *driveway* well before you turned into the *driveway* from the street."

"Driveway, shmiveway." Smith laughed coarsely, and then said, "Prove it, hotshot."

Dr. Fairchild sighed and placed his hands on his hips. He shook his head sadly. Talking to Smith was an exercise in futility. "You don't want to listen," he said. "I don't see what more I can do if you're unwilling to be reasonable."

"Tell me, Dr. Terrific, what's being reasonable?"

"A recognition of what's fair," Dr. Fairchild shot back with an emphasis on the word "fair."

"Prove it."

Dr. Fairchild stared into Smith's nervous, twitching eyes. The doctor could only speculate on what was coursing through the man's half-baked brain. He seized the moment to press home his point.

"Consider the position of our vehicles. Mine is about ten yards beyond the neck of the entrance into the driveway, while yours is about the same distance from the street. Now the lot extends back some fifty yards or so. To reach this point, I had to drive sixty yards. If you had turned in from the street at the same moment when I had turned to leave the lot, you would have been into it well before I had reached the neck of the driveway. Smith, open your eyes! Pay attention! Now clearly there's your proof that the right of way belongs to me."

Smith yawned mightily, and then said, "Mac, your mathematics sucks."

Dr. Fairchild shrugged. It was discouraging to be a saint in a world of sinners. He might as well have been talking to the machine as to the man.

"There's something I didn't tell you before," Dr. Fairchild said. "I withheld this information as a matter of principle." A Machiavellian smile crossed Smith's face, which at the moment the doctor dismissed as having no special importance. "You see," the doctor went on, "your driving into the parking lot is pointless because there are no parking places available. You're going to wind up parking in the street the same as I am. We're in the same boat, Smith, two peas in a pod, if you don't mind my little simile."

"Peas, my ass. I don' believe nothin' you got to say. Back up, and let me see for myself."

Dr. Fairchild threw up his arms in despair. "I don't know what's the matter with you," he cried, and went back to his car.

Once inside the Mercedes, he leaned against the seat and closed his eyes. Within seconds he dozed off and dreamt of fractured bones dancing on the operating table— disjointed pieces of femurs, tibias, ulnas, vertebrae, shimmying to the syncopated sounds of coughing auto-mobile motors and honking horns.

When he awakened, he was surprised to discover that the dark night had given way to a pre-dawn gray, and that behind him another automobile was blasting its horn. Looking straight ahead he couldn't believe that Smith's Thunderbird was still there, as if rooted in the concrete.

The honking of the car behind ceased and a voice called out, "Hey, Doc, move your car? You're blocking me." The voice belonged to Harold Livingston, another condo owner who lived on the floor below him. Dr. Fairchild would sometimes meet Livingston and his wife, a flashy blonde, on the elevator, and over the years had formed a nodding acquaintanceship with them.

Dr. Fairchild lowered his window and called out "I'm sorry, but I can't."

Livingston stepped from his car and made his way over to the Mercedes. "Car troubles?" he asked the doctor. "Can I help?"

The doctor pointed a finger at Smith, whose face was an emerging shadow in the shimmering pre-dawn light.

"He refuses to move his car. I'm stuck here."

"Something the matter with his car?" asked a puzzled Livingston.

"There are those who prefer to live according to the Law of the Jungle."

"Is that so? Why don't we talk with him?"

"I've tried. Believe me, I've tried. Perhaps you might have a go at it."

Livingston strode toward Smith, who promptly rolled down his window. Dr. Fairchild observed that Smith did most of the talking, his thin, transparent lips moving rapidly, his hands gesticulating wildly. Finally, Livingston returned wearing a dazed expression.

Dr. Fairchild said to Livingston, "Now, perhaps you can appreciate what I'm up against."

"I can't quite figure out what's going on here," Livingston said. "None of it makes any sense."

Dr. Fairchild attempted to explain the principle involved in his dispute with Smith, and then added, "To give in to his demand would be base appeasement."

"I see your point," Livingston reluctantly conceded. "But to tell you the truth, I've got to be in Pittsburgh by noon. That's three hundred and sixty miles of hard driving. So have a heart, Doc."

"I'd like to accommodate you, Livingston, but if he doesn't move, where can I go?"

"I'll back up, then you can back up and drive into my vacated spot."

Dr. Fairchild shook his head from side to side. "That won't work. As soon as I'm clear of the driveway, he'll shoot in and grab the spot before I can turn around."

"It's a possibility," Livingston conceded. "You'd have to hustle."

"Livingston, this is your battle as well as mine. We all stand to lose when principle is allowed to drown in a well of complacency. In effect, we all become a part of the conspiracy."

The entrance of another car turning in from the street distracted the attention of both men. Blocked by Smith's car, the driver blew his horn like a maniac. Heads popped out of the windows from the adjacent buildings hurling obscenities into the early morning dusk.

Smith jumped out of his car and began to talk to the new driver. A few moments later Smith and the new man were headed in the doctor's direction. The new man introduced himself as Blumberg.

"I'll come straight to the point," said Blumberg. "Your car is blocking the alleyway—"

"—Driveway," Dr. Fairchild said, not caring for this intruder's nasal, unfriendly tone.

"Whatever!" cried Blumberg. "Are you some sort of nut?"

"Ripples grow into tidal waves, Mr. Blumberg," retorted Dr. Fairchild. "When the general well being of a community is threatened, no matter how trivial the threat may appear at the time, its citizenry must stand firmly together to combat it, or ultimately suffer the consequences of its indifference."

"Call out the guys in the white suits," said Blumberg.

"You're wasting your time, Blumberg," said Dr. Fairchild. "The lot's full up. You might as well park in the street."

"I'd like to check that for myself, if you don't mind."

Livingston stepped forward. "You know, Dr. Fairchild, it seems to me that your principle lacks depth. Surely, it's not worth the inconvenience that it's causing all of us."

"Here, here," cried a jovial Smith.

"A principle cannot be measured qualitatively," said Dr. Fairchild feeling refreshed from his few hours of sleep.

"Admittedly some are good and some are bad, depending on the men who make them. In this instance I think the facts speak for themselves."

"Yeah, well here's a fact for you, pal," began an irate Blumberg. "I've been working all night, and if I don't catch a little shut-eye, I'm going to get a little crazy."

Smith pointed a finger at Dr. Fairchild. "You see, Mr. Hotshot, everybody's against you. Now back up and let us through."

Dr. Fairchild shouted at Smith, "I'll not take orders from you. You're nothing but an—an *Immoralist*.

Livingston pleaded, "Have a heart, Doc? Pittsburgh by noon. Remember?"

Fresh waves of righteous indignation swept over the doctor. He was alone, but not without courage. He said to Blumberg and Livingston, "Why is it you demand that I be the one to move? Why not *him*?" He glared at Smith, who responded with one of his sleazy smirks.

Then Livingston said, "Why don't you both back up? After Blumberg and I are out of the way, you and Smith can solve your dispute any way you want to. By doing this, you'd not be interfering with our rights. That is also a principle to be considered."

Suddenly Smith banged a fist against a fender. "All right, I'll do it," he exclaimed. "I'll move."

All eyes became riveted on Dr. Fairchild, who, feeling the weight of their unanimous gazes, shook his head sadly. Then slowly his shoulders drooped, and he experienced a deep sense of loss.

"Okay," he finally said, "but no tricks, Smith."

The men went back to their automobiles. Motors were cranked on simultaneously, and the driveway, enclosed on both sides by buildings, echoed the roar of the engines, a sound that could have been mistaken for the start of a racing car event.

Dr. Fairchild looked into the rear view mirror, then ahead. Both Blumberg and Livingston had already backed up. Now it was up to Smith and himself. He threw his transmission into REVERSE.

He was about to press down on the accelerator when he once again considered the possibility that if Smith reneged and didn't back up into the street as he had promised, he'd beat him to Livingston's vacated spot.

"Go," the doctor cried out the window to Smith.

"Go ahead yourself!"

"We'll do it together."

Both men stared defiantly at each other, waiting for the other to make the first move. Dr. Fairchild gripped the wheel tightly, his body growing rigid, his heart beating hard and fast. His head began to whirl, and for a fraction of a second he again saw the bones, fractured and dancing at dazzling speeds. Suddenly he didn't care about beating Smith for the vacated parking space. Only the *Principle* mattered.

Dr. Fairchild threw the Mercedes back into DRIVE, released the hand break, and slowly inched forward. Smith accepted the challenge. The two powerful machines crept closer, the gap closing between them at a microcosmic pace, until finally their front bumpers made contact.

Experiencing an exhilarating catharsis of flesh and spirit, Dr. Fairchild pressed his foot down hard on the accelerator. His magnificent automobile, well oiled and bursting with power, responded perfectly to his touch, and the two vehicles merged into each other, bumpers, grills, fenders, all fusing into one cohesive mass until it was impossible to distinguish where one car ended and the other began.

"Run to the Hills" is a fictionalized account of a tragedy that occurred at the Watchung Reservoir some twenty years ago. Two of the boys involved were friends of my son.

It is the sort of incident that has been dramatized in one form or another numerous times over the years, which makes this particular story no less poignant or diminishes in any way the failure of a suburban society, even today, to understand a mentality that has taken hold of its teen-age children.

RUN TO THE HILLS

In the entire eleventh grade at Clark High School, I was probably the only person willing to hang out with Eugene Heiber. When asked by my classmates why I bothered to hang out with such a loser, I had no answer other than to say that Eugene wasn't all that obnoxious once you got to know him. I think what appealed to me most about Eugene was that he didn't seem to care that everyone thought he was a little shit.

What also appealed to me was Eugene's wheels— not ordinary wheels, but a flaming red, deluxe brand new 1981 Corvette, in remarkably good condition, especially when you consider that fifty percent of the time when Eugene was driving, he was totally stoned.

On the last Sunday in March, fortified with two six-packs and three joints, Eugene and I decided to motor to the reservoir where we figured everybody would be getting high to celebrate the passing of another ass-freezing New Jersey winter.

We could barely hear each other over Iron Maiden's heavy metal blasting from the eight-track cassette player while we drove toward the highway. *"White man came across the sea, brought us pain and misery. . . Run to the hills run for your lives—"*

My mind settled into the music, Dave Murray's electric guitar drifting in and out, a hard, dissonant sound that expressed an almost paranoid anger toward an indifferent establishment. And Bruce Dickinson's screaming wail, the Air Raid Siren's personal protest: *"We fought him hard we fought him well. . . Run to the hills, run for your lives."*

"You want a joint?" asked Eugene, breaking my train of thought.

"I don't like to mix weed with beer," I said.

"What's the big deal?"

"No big deal. I just don't like to mix it." It wouldn't have been cool to admit to Eugene that the combination of alcohol and grass always made me a little sick, like there was a giant elastic band inside my brain stretching it apart. In those high school days, friendship was all mixed up with drugs and alcohol.

For nothing, we began to talk about our parents. Bitching about parents was one of our most popular topics of conversation, next to knocking classmates. You couldn't blame my parents for always getting on my case, especially since my last report card was a string of C's. My trademark was mediocrity. With Eugene it was a different story. He had decent grades, but since he was supposed to have an IQ over 140, his parents expected him to be an honor student.

"All they care about are their possessions," said Eugene. "They want to line me up with their expensive furniture, their His and Hers Mercedes', the summer home in Martha's Vineyard and I don't measure up. If they can't brag about it, it has no value."

"What're you bitchin' about?" I said. "They gave you this car. You ought to get down on your knees and kiss their collective asses."

"It was just a goddamn bribe. I promised I'd give up all the dope and stuff after the last time I got wasted and the cops picked me up."

"A fucking Corvette. I still can't get over it."

"My father writes it off through the business."

"How do you write off a car?"

"Taxes, jerk-off. He depreciates the car, then after a couple of years sells it and makes a profit."

"What are you talking about?"

"You're ignorant, Grossman. Tax loopholes. You got to know the angles or you wind up giving everything to 'Uncle.'"

The Corvette slowed to twenty behind a banged-up '68 Dodge. Without hesitation, Eugene crossed the double line and shot around the Dodge, narrowly missing an oncoming pick-up.

"If you want to kill yourself," I said, "don't include me in your plans."

Two months ago my father confiscated my driver's license after I'd been accused of a hit and run. The case was supposed to come up in court in two weeks. Some weasel reported that I'd backed into a pick-up in the parking lot outside of Caldor's. The pick-up had been parked at this crazy angle and I never saw it. The driver must have been as drunk as I was.

Having no wheels was like being confined to a hospital bed.

Eugene hit the gas to beat the red and crossed over to the highway. In a matter of seconds, he had accelerated the Corvette to sixty-five, weaving in and out of the Sunday traffic like a stock car racer. A young woman shook a fist at him after he had tailgated her BMW, and then passed her with a burst of speed. "Rich bitch!" he cried before he waved his middle finger at her.

"Why are you angry at her?" I asked. "You almost ran her off the road."

"It wasn't even close."

"You're gonna get busted," I warned him.

"Who cares?"

"You think your father's gonna get you out of every jam?"

Last month, the high school tried to suspend Eugene for smoking weed in the john. Eugene wound up doing Saturday detention for two weeks after his father met with the head of the Board of Education, an old law school friend.

"He's gotta, or the old lady will make him sleep by himself in the guest room."

The idea that his mother might withhold sexual favors from his father was so hilarious to Eugene that he threw up his hands as he laughed, the Corvette narrowly missing the center divider before he regained control of the wheel.

The tape droned on: *"Riding through dust clouds and barren wastes. . . Fighting them at their own game. . Run to the hills, run for your lives."*

"You play the same tape over and over," I said.

"Yeah, well I happen to think it's a great tape."

"You're such a fool, Heiber."

Eugene shrugged, and then began to sing the tape's lyrics. After a while, he said, "Later, you want to do some coke? I know where we can get good stuff cheap."

"I'm not into coke."

Several months ago, I was at a party in Scotch Plains and was goaded into doing a line. The high was terrific, but the cost was twenty dollars and the drug made my heart beat so hard I thought I was going to have a heart attack. To pay off the dealer, I stole the twenty out of my mother's purse. When she discovered she was missing the money, she accused me of taking it.

"You don't have any goddamn proof!" I shouted at her. I never shouted at my mother, who was really a very nice person. Afterwards, I felt like a complete shit, and vowed I'd never steal from her again, a promise I'm ashamed to admit I did not keep.

"You know, I don't give a damn what anyone thinks of me," Eugene said. "I'm goin' to live my life the way I want to live it."

"You gotta have friends," I said.

"You gotta stand up for what you think is right, or you're nothing but a worm."

A month ago, Eugene and I were strolling down the hallway at the high school when Eugene spotted Zeke Krowicki patting Amy Levenson's nice, round butt as she walked by him. Amy never broke stride. Eugene, who has openly acknowledged to having a hardon for Amy since the fifth grade, called Krowicki *an asshole.* Zeke, an all-county offensive tackle, two hundred and ten pounds of bone and muscle, grabbed Eugene by the throat.

Eugene whispered to Zeke that if he didn't get his *fucking* hands off his *fucking* throat, one day he would cut off his *fucking* balls. Everyone, including Zeke, knew how crazy Eugene was, and, after a moment's reflection, Zeke let go of Eugene's neck. Still, you had to wonder how long Eugene could get away with such *chutzpah* before someone like Zeke changed the anatomy of his face.

By the time we arrived at the reservoir, we had already consumed more than half a six-pack. Just as we figured, the grassy mall was jammed with kids from all over Union and Morris County. Music was everywhere, mostly disco, what we'd refer to as *voodoo* stuff. One could dance to disco music, but personally, I found it boring. *Heavy metal* was loud, hard, and fast. When my friends and I were on a high, we wanted *heavy metal.*

We weaved our way in and out of groups of teens, only a few of whom we recognized from the Clark area, until we entered the woods and found a secluded clearing near the lake. The music from Eugene's portable stereo blasted away, creating a sound barrier against all outside noises. We broke open another two cans of Bud and settled down to enjoy the music and the good, clean spring air.

With the fourth can of beer, my head began to buzz. I stretched backwards and closed my eyes, blocking out parents and teachers who liked to keep reminding me what a dumb shit I was. ("Benjamin is not living up to expectations. He could do much better if he wanted to," was the standard note sent home at each marking period to my parents.)

"On the run kill to eat. . .Do what I want, as I please—"

Eugene rolled over on his back and did a shoulder stand. "I can hold this position for five minutes," he bragged. The cigarette that had been hanging out of the corner of his mouth dropped to the ground.

I barely managed to crush the smoldering butt with my beer can before it singed Eugene's nose. "You're a freak, Eugene."

"I'm meditating."

Two girls walked by. Eugene chirped like a bird, and then called out to them. "Want a beer?"

One of the girls, a pale, red-haired teen-ager, stopped and stared at Eugene. "Who's your upside-down friend?" she asked me. She was chomping on a huge wad of bubble gum.

"He just landed," I said. "Where you hanging out?"

"Around the bend," said the redhead. "Have I seen you before?"

Eugene dropped down from his shoulder stand. "At the zoo," he said.

"Your upside down friend is a comedian," the other girl said. She was short and stocky and her blue jeans seemed painted to her body. She appeared eager to move on.

"Yeah, man, I be de funniest guy in de whole world," said Eugene.

"Ignore the spaceman," I said. "Where you from?"

"Roselle Park, " said the redhead.

"Roselle Park!" Eugene cried. "Not *the* Roselle Park. My God, *senorita*, you must be a celebrity."

The redhead suppressed a giggle, then blew a gigantic bubble. "See you," she said, and trotted after her friend.

I stared at them until they edged past a cluster of trees and disappeared. "You've got a great line, Eugene. You really know how to attract women."

"Women!" Eugene guffawed. "That, my dear partner in crime, is jailbait."

Eugene lit a joint and took a long drag before passing it over to me. Once again I turned down the joint, this time without explanation.

"I'll bet little Miss Roselle Park wouldn't mind sharing this weed with the comedian from Clark," Eugene said.

"Why don't you go ask her?"

A squadron of blue and white ducks swam to the shore. Almost all the ice on the lake had melted, and I wondered how ducks survived during the worst part of the winter when the lake was iced over. It was nice lying next to the water, watching the ducks and all. Even if

Eugene was a pain in the butt, I was glad to be with him, glad to be out of the house, away from my parents, sitting under an open sky.

Eugene stood up, his portable stereo in one hand, the joint in another. "Let's find those little titties from Roselle Park," he said.

"Do we have to?" I asked, at the moment feeling comfortably grooved. "Why don't you find them and bring them back here."

"Grab the six pack and let's go."

Eugene started down the side of the lake in the direction that the girls had come from. Reluctantly, I followed, figuring that I'd better stay close to Eugene if I wanted a ride home.

Sitting around a small campfire were three boys and the redhead. The girl in the tight jeans was leaning up against a tree, smoking a cigarette. The boys were passing around a pint of Seagrams Seven.

The redhead stood up. "Look what's arrived—the hit men from Clark."

"Hi yo, Silver," Eugene said.

Without waiting for an invitation, Eugene marched up to the campfire and flopped down between the redhead and a tall boy. I sat just beyond the ring, behind one of the other boys, a husky mutant with a crew haircut that looked like someone had implanted a big, round wire brush in his scalp. I eyed the girl against the tree, but she didn't seem to notice me, her gaze fixed upwards at the spiraling branches.

"Trade you," Eugene said to the tall boy next to him. He dragged on the joint, and then passed it over to him.

The boy examined it carefully, sniffing it before smoking it. "Very good stuff," he said, before he coughed hard several times. He passed over what was left in the pint of whiskey to Eugene. "I'm Donny." He held out a hand to shake.

"Yeah, man," said Eugene, so bombed that he didn't notice the hand. "Very invigorating." He finished off the pint in one gulp.

Donny reached into a paper bag and produced an unopened pint. "Fear not, hit man from Clark, we come well-prepared."

I opened a new can of beer. I tried to remember how many beers I had already drunk. The hell with it, I thought. Have fun and worry about getting sick when it happens.

I tried to make conversation with the big ape sitting in front of me. He owned a peculiar grimace that seemed permanently imprinted on his face. "Are you from around here?" I asked him.

"Yeah," the boy grunted. He was enormously broad-shouldered and wore a velvet jacket decorated on the back with a golden football and beneath, the word VARSITY.

I took a long swig from the beer can. "I'm Benjy Grossman."

The boy shrugged. "Excellent," he said, "so you're Benjy Grossman." Then he turned and faced me directly. Beneath the grimace was a menacing look on his big, square face. I didn't know what his problem was but then, to my relief, the boy-ape said more affably, "I'm Charley Appel."

"Who are the girls?" I asked.

"Jailbait," said Charley Appel.

Eugene had also said *jailbait*. Who in this group wasn't *jailbait*? I looked toward Eugene, who was talking non-stop to the redhead. The tall boy, Donny, was staring at Eugene with an amused smirk on his face. I could tell that Eugene was showing off when he began to insert obscenities into the conversation. The third boy, who, I was later to discover was named Ziggy, kept staring at Eugene when he wasn't glancing at his biceps, bared as a result of a constant rerolling up of his shirt-sleeves.

"You got more beer?" Charley Appel asked me.

I handed him my last can. New friendship demanded sacrifice.

Charley tore open the top of the can and quickly consumed it. Not even a small "thanks." The guy was a cretin.

Eugene turned up the volume of his portable stereo, and the exaggerated, feverish sound of Iron Maiden immediately dominated the atmosphere, just about stifling all conversation. *"On the run, kill to eat. . . Do what I want as I please—"*

Two men approached the group, slowing down as they neared it. Stopping, they stared at the teen-agers, and then went on without a word. Undercover cops, I wondered, or a couple of curious adults checking the party habits of the younger generation? If they were cops, the party was *finis*. Signs prohibiting alcohol were posted all over the reservoir.

"—Now you see me, now you don't—"

"Christ Almighty, does he have to play the music so goddamn loud?" asked Charley.

"That's the way Eugene likes his Iron Maiden,*"* I said. "He thinks everybody likes it that way."

"Eugene? What kind of faggot name is Eugene?" Charley asked.

I shook my head. Was *Charley* any less of a faggot name than *Eugene*? And what about *Benjy*? What about anyone's name? I finished my beer, then remembered that Charley, the Neanderthal hulk from Roselle Park, had drunk my last one.

An argument erupted between Eugene and Donny. I didn't hear what had prompted the shouting, but figured it probably had something to do with the redhead. The *"fuck yous"* began to fly freely between the two boys after they jumped to their feet. Eugene stared up at the bigger Donny. His fists were clenched, and his eyes were blazing.

Before I could interfere, Eugene shoved Donny hard, but the shove hardly budged Donny, who nonchalantly took a step backwards. Donny began to laugh demonically. "You little shit," he shouted, and, without warning, booted Eugene's portable stereo. Instantly, Iron Maiden was muted.

Ziggy, in an apparent need to demonstrate group solidarity, stepped up and finished off the stereo with a wicked kick of his own.

Eugene was stunned. Looking forlornly at his broken player, he picked it up and observed that one side of the machine had completely caved in; transistors and wires poked out of the huge hole like the guts from an injured animal.

"Hey, Eugene, you gotta name like a faggot," called Charley, rising to his feet. I noted that a standing Charlie was an impressive sight. His varsity football jacket could have been earned by his mere presence on the football field.

There followed another series of *"fuck yous"* from Eugene while staring at his ruined stereo, his loud-mouthed child that would no longer provide him untold hours of pleasure in the solitude of his room where all existence began and left with Iron Maiden's syncopated message of life and death. *"Fuck* all of you!" he shouted.

I went to Eugene's side. "Come on, Eugene," I whispered. "Let's get out of here." I nudged his shoulder hard.

"Yeah, get the creep out of here," Ziggy said, as he once again rolled up his sleeves.

"I ain't going nowhere," said Eugene, "not until you bastards pay for the damage to this box. You hear me; I want damages. Eight-eight dollars and fifty cents, to be exact."

"It's a piece of second-hand shit," said Donny. "Get it fixed and I'll give you five bucks."

Ziggy and Charley laughed. Donny was clearly the tribal wit.

"It was brand new," Eugene said. "Eighty-eight dollars and fifty cents." He dropped the broken stereo and solidly planted his feet on the muddy earth.

"Eugene, let's get out of here. Please," I pleaded with him.

Charley had moved in behind Donny. How come Donny, Charley and Ziggy didn't appear as formidable to Eugene as they did to me? But you had to admire Eugene's courage, even if it was suicidal. "Listen, we came here to relax and have a little fun," I said to the trio of boys from Roselle Park. "Not to fight."

"We're having fun," said Donny.

The redhead threw up her hands in disgust. "Big shots," she said, and went over to her girlfriend, who seemed more interested in smoking Eugene's joint than in the argument.

"Bastards," Eugene said. "You think you can destroy someone's property and not be responsible?"

Quite remarkably, I saw that Eugene had suddenly metamorphosed into his lawyer father's son.

I grabbed Eugene's arm, but Eugene shrugged me off and continued to shout at Donny: "You lousy mothers, you know how many goddamn hours I had to work at MacDonald's to buy that box? I want my money or I'm getting the cops."

As far as I knew, Eugene had never as much as set a foot into a MacDonald's for fear of food poisoning, let alone cook Big Macs at a minimum wage.

"Come on, Eugene," I implored him. "Let's go."

Too late! Without warning, Donny took hold of Eugene by the shoulders and spun him around, then kept pushing him until Eugene stumbled into a small clump of bushes. Then Donny picked up the broken stereo and heaved it after Eugene, the already mangled player striking against the tree, its back end splitting in half—a final, fatal blow to Eugene's eighty-eight dollars and fifty cents instrument of joy.

I grabbed Donny around the neck, but Charley and Ziggy sent me spinning toward the burnt-out fireplace. I wound up on my backside, staring at that naked blue sky that had seemed so peaceful moments before. Slowly, I sat up, the fight having been quickly knocked out of me and I watched in dismay as Eugene, once again on his feet, charged Donny, the swiftness and suddenness of the attack surprising the larger boy and knocking him down. A stunned Donny looked up at Eugene in disbelief, and then he jumped up and, with the help of Charley and Ziggy, grabbed Eugene and carried him down to the lake, where they tossed him into the near-freezing water.

Furiously, Eugene tried to scramble up the short, steep embankment, but was immediately thrown back into the water by the three boys.

"Cool off!" shouted Donny.

Mud clinging to his pants, Eugene sloshed his way through the knee-deep water along the embankment, looking for a new way up. But the boys followed him and continued their game of pushing him back into the lake whenever he tried to climb the embankment until Eugene, in frustration, gave up. Standing in waist-high water, he put his hands on his hips and cursed them in three different languages.

"That's enough," I cried.

I jumped to my feet and ran between the boys to try and haul Eugene out of the water. After a lot of pushing and shoving, the boys threw me into the water as well.

Slowly, I dragged myself to my feet. The icy water cut through my pants and my balls felt as if they were on fire. Though weighted down by the mud on my shoes and pants, I clawed my way back up the embankment, only to be met and thrown back into the water by Charley Appel. Standing next to Eugene, I shouted, "Cut it out already, goddammit!"

The boys laughed. "Take a swim," said Donny.

"Yeah, take a swim," echoed Ziggy.

Charley alone would have been an insurmountable barrier to climb around, let alone all three boys. I looked for help and noticed an opening in the woods about twenty yards down the embankment.

"Come on, Eugene," I said, but Eugene wasn't listening. His entire body covered with mud, he looked like a World War II commando. Undaunted, he once again forged up the embankment, swinging and kicking, only to be beaten back into the freezing water.

I dragged myself away, sloshing along the lake's edge. Ziggy pursued me for a few yards, but then went back to continue to harass Eugene.

Once past the clearing, I discovered several teen-agers sitting around listening to music and smoking cigarettes. One of the boys came over and helped me up the embankment.

"Hey," he cried back to the others, "he must be from Atlantis." Then he said to me, "You okay, man?"

Exhausted, I looked back toward where I had left Eugene, hoping that Eugene had decided to follow me.

Instead, I saw Donny at the water's edge, hollering at Eugene. "Hey, stupid, come on back. We give up." And there was Eugene, looking like some giant, sluggish reptile, about twenty yards into the water, inching his way across the narrow lake.

Eugene raised both his fists above his head in defiance, until to everyone's astonishment, he slipped out of sight, the waters reaching up and swallowing him without warning. For a fraction of a second, those same fists reappeared, but then there was a giant thrashing sound and, unbelievably, Eugene disappeared completely. Moments later the water's surface assumed a deadly, calm appearance.

Donny dashed into the lake, but before he had taken more than ten steps, he fell on his face and began to sink in the mud. Big Charley went after him and hauled him to his feet. Fearlessly, Donny again set out in the direction where Eugene had gone under, and once again Charley went after him and had to pull him back in.

I was on my feet. "Eugene, Eugene!" I hollered.

I started back down the embankment, but I had lost all feeling in my legs and couldn't sustain my balance. Two of the boys grabbed me as I was rolling into the water and helped me back up to the clearing. I collapsed against the trunk of a large oak.

I had trouble breathing, and for a moment thought I was going pass out. I looked out across the lake, once again searching for Eugene.

"Damn you, Eugene," I cried. "Stop fooling around."

I don't know how long I lay propped up against that hard oak tree before I realized there was a major commotion going on, teens running from everywhere toward the lake, the sounds of sirens in the distance. Then I spotted a couple of cops standing at the edge of the embankment looking out over the lake.

I held my breath, hoping for the miracle of a defiant, nasty, disagreeable Eugene, alive with his Iron Maiden, jumping up and down on the opposite shore threatening to get even.

"Spit in your eye, I will defy. . . Run to the Hills, Run to the Hills."

Standing up, I slowly made my way toward the water's edge near where the cops were standing. One of them was pointing toward the middle of the lake. From out of nowhere, a formation of geese skimmed across the surface of the water landing just beyond the point where Eugene had disappeared, almost as if they had been consigned to mark the spot. The water rippled concentrically in their wake before the geese took off again, and then, after a few seconds, all was as still as death itself.

I lived the first seventeen years of my life with my family in a six-room apartment in the city of Newark. Backyards were all concrete and, except for an occasional potted plant sitting on a window sill, you had to ride to the park to find any greenery. Once in a while, neighbors would go at each other over the garbage and debris that would accumulate by the curbs and clog the sewers, but for the most part, nobody really seemed to care very much about the condition of the sidewalk and alleyway that surrounded the building in which you lived.

I was, therefore, totally unprepared when later in life I bought a home in the suburbs and discovered that suburbanites regarded the maintenance of their property and the property of those living around them as a guiding principle of their lives.

Flowing green lawns and exotic shrubbery defined a community, frequently taking precedence over serious social issues. If you were to question that principle, you, your wife, your children and even your dog became the enemy.

Dinga Goes To Trial

I was enjoying a peaceful moment in the den reading a John Gresham novel and listening to a new recording of Beethoven's Ninth when my wife, Helen, stormed into the room, her nice round face all flushed with rage.

"Richard, I want you to get rid of Dinga immediately."

When Helen called me by my proper name 'Richard' instead of the usual 'Dick' or 'Hon', I knew she meant business.

"What do you mean 'Get rid of Dinga'?"

"I refuse to live in the same house with that dog one more day," she cried.

Dinga Goes To Trial

These were harsh words from an easy-going, even-tempered woman, since we were talking about an animal that had been an integral part of our household for the past eight years. Being a wise guy, I considered a wise crack, given the nature of this extreme demand, and then I realized that this wife of mine for the past forty-four years, a person I would run into a burning house to save, was on the verge of tears.

"Calm down," I said, "and tell me what's going on." I mean even Dinga, a mongrel who admittedly lived according to her own rules, should be allowed to tell her side of the story before being kicked out of the house, notwithstanding that it was her accuser who was doing the telling.

"Didn't you hear all the shouting outside?"

"I must have blocked it out."

I'm good at that, an old habit acquired in the early part of my life when I was forced to study in a room where even with the windows shut, the sounds of the city could be deafening.

"I was raking leaves in the front when Dinga flew out of the front door and raced by me as if I didn't exist."

"Don't tell me she did it again."

The 'again' was a reference to a year ago when Dinga had escaped the house and used as her designated toilet the lawn three doors down the block. One of the new owners of the house came storming over, banging on our front door, not bothering with the doorbell. Upon opening the door, I encountered a young woman, her handsome features all contorted in anger.

Without bothering to introduce herself, she declared our dog to be a serious menace to the community, and then went on to state that she did not deserve to have her lawn obliterated because we exercised no control over our animal, and finally that she was going to report the crime to the police. Our dog would never be allowed to deface her property again. Before I had an opportunity to respond, she turned and tramped across my lawn to the street.

133

Our home is in Scotch Plains, New Jersey, a quiet, suburban community about fifteen miles southwest of Newark where policemen are trained to be overly polite to the residents. I was, therefore, not surprised when the policeman, who knocked on our door thirty minutes later, apologized four different times in the course of explaining that he was required to respond to all calls. He seemed greatly relieved when I confessed that Dinga was guilty as charged and assured him that it would never happen again.

The next day we received a summons from the town and I immediately went down to the police station and paid a twenty-dollar fine.

Following that incident, our clan, which included children and grandchildren, who moved in and out of our nest like gypsies, gathered together and we all agreed to be especially careful not to leave open a door that would allow our villainous cur to escape the house without being leashed.

I must confess that Dinga running around the neighborhood was not a recent phenomena. About eight years ago, my daughter, Debbie, had brought home this mangy, malnutritioned, abused mongrel, whom my grandchildren named Dinga because they claimed she resembled the Australian wild dog, though in fact she had a soft brown coat and a big bushy tail and looked to me more like a fox than a dingo.

We resuscitated her back to life, but were never able to completely train her. She remained always this spirited animal who preferred the freedom of the streets to the confinement of a house. Though over the years, she had tempered her need to run loose, now and then, when given the opportunity, she'd break out, not returning to the house until she became hungry. A stray dog was not an uncommon sight in our neighborhood, but to my knowledge, this new neighbor, who turned out to have the curious name of Barbara Brothels, was the first one to file a complaint with the police.

"How could it have happened?" I asked. "We've been so careful."

"It happened."

"Where's Dinga now?"

"I went and got her. While I was cleaning up her mess, that horrible woman stepped out of the house and began to scream and curse at me. I never was so embarrassed."

"What did you do?"

"Do? What could I do? I had to suffer that woman's abuse because of your dog."

My dog? Not rational, but who could blame Helen for being a little irrational after such an experience. "You should have thrown the stuff back into her face," I said.

"I was so embarrassed I wanted to die." And then my sweet, little wife rose up on her toes and shouted: "Now you get rid of that dog forever, Richard. Do you hear me? Put down that stupid book and get rid of that dog."

Helen never shouts. I was being asked to make a choice where there was no choice.

"Okay, I'll do it," I said. "Now please try and calm down."

What was going on in this suburban nightmare in which we lived when a civilized thirty-year old woman could whack out over a dog turd on her lawn and publicly humiliate a sixty-five year old woman, who I knew to be one of the kindest women on this planet? I wondered if Barbara Brothels was just as maniacal over the industrial pollutants that defiled our air, air that her children, all of our children, breathed on a daily basis. My next-door neighbor, in his own way probably the most generous man on the block, labored for hours each day trimming his lawn, and in the process spewed hundreds of gallons of toxic gasoline fumes into the atmosphere. Neighbors across the street, rather than offend him, spent hundreds of dollars putting in an electronic fence to contain their two dogs. There was probably more than a dozen landscaping and lawn mowing companies operating in our town, the roar of huge, commercial lawn mowers a constant on our block.

After putting together medical records and a week's supply of dog food, I drove Dinga to the nearest dog pound, which turned out to be off Route 22 in Plainfield.

"Can you find her a home?" I asked this very nice young woman who worked the front desk at the pound. You could tell after the briefest of conversations that she loved animals more than humans.

The woman came around the counter and squatted next to my Dinga and petted her gently. "She's an old one, isn't she?" she said.

"She doesn't eat much and she's still a terrific watch dog." I think I must have sounded like some ancient, over-the hill-salesman desperate to sell a useless product.

"I doubt if we'll be able to place her," the woman said with a certain real regret. "You might want to try and put an ad in the paper. Or you could even advertise her over the internet."

"I can't take her home." I was about to launch into the reasons why, but this woman wasn't the sort of person to whom one would find a sympathetic audience when it came to explaining why you didn't want a dog around anymore. Then I asked with trepidation, since I already knew the answer, "What happens if I leave her here and you can't find her a home?"

She handed me a two-page pamphlet. "We do our best, but we have space limitations. It's all explained in there."

I gave her the dog food and medical records, and paid an eight-dollar fee. On my way out of the building, I turned and watched the woman lead Dinga through a side door into the kennels. I stopped for a moment and thought I ought to make sure that Dinga wasn't going to be housed in some four-by-four cage where she'd hardly have room to turn around, but what would be the point of torturing myself further. Driving home without Dinga lounging in the back seat was not one of the high points of my life.

Dinga Goes To Trial

At home, I handed Helen the pamphlet the woman from the pound had given me and then, without a word went upstairs to my room and took out my violin, my best escape in a world gone mad.

About an hour later, Helen interrupted me.

"Now what," I said.

"We're going back."

"I don't get it."

"Didn't you read the pamphlet?"

I shrugged. "What was there to read?"

"Don't you understand? If they don't find a home for Dinga, they're going to gas her. How could you leave her in a place like that? What's the matter with you, Richard? Have you completely lost your mind?"

"But—"

"Put away that awful violin and let's get going?"

"It's past five. There may be no one there now. Why don't we go tomorrow morning?"

"Are you crazy? They could be marching her right now into the ovens. That place is no better than Auschwitz."

If one were to judge by the way Dinga was relaxing in her little cubicle, you'd have to conclude that she wasn't too concerned about any *final solutions*. She gazed up at us with an indifferent look, asking us, I think, where've we been and why had it taken us so long to come back and retrieve her.

Okay, so Dinga had been liberated from the dog pound, but now what? What would happen if she got out of the house and once again wound up squatting on that woman's lawn? Dinga, that neurotic monster, half-fox, half-dingo, had turned our house into domestic chaos.

After a heated debate, we settled on our own *final solution,* which wound up costing a mere twelve hundred bucks between the fence in the backyard, and the electronic collar and power transmitter that was mounted on the wall next to the front door.

137

Dinga Goes To Trial

Debbie was the first one through the front door with the transmitter turned on. Dinga, as was her custom, made a beeline for her. Once within range of the transmitter, the poor animal's hair stood up on end before she turned and raced upstairs as if she had been shot from a canon. She crawled under our bed and refused to move for the next day and a half.

Cruel, yes, but what was our alternative short of the gas pipe. Happily, after a while, we were able to turn off the transmitter. Dinga had responded to the negative stimuli as if Pavlov, himself, were conducting his famous experiment on animal conditioning. All it took was that one jolt. She would never again venture to within twenty feet of the front door. Hallelujah! No more chasing her through the streets, no more dealing with that *Madwoman of Chaillot* three doors down the block, no more fines to pay.

Ten months later, on a bitter, wintry day late in January, we received in the mail the following four official documents from the Municipal Court of the Township of Scotch Plains:

1. Control of dog defecating. Violation 5-8.7
2. Dog trespassing. Violation 5-8.5
3. Dog running at large. Violation 5-8.4
4. Dog to be accompanied when defecating. Violation 5-8.6

The complainant was Barbara Brothels.

All four violations were dated as occurring on the previous Sunday. Since on the day in question, Dinga had been either sleeping upstairs or lying at my feet while I was watching the football game, we became righteously indignant.

I called the clerk at the Municipal Court and informed her that we would be entering a not-guilty plea to the charges and would appear in court on the day indicated on the summonses. Out of curiosity, I asked her how the township felt about this unusual string of charges.

"It's a lot of paper work," the woman replied sourly. "I told Mrs. Brothels that we like to take these types of complaints to arbitration. Her reply was that she had evidence."

"What kind of evidence?"

"She said she had pictures."

"Did she show them to you?"

"She said she's saving them for the judge."

"What kind of arbitration are we talking about?"

The clerk went on to explain that the town had established procedures to settle disputes between neighbors rather than waste the court's time. Which seemed reasonable to me, but unfortunately, not to Mrs. Brothels, who was apparently determined to prove that Dinga was guilty as charged on all four ordinances.

On the day of the court proceedings, I spoke to the Prosecuting Attorney and requested that he talk to Mrs. Brothels, ask her to drop the charges and accept the town's invitation to arbitrate our differences. He said he would consider it, but, at this point, unless Mrs. Brothels changed her mind, I would first have to go before the judge and enter a plea of not guilty.

While I was hanging around in the hallway outside the court waiting for the judge to complete his recitation on the rights of the accused, I spotted Mrs. Brothels and a young child. Our neighbor seemed confused as to what was going on and what her role was in this preliminary hearing. I walked over to her thinking that one never knew the possible effect a few conciliatory words might evoke, not to mention that I was less than keen about sitting in a courthouse for hours before my name would be called.

"Hi," I said to both her and her little son.

Once again I witnessed a rather pretty face turn into a snarling, angry mask.

"Can we try and talk for a moment?" I asked.

"There's nothing to talk about."

"But my dog is innocent. By pressing these charges, you'll be forced to spend hours in court."

"Don't worry, I have the proof." She waved an envelope containing several pictures in front of me.

"Let me see the pictures," I said. "If you've got the goods on Dinga, I'll plead guilty, pay the fines and we can all go home."

"All right," she said triumphantly, removing the colored prints from the envelope. "Take a good look."

And there it was for all to see: two colored prints, each one taken at a slightly different angle. On each print was a well-formed, perhaps three or four inch turd lying unceremoniously on Barbara Brothel's meticulously cultivated front lawn.

"This is your proof?" I exclaimed.

"It belongs to your dog!"

"But it could belong to anyone's dog. It could even be your own."

And then Barbara Brothels freaked out and went into a crazed tirade, her hands moving up and down furiously like the conductor of a symphony orchestra. "You know how much money we've spent on our lawn? It hasn't been easy you know. We try to be good neighbors and keep our place beautiful. You don't give a damn. You let your dog run all over the place ruining lawns. Well I'm going to put a stop to this. You'll see. The judge will know what's going on here. By the time I'm finished with you and your dog, you'll want to move out of the neighborhood."

I could have told her that she was deranged and ought to consult with a psychiatrist before she wound up caged in the mental ward at Muhlenberg, but I decided that my best course of action was to get as far away from Barbara Brothels as possible and go back into the courtroom and wait for my name to be called.

Two hours later, I stood before the judge. He read me the charges. "My dog is innocent, your honor."

Dinga Goes To Trial

"The charges are against you, Dr. Karlen."

"Dinga and I are both innocent."

"Do you wish to be represented by counsel?"

"We'll defend ourselves."

I glanced over at the Prosecuting Attorney and then back to the judge. The whole procedure went forth with the sort of gravity one might associate with the mugging of an old lady. Wasn't there anyone inside that courtroom to crack a smile? It appeared that suburban lawns required the full protection of the courts against any four-legged creature that would dare to desecrate them, and it was no laughing matter.

Three weeks later I was back in court accompanied by my wife, my only witness that Dinga had not strayed from our house on that fateful Sunday. The Prosecuting Attorney offered me a plea bargain. If I would agree to plead guilty to one of the charges, he would drop the other three. He even offered to drop court costs. "For twenty bucks, you are free to spend the afternoon in the comfort of your home rather than in court," he said.

The Prosecuting Attorney, a big, bear of a man, was soft spoken and trying to be considerate and I hated to turn him down. "Nothing would please me more," I said, "than to spend the afternoon at home instead of in a courtroom, but you're asking Dinga to plead guilty to a charge to which she is innocent. I am obliged to defend her honor and thus forced to turn down your generous offer."

The Prosecuting Attorney then went into session with Mrs. Brothel, and when she wouldn't withdraw the charges, the scene was set for Dinga's trial. The judge agreed to try the case as the final piece of court business of the day.

While we were forced to wait for every case on the day's calendar to be concluded, my wife went shopping, and I drank coffee and continued to read John Gresham in the small restaurant across the street from the courthouse. Around 4 P.M. we were back in court and the trial of Dinga versus the Township of Scotch Plains got under way.

As the township's only witness, Mrs. Brothel was called to the stand. In a surprisingly timid voice, she stated that she had witnessed a brown-haired dog with a bushy tail, whom she had instantly recognized as the dog that belonged to Dr. and Mrs. Karlen, defecating on her front lawn at approximately 2 PM on the 27th day of January in the year 2002.

I was then allowed to cross-examine the witness. As I approached the witness stand, I experienced a curious exhilaration comparable to the time when I once held four aces in a nickel-dime poker game of seven-card stud, three of them in the hole.

I began my questioning of the witness using a placating, reasonable tone. You don't read John Gresham and watch old Perry Mason reruns on TV without learning a trick or two on how to throw a witness off guard. "Before this incident, had this bushy tailed dog ever defecated on your lawn?" I asked Mrs. Brothel.

"You bet," she exclaimed, delighted that I had given her the opportunity to express her wrath against a beast that would continue to defile her property unless the court once and for all put a stop to her.

"And this made you pretty angry, didn't it?"

"How would you feel?"

At this point the judge, a middle-aged, contemplative man, one who listened well and spoke precisely, directed the witness to answer the question.

"Yes, it made me angry," Mrs. Brothel said, accompanied by an expression of disappointment since she wasn't going to be allowed to elaborate on the reasons.

"And you never stopped feeling angry toward my wife and myself, have you?" I moved my voice ever so slightly from reasonable to cautiously argumentative.

"I don't need your dog ruining my lawn."

Once again the judge told the witness that she must answer the question.

"Yes, I'm angry at you and your wife."

"Now isn't it true that when our dog defecated on your lawn about a year ago, my wife went over to your house to retrieve the animal and clean up the mess."

Mrs. Brothel was about to expound on the incident, and then glanced toward the judge and thought better of it. "Yes, it's true," she answered.

"Do you also remember that while my wife was on her knees picking up the dog's droppings, you screamed and cursed at her as if she had just robbed your house and assaulted your children?"

"No, no, I never did that."

"Admit it, Mrs. Brothel, you publicly humiliated her, now didn't you?"

Barbara Brothel's complexion turned ashen. She began to hyperventilate and I was afraid for a moment that she might pass out. In the tradition of Perry Mason, I pressed my advantage. "How did it feel to demean a decent, sixty-five-year old woman, a woman old enough to be your mother, who was only trying to do the neighborly thing and make amends for her dog's indiscretion."

"I was cursing at the dog, not your wife," Mrs. Brothel finally said.

I paused to note with a certain degree of satisfaction the observant, interested look on the judge's face. Before we started the trial, I had feared that he might show a minor prejudice toward me because I had refused the Prosecuting Attorney's plea bargain, requiring him to hang around the courthouse thirty minutes longer than I'm sure he would have liked to. On the other hand the Prosecuting Attorney was looking off in the other direction and I had the distinct feeling that his interest in the proceedings was minimal.

I went on: "Are you aware, Mrs. Brothel, that since that incident a year ago, we built a fence around our back-yard for the sole purpose of preventing the dog from escaping our premises through the kitchen door?"

"How would I know that?"

"So you didn't know?"

"No, I didn't know."

"We could save time here if you'd answer my questions directly." I glanced at the judge with the faintest of grins.

Next I asked the witness: "And are you aware that after last year's incident we bought an electronic collar that we hung around the dog's neck and placed a power transmitter next to the front door so that if the dog goes within ten feet of the front door, she gets zapped?"

"I didn't know that."

"Now that you've been informed that our dog, Dinga, couldn't possibly have left the premises, do you think you might have been mistaken and seen a dog that resembled Dinga defecating on your lawn?"

"No," cried Mrs. Brothel. "It was definitely that dog."

"Is it possible that you never saw any dog defecating on your property but because of your anger toward us you assumed that it was our dog when you discovered the droppings? Now remember, Mrs. Brothel, you're under oath."

"It was that dog," she hissed. "Your dog."

I was considering hammering away at her, trying to make her confess that she had lied, but I backed away satisfied that the judge had probably already decided on what kind of a person Barbara Brothels was. To continue questioning her would only denigrate my own persona. I looked at the judge and declared, "I have no more questions at this time, your honor." Perry Mason rested his case.

The judge then asked me if I wished to testify on my own behalf after advising me the Township could not insist that I take the witness stand.

"I would be happy to testify on behalf on Dinga," I said and moved to the witness stand. After I was sworn in, the Prosecutor, without bothering to move an inch in his seat allowed me to defend Dinga without interruption.

After I had denied that it was Dinga who had defecated on Mrs. Brothel's lawn, I offered to the court pictures of our backyard fence, and the power transmitter that was mounted by our front door, along with the receipts dating their purchase.

"We believe you, Dr. Karlen," said the judge, who waived off the evidence.

The case having been concluded, the judge rendered an almost immediate decision. He cited prior decisions involving cases where it was also a question of one person's word against the other. Since the burden of proof lay with the prosecution and in this particular case there was a reasonable doubt as to whether the dog in question was in fact the one who had violated the town ordinances, he declared that the defendant was not guilty and dismissed all charges.

Hooray for Dinga. Hooray for all those four-legged creatures who are trapped inside painted sheetrock and floral wallpaper like prisoners and whose only link to the outside world are when they are granted a little walk around the block while harnessed to a leash. And if once in a while one of them escapes her cage and romps about without restraints, should we not rejoice for her moment of freedom? Won't our precious lawns survive her occasional, harmless misdemeanor?

My wife and I were standing at the back door leading into the parking lot behind the police station when Mrs. Brothel and her son passed. We could hear her whisper to the boy, "Next time we'll take pictures of that dog. We'll fix them."

Good for you, Mrs. Brothel, I thought, but I warn you: Dinga is a dog to be reckoned with. I'd advise you, Mrs. Brothel, to keep your camera ready at all times. Before that old dog dies, I guarantee that she'll find a way to get past chain link fences and electronic transmitters and once again deliver on your sparkling carpet of green a final, definitive statement acknowledging that she knows who in this world most deserves to be shit upon.

I served a year in South Korea (1957-1958) as an Air Force dentist. Though the Korean War had ended four years before, the country was destitute, and a significant part of the economy was dependent on the fifty-thousand American troops stationed within its borders.

The primary service the Koreans sold to the Americans was prostitution. From the money the prostitutes fed into the economy, the Koreans bought American goods through the Black Market. Thus, the mentality of a proud, venerable, four-thousand-year-old culture was reduced in a single generation to a wretched, sickening shell of its former self.

ANOPHELES

A mosquito circles above Sam Meyers' head. He fans her away, but she is arrogant and lands on the stationary in front of him. He studies the motionless insect and feels an immediate revulsion; yet for the moment he is fascinated by the terror he knows she is capable of inflicting on a human being, her potential to transmit a fatal disease to her host.

He whispers her name, "Anopheles," then seeks vengeance. He puts down the ballpoint pen being held aimlessly between his fingertips and slowly edges a lethal hand over the unsuspecting life.

The insect twitches, the final drama, stylets itching to tear into flesh, absorb nutrients, maintain reproductive schemes.

"An eye for an eye!"

Meyers squashes her and flicks her away, all in the same motion.

There is a spot of blood left on the corner of the blank stationery. Did the mosquito get him first? He crumples the paper and drops it on the floor. He is sweating, not just on the forehead, but under his armpits, down his back, inside his crotch.

Meyers has been sitting at his desk in his BOQ (Bachelor Officer's Quarters) room for the past thirty minutes trying to compose a letter to his wife, Marge. It was an exercise in frustration. He'd write the date: August 4, 1957, the place: Kimpo Air Base, South Korea, the time: 1930 (7:30 P.M.) now 2000 (8:00 P.M.), then a variety of sentences: "Sorry I haven't written sooner—" "I wonder about you and the girls—" "The weather is sizzling hot. We've got an encephalitis epidemic and we're confined to the base—" Rip, next sheet, rip. Marks filling up space, no thoughts to express, no emotions to convey, unless the unwritten is an emotion. How do you express loving concern when you've lost your soul?

He had opted for the Korean tour of one year, which meant being separated from his family, in the hope that by the time he returned to New Jersey he could work out of the depression that had been insidiously enveloping him the past few years. What he couldn't have foreseen was a weakness of character that had nothing to do with depression.

He rereads Marge's most recent letter to try and stimulate the simplest mechanical operation of his brain. "Three weeks since your last letter. The girls say nothing, but what are they feeling? How much longer do we have to wait before we begin to worry that there's something physically the matter with you?" Her writing flows in swirling artistic waves. Even when angry, Marge's hand is a fine brush that moves with its own special rhythm.

He runs out of stationery and searches a bottom desk drawer. Amidst the clutter of old orders and Air Force documents he finds a buried sheet. He's surprised to discover that "Dear," has already been written at the top. He adds "Marge," then arises and walks to a small window, sidling past a large pot-bellied kerosene stove, a giant piece of iron foliage planted in the center of the narrow room. He stares into the twilight sun, a hot Korean ball of fire settling behind a distant peak. Streaks of orange flash across a purple sky, daytime's final ruptured message before the sticky dampness of the August night sets in and *Anopheles* awakens and seeks nourishment.

To his left is the dispensary, a long, green quonset, where he performs his medical chores with a skill born of eighteen years experience. Now a lieutenant-colonel, Meyers was a captain in 1950 when he had first arrived at Kimpo Air Base and witnessed a dozen South Korean medics swinging by their necks from the rafters in the dispensary waiting room, a vendetta from an enraged North Korean high command because its dreams of a quick victory over the South Korean and United Nations' armies had been upended by MacArthur's counterattack at Inchon.

Why come back to Korea? With his rank and years in service, he could have requested a different assignment. Had returning to Korea for a year's tour been an unconscious act of penance?

He hears a jeep pulling up in front of the BOQ. There is a light inside the dispensary. He assumes one of the medics, probably O'Brien, is on duty to handle evening emergencies. If it is O'Brien, Meyers will be able to enjoy a quiet evening with Yung Sook, for Sergeant O'Brien is not only his best band-aid and aspirin medic, but he knows how to keep his mouth shut.

Meyers searches the road for the jeep he thought he has heard. The dispensary jeep carrying Yung Sook should have arrived thirty minutes ago. Chet, the BOQ

Korean houseboy, is driving her. Meyers trusts Chet, an attitude not shared by the other dispensary officers, who include, besides Meyers, Axel Harris, the dentist, George Santoro, the vet, and Raymond Brown, the medical adjutant. "Watch out," they warn him. "If a suspicious AP at the main gate should ask the wrong questions, Chet will cut and run."

Back at his desk, Meyers continues to ponder his unfinished letter. He picks up a snapshot of Marge, the girls and himself, the one taken two months before he had departed for Korea. The photograph had arrived with Marge's last letter, her personal way of reminding him that he was still part of a family. The girls stand tall and relaxed, unafraid of the camera. Marge is too erect, too well posed. Her smile is half-baked, a wry little grin. Meyers seems unnaturally bent, his slender frame slipping forward, an unwilling subject. Could one already read the look of guilt on his face?

He has forgotten the mustache he had worn for a little more than a year. It amuses him to remember how he had pampered it, trimming it meticulously, observing the way it had divided his angular face in half. Marge had hated the mustache. All those whiskers didn't suit him, she said. In the end he had shaved it off to please her.

The picture slips through his fingertips, floating to the floor. As he is about to pick it up, there is a sharp rap on the door.

"Come in."

"Colonel, Chet is here!"

Meyers faces a small, dark Korean with straight black hair that stands on end and at times seems to give him a surprised look. Chet, the BOQ houseboy, is no boy. At age twenty-five, Chet, an ex-ROK infantry man, is a short, squarely-built man, who walks with a slight limp, the result of losing two toes on his right foot from gangrene incurred during the winter campaign near the Yalu in 1951. His ripped tee shirt and frayed khakis are smeared by bits of shoe polish. He refers to himself in the third person; the avoidance of the "I," according to Harris, is a phony deference to power. Chet shines shoes, make beds, and does 'special favors.' Despite Harris's misgivings, Meyers has never found a reason to distrust him.

"Chet brings Yung Sook," Chet says. He often whispers, for everywhere there are spies and communists and he is a petty gangster.

A slender, young Korean woman, wearing a Chinese dress, a faded, pink silk brocade, pushes her way past Chet before closing the door, almost crushing his arm. He curses her as he falls backwards into the hallway. Grunting angrily, he limps toward the outside door. The woman shrugs indifferently.

"He gives me hard time," she says. "You speak to him. You tell him to be nice to Yung Sook. I no have to take his shit."

"I'll talk to him," Meyers said, though he has no idea what he will say to Chet. How does Chet treat her badly? Does he beat her, double-deal her? Is it any of Meyers' business what goes on between pimp and prostitute?

Yung Sook wraps both arms around his neck. "Sorry to be late." She kisses a cheek and licks an ear lobe. He wants to hug her, but she pushes him away and leads him to the bed. In an instant there is a bodily fusion of legs, hips, stomachs and chests. He sits up. He doesn't like the way she is rushing things.

"I was writing a letter to my wife," he tells her. A peculiar half-lie. That particular fact means nothing to her. He is telling it to himself, an almost conscious braking action. He knows that thoughts of Marge will affect his libido.

"Men write letters to wives. You want good time, you get Korean girl." Yung Sook speaks English with surprising clarity. She refuses to talk about herself, but Meyers suspects that she is too well educated to have always been a prostitute.

In the Air Force men are constantly being separated from their families; sexual vagaries are a way of life. One learns to categorize emotions: make the distinction between duty and pleasure, love and sex.

Meyers liked to believe that he was the exception. No matter where he had been stationed, he had always been faithful to Marge. Until this year, in Korea, with Yung Sook. His feelings toward the girl were out of control, no different that if he had become addicted to heroin.

"We have good time today," Yung Sook says as she fumbles with his fly.

Meyers slips a hand down her back and feels the smooth, olive skin under her dress. "I was hoping you'd come tonight."

Since Chet first brought Yung Sook several months ago, Meyers finds himself constantly thinking about her. He has given up trying to analyze his obsession for her. He could be examining a patient, or filling out a report and her face would intrude—a smiling, taunting face, white teeth bared, signaling him. He'd wonder—who was she with, what was she doing? He had problems dealing with commonplace troubles: a sphygmo-manometer out of whack, an over-developed X-ray, a misplaced key to the narcotics box.

Earlier in the day, Santoro, the vet, had called him. John Edwards, the Deputy Base Commander, had informed Santoro via an official communiqué that he had been assigned to the job of Base Public Health Officer in charge of indigenous personnel. Santoro reminded Meyers that aside from his usual veterinary duties, which included the care of twelve guard dogs, he inspected all food sold at the Commissary, as well as food used by the service clubs. He complained that he hardly had time for a decent fuck.

"Chet thinks I've become queer. Please, Colonel," he exhorted Meyers, "get that piece of bullshit rescinded."

Meyers phoned Edwards. Military courtesy demanded that Edwards should have consulted with him before issuing such a direct order. Beneath the familiarity of their greetings, the two Lieutenant Colonels sparred. They don't like each other, but are careful to conceal their feelings. They decided to air out Santoro's gripe over dinner in the near future. A temporary truce had been put into place.

This afternoon, there was another case of encephalitis, Japanese B. To be certain of the diagnosis Meyers needed a spinal. The patient would have to be transported to the army hospital at Ascom City, but the only decent ambulance had a flat and the spare was bald. The patient, a young flight lieutenant, was half-comatose.

"I'm going to die," he kept repeating.

The lieutenant's fears were real enough. Meyers thought about his own anxiety, the constant vibe of a nervous system out of whack, until finally, the day would be over and he'd return to the BOQ and await Yung Sook.

He was two months into his tour when Chet had approached him: "The colonel needs a woman to make the year pass quickly."

Meyers wasn't interested. His tour in Korea was to be a time for reflection, a time to try and come to grips with what was ailing him, those inner fears that seemed to come and go without rhyme or reason. He was going to listen to music, read old medical journals that had been piling up for months on the upper shelf of his bedroom bookcase. In short, he would practice his profession and live like a monk. Abstinence would be a part of it.

"No good," Chet had argued. "Colonel needs woman to balance mind and body. Chet has perfect woman. If the Colonel doesn't like Yung Sook, then Chet brings him another girl. But the Colonel will like Yung Sook, for she is smartest and prettiest girl in Kimpo."

One evening Chet knocked on his BOQ door. "I bring Yung Sook," he said.

"I told you, I wasn't interested."

All his vows of abstinence flew out the window when the girl strolled into the room and sat down on his bed and crossed her legs. She was absolutely exquisite, the most beautiful woman he had ever laid his eyes on.

"Hi," she said simply. "I'm Yung Sook. Don't be afraid, I not eat you."

Now, three months later, though the relationship had become narrow and unsatisfying, and often left him empty and frustrated, he cannot do without her.

Meyers is not such a fool to believe that Yung Sook could ever feel any genuine affection toward him. The problem is within himself since it is his nature to want to love a woman he sleeps with.

"What do you do after you leave here?" he had once asked her. He wonders about whom she lives with, who are her friends, those small habits that define a person.

Anopheles

"I go home." Her voice had suggested neither surprise nor understanding of any deeper meaning in the question. She added, "I wash my face and go to sleep."

"I've never seen you sleep."

She shrugged as if to say: "What does it matter?"

Before the encephalitis epidemic, airmen and non-commissioned officers would routinely live with their girls in the village. Many of them, hardly more than adolescents, would sneak out after duty through a dozen different routes and return in the morning. Though it was common knowledge what was going on, it was unofficially tolerated. Consorting with the "indigenous" population was considered good for morale. VD was an unfortunate fall-out, but the impact was minimized since treatment with antibiotics was almost always effective.

Officers, particularly senior grades, however, were required to maintain a higher moral standard: the price one paid for privilege, for rank. An officer risked a serious reprimand if he was caught outside the base with a woman. One quickly learned how best to work around the system.

Yung Sook unzips Meyers' fly, her thin fingers slipping their way through his pants. His body becomes alive and he pushes her down on the bed and kisses her. She arches a leg and swings it around his body, her dress sliding up to her waist. He runs a hand along her thigh, squeezing it.

"You hurt," she says.

"Sorry."

He is momentarily distracted by the sounds of a C-125 as it circles the airstrip. It is a giant with a bellyache descending earthward. On the plane are a hundred and fifty airmen, most of whom are probably still remembering the few days spent in Japan with its neon lights and iniquitous bars, and wondering what their Korean tour of duty has to offer. Rumors circulate that Korea is a land of unpleasant temperatures, diseased women, desolate bases. After a while, out of boredom, the more adventurous will wander into the village, to be rewarded when they discover an ancient, complex society. The less courageous will brood and curse their bad luck and go to old movies on base when they aren't drinking and gambling.

"I think you not like to see Yung Sook today," Yung Sook says. "Maybe I do something wrong. Maybe you not like the way I talk with Chet."

He disengages himself from her and they sit up. "No, no," he says. "nothing's the matter."

"Chet is okay. But sometimes he is ignorant, stupid man."

The quonset shakes from the roar of the plane's engines as the aircraft zeroes in for a landing. Meyers hopes that amongst those one hundred and fifty passengers will be a young MD eager for the experience of sharing a workload on a base of twelve hundred men. The dispensary roster calls for two physicians, yet for months he has received no orders when another would be coming.

Outside the base, in the village, the encephalitis epidemic is becoming worse. On the base he has already diagnosed fifteen cases. Six men have died. He sent a memo to Fifth Air Force Command Operations at Fuchu that he needed help right away, but he was given only the usual promises that another doctor would be sent in the near future.

"We have big time, Colonel," Yung Sook says. *Big time* is one of her favorite expressions, along with *baby, no sweat,* and *hot stuff,* the latter aphorism enjoying a multitude of meanings, depending upon the particular time and situation.

"Let's get undressed," she says.

"In a few minutes."

She leans on his shoulder and fiddles with one of his ear lobes. "I think something the matter, but it's okay, baby. Every time you cannot be happy to see me. Maybe we see each other too much."

"I always want to see you."

The hand that has been playing with his ear has dropped to unbuckle his pants belt.

"I'll do it," he says.

Both stand up. He undresses himself, and then goes back to the cot. She slips out of the upper part of her dress, and then reaches around to unsnap her bra. She tosses the bra into his lap, shakes her small high breasts while shimmying out of her tight Chinese dress and finally kicks off her high heels. He reaches to pull off her panties; she squirms and lets him do it, before she flops back on the bed. The way she undresses has become ritualistic, the same sequence of disrobing, the same seductive movements

He kneels before her outstretched body and marvels at the long, black, silky hair that spreads across the pillow, the thin, pinched waist, the smooth, hairless thighs. Her neck is slender, elegant, her face, regal, with imposing, high cheekbones and full, curved lips. Where did she come from? What God made her?

He lies down beside her and touches her neck; his fingers circle a pattern toward the nape. He kisses her delicately, affectionately, but she breaks off the kiss abruptly.

She reaches down. "Come on already," she whispers.

She grinds her hips. He knows she wants to bring him to orgasm as quickly as possible. She squeals and cries "fuck me." This is part of her act. Actually, she exhibits little excitement, virtually no passion. He tries to respond to what little she offers.

"Not yet," he says.

He grabs her from behind to hold her immobile, to try and prevent her from bringing him too quickly to orgasm. But he is too late. It is over and he collapses in her arms.

He struggles to catch his breath, then her inevitable, "Hot stuff," before she strokes his back in a surprising moment of tenderness.

He becomes depressed; the gratification has been too intense in spite of her indifference. Already her eyes have turned blank; her smile is forced.

He thinks of Marge and the two letters, hers and his own unfinished one, both lying like weighted stones on his desk. He closes his eyes. Marge is sitting in front of her easel, brush in hand, her head arched ever so slightly as she contemplates her unfinished watercolor. Her splendid, long legs uncross themselves; the knees are exposed from between the folds of her housecoat. She turns and looks at him, catching his glance, and then smiles back at him. He tells her that he is sorry, that he still loves her. She doesn't hear him.

"I have to go early," Yung Sook says.

"Why?" He is unable to conceal his disappointment. "Chet can bring us dinner if you don't wish to go to the club."

"I'll come tomorrow." She slithers out from beneath him and rolls free. He stretches an arm in protest, but she is already sitting at the edge of the bed, dressing.

There are sharp footsteps down the hallway, then a knock on the door. "Sergeant O'Brien, sir," a rough voice calls out. "We have a man with a hundred and five temp. Could be Jap B, sir."

Meyers jumps to his feet. "In a minute." He picks up his clothes off the floor. Yung Sook stands before him fully dressed. "I have to pay rent," she says.

He removes his wallet from a bureau drawer and hands her two ten-dollar m.p.c., military pay currency. "Maybe you can come back later?" he asks.

She slips the bills into her bra. "Tomorrow," she says. "Chet waits for me."

He gives her a can of DDT. "This will kill the mosquitos."

"You give me DDT last week."

"I had forgotten. Take the extra can. Give it to a neighbor."

She looks at him curiously. "You are good person, Colonel," she says, and then leaves.

He picks up the fallen picture of his family from the floor and places it neatly inside the desk drawer. He thinks of Yung Sook telling him that *he is a good person.* In her voice he thought he detected a moment of honest affection and hoped that, perhaps, she realized that he was more than just someone who paid the rent

Moments later, he is standing in front of the dispensary looking down the road toward the main gate. Dusk has given way to darkness. He sees the headlights from the dispensary jeep as it rolls past the NCO club, and wonders how Yung Sook and Chet will split the twenty.

What difference does it make, he says to himself? His mind returns to the business of dealing with disease and human misery. It was, after all, what he did best. He hurries into the dispensary.

In forty-three years of marriage we have always had a dog in our home. It has often fallen to my wife to walk, the dog, feed the dog, and vacuum the globs of hair that every one of our dogs would shed. She has always claim-ed that she hates dogs and would never have married me if she knew that there would forever be a dog in her life. But sometimes, when she doesn't realize I'm around, I hear her talking to the dog—a nice little conversation, even if it is a one-way dialogue.

I think I am living with a dog lover, who hasn't come out of the closet.

SEBASTIAN

New Jersey, 1957

Marge Meyers sat at the kitchen table drinking black coffee and smoking a cigarette. Though it was almost noon, she was still in her housecoat. She felt bound in, listless, a victim of her own morbid thoughts, most of which were centered about her husband, Sam, who was stationed in South Korea. She peered out the window and wondered if the sky in South Korea was as bleak and gray as the one at McGuire Air Force Base. Let it rain, let it rain like hell.

In the corner a can of paint remained unopened. She had bought it two days ago at the Base Commissary with the intention of sprucing up the kitchen wall, a small demonstration to her two girls, as well as to herself, that she could still be useful. Today, however, was the same as yesterday—another lousy night's sleep, and then, on rising, a nagging headache. Her limbs felt palsied. She might as well be living in a wheelchair.

Sebastian

The phone rang a dozen times before she picked it up. It was Vinnie Tortorello, wife of Brigadier General Ernest Tortorello, second in command of the Twenty-first Air Force of the Military Airlift Command, more commonly known as MAC. The Tortorellos occupied a large, brick three-bedroom ranch on the next corner in the community just outside the air base.

Vinnie was upset, her usual contralto cracking and rising to an unnatural mezzo pitch. "I couldn't hold Claudia," she cried.

Her breath sounded short and wheezy and Marge worried that she was about to suffer one of her celebrated asthmatic attacks.

"Calm down, Vinnie," Marge said.

But Vinnie was inconsolable. "When Claudia saw Sebastian, there was no holding her. She broke away from the leash and knocked me on my butt," she said, then quickly added, "My God, Marge, you promised to keep Sebastian fenced in."

Marge stared at the receiver, then studied the breakfast dishes piled in the sink. The wall clock read eleven forty-eight. In twenty-seven minutes the girls would be home for lunch. She decided that she might as well wash all the dishes after lunch. "Is Claudia in heat?" Marge asked.

"I distinctly remember telling you, Marge. It was last week at the club luncheon."

Vinnie's powers of recollection were beyond dispute. But who paid attention to the chitchat that poured from the mouths of those bored, restless officers' wives.

"Vinnie, you can't be sure it will happen."

Marge couldn't restrain a sardonic half-smile as she imagined mangy Sebastian copulating with General Tortorello's prize golden retriever, Claudia d'Antoinette,III.

Scattered drops of rain continued to streak down the window. Let it rain, let it pour while Sebastian revitalized Claudia's youthful, golden soul, the rain, a joyful expurgation for the lovers.

"The general will have my ass," Vinnie said.

Air Force protocol demanded that a lieutenant colonel's wife pay homage to a brigadier general's, but Marge wasn't in the mood to be deferential. "It just goes to show you, Vinnie, that even a honey like Claudia can't be trusted." Actually Marge liked Vinnie, for in spite of certain insensitivities, Vinnie spoke her mind with an honesty that Marge admired.

"But with Sebastian—ich!" There was the faint sound of a chuckle, a lessening of the crisis. Then Vinnie said, "Do you know, my dear, what it's like being married to a man who loves his four-legged bitch more than his two-legged one?"

Claudia and Sebastian. Beauty and the beast. Who could have predicted that the stray, abused puppy that Sam had picked up out of the gutter three years ago would grow into an eighty-pound Goliath? Though he slobbered excessively and twice a year shed globs of mangy brown hair, Sebastian had been awarded the role of household pet. To please their neighbors, who were wary of the big animal, Sam had bought a post-hole digger and spent two months building a fence.

Sam had promised to repair the fence before departing for Korea. A small task, a few loose boards, something she could have managed herself, but Sam had insisted on doing it, a job for a Sunday afternoon. But he had forgotten; they both had forgotten. Those last few weeks before he had left, he had grown incessantly irritable, nagging her almost daily over no-account household details, unreasonably criticizing the girls. It made no sense to fight back; it wasn't a fight you could win. Sam Meyers was a man with a guilty conscience; a man about to desert his family for a year.

"Maybe the vet can fix it," Marge suggested.

Another silence, then a gasp. "They're doing it right now, Marge," Vinnie said. "I can see them out the window."

Marge heard the sound of the phone receiver banging against the floor, then a distant "Claudia!" Moments later, Vinnie's agitated voice: "Too late, Marge. At this very moment, that awful dog of yours has tied himself to Claudia in the middle of the street. It's not a pretty sight, dearie."

A rustling at the front door. The postman? A letter from Sam? She waited for the doorbell, but there was only the sounds of departing footsteps. She laid the receiver on the table, Vinnie's voice blowing through it like a stream of vacant air, and ran down the five short steps to the front door. The Air Force Weekly was stretched diagonally across the WELCOME mat. Slowly, she retraced her steps back to the phone.

"Marge, are you listening to me?"

"I was getting a cigarette." The lie invoked a sudden need. She searched the ashtray for a butt.

"I can't see them anymore. They've run off." Vinnie's tone suggested resignation. "The damage has been done. *C'est la vie.*"

Vinnie's ability to move in and out of emotional confrontations with no apparent aftereffects was probably her greatest virtue. Unlike other generals' wives Marge had known over the years, Vinnie thrived on crises.

"Are you coming to the club social, Saturday?" Vinnie asked. Her mood had shifted; Sebastian and Claudia, doomed lovers, had played out their scene. She would manage the General at the appropriate time.

"I don't think so," Marge said.

"Marge, it's no good sitting around by yourself." Vinnie had turned matriarchal, her privilege by rank. "You know dearie, you're not the first woman who ever had to wait it out a year."

Marge had never complained before, not even during those eighteen months Sam was away during the Korean war. It was different then; Sam was different. *Then*, it wasn't his idea to go to Korea.

"Marge, I insist you come to the social," Vinnie said. "I don't think Sam would like you to wither away like a beached starfish. I'm sure *he's* not withering away."

Did rage make one wither? She had a right to be angry. Sam had left her and the children. Oh, yes, he said he was coming back; a year's tour of duty in Korea, he claimed, was preferable to three in Europe or Japan, even though the Air Force would have allowed his family to accompany him on those types of tours.

"If you insist on the Orient, why not Japan," she had argued.

They had never been to Japan before. What had happened to their old sense of adventure? Seeing the world together was supposed to be the reason Sam had decided to make a career out of the Air Force in the first place. Who volunteered to go to Korea. The country was still in shambles. Korea had been Sam's personal nightmare and now he had volunteered to go back for a year. Why? He wouldn't talk about it. He said she would never understand.

Sam always made the big decisions in their lives. In 1946, after returning from Germany, he had announced that he was remaining in the service. He didn't think he could abide going into private practice and settling down in one place for the rest of his life. Phyllis was almost three and within a month Marge had become pregnant with Janet.

Marge pleaded with him to go into private practice. What was so terrible about living in their own house, in a decent community where she could raise her children without the anxiety of being transferred from base to base every few years?

He countered with: "Please give it a try. Think of the adventure for all of us. We'd be able to live in parts of the world that are nothing more than dots on the old Rand McNally map hanging over our bed. If it doesn't work out, I can always resign and try out that other world."

Jessica was born in Paris; Phyllis had her tonsils removed in Barcelona. Marge spent days wandering through the Louvre and the Prado, went to the opera in Rome and Milan, skied in Zermatt. Oh, yes, there was the other, the disagreeable part of the Air Force that she feared—the constant uprooting, those special luncheons at the Officers' clubs.

Life was compromise. The most important thing was to be with those you loved. With plenty of time on her hands, she went back to painting, buried her insecurities in her oils and watercolors. With Sam around, she never worried. Above all else he was dependable.

"Maybe another time," Marge said to Vinnie. "Anyway, I don't see the point."

She was staring through the doorway into the living room at an old oil painting that hung above the clarinet stand. She had been seventeen when she had painted the self-portrait, a triangular face split in two by sharp, bold lines, then dissected into square blocks with reds and oranges mixing with the dark purples and blacks. Did the artist, like the face in the painting, possess the same schizoid view of reality?

"The point is people," Vinnie said. She paused, and then added, "Charlie will be sitting with us."

Major Charles Lennox, hospital adjutant, graying sideburns, porcelain smile, forever stepping out of an *Esquire* underwear ad. Charlie gave neck massages with one hand while eating tossed salad with the other. In whispers he claimed to be good where it counted most.

"Save Charlie for another night," Marge said.

Vinnie laughed provocatively. "Charlie notices you," she said.

Marge grinned. She suspected that Charlie had noticed Vinnie more than once when the General was on one his top-secret missions. Vinnie could be generous that way. Marge berated herself: Don't be so damn self-righteous about Vinnie. Who knew what really went on between married people? Look what was happening with Sam and herself.

The conversation dwindled; Vinnie grew weary and said goodbye. After hanging up, Marge squashed the cigarette butt in a coffee cup, then stood up and remembering her old childhood ballet lessons moved into the first position, heels together, toes turned outward until her feet were in a straight line, her hands cupped and held loosely at her waist. She tried a pirouette, and fell awkwardly against the table. She was in miserable shape. She smoked too much; she had stopped exercising. Sam had sucked the life out of her.

Through the window, she viewed the hole in the fence through which Sebastian must have escaped. Two boards had been ripped clean out of their slots. She recalled the last time Sam had been patching up another hole Sebastian had made. He had cursed each blow of the hammer, while the big mongrel sat by his side wagging his tail. He said he was fed up, crazy to put up with an animal that caused him nothing but grief from his neighbors. Yet Sebastian remained.

The doorbell! Move slowly, she cautioned herself, don't allow a mailman to control your life. Sam was never much of a writer, even when he had a reason to write.

There was a handful of letters in the box. She flipped them over quickly: The American Indian Fund, Sears, the PTA, UJA, Project Hope. Back in the foyer she re-checked the mail before dropping it on the floor.

Her face in her hands, she gave her cheeks a small dig with her fingernails, then mentally drew up a list of things to do: dress, beds, vacuum, dishes, lunch for the girls, repair the fence, practice the clarinet, start a new canvas. That was the order of things. Grow up, Marge, you weren't born yesterday.

She went as far as the bedroom, where instead of making the bed, she flopped down on it.

She awakened from the short nap in a sweat. She wasn't certain whether she had dreamed or daydreamed. Sam was lying naked with an Oriental girl. Heavy rain beat against the roof of the room. The roof began to collapse and she screamed, but no one heard her.

She went back to the kitchen table. She needed to collect her wits with another cigarette and a hot cup of coffee. She could hear the next-door neighbor slamming shut the car door, then gunning the engine. Ann Peters, a captain's wife, young, energetic, drove like a stock car racer, probably off to Trenton to shop for a smart dress in which to drape her sexy, youthful body.

"What a great ass," Sam had once commented. "Too bad she's got the brains of a camel." Captain George Peters didn't think his wife had the brains of a camel.

The phone rang.

"Claudia has come home," Vinnie said. "Her coat is disgusting, a dirty, wet tangle, her nose is gooey and her eyes look as if she had just survived a twister." She laughed gaily. "My, how she is wagging her tail."

"About the social," Marge said. "I've changed my mind. Save me a seat at your table."

What the hell, who was it going to hurt if Major Charlie Peters wanted to try out a few of his famous, coveted moves on her? "For chrissake, I'm only forty years old, Sam," she said into her cup after saying her goodbyes to Vinnie.

She went into the living room and practiced a little Mozart. Not too bad, she thought, before shifting over to the sofa, where with her feet perched on the coffee table, she slid into a soft rendition of *Blue Moon*. She was interrupted by a familiar scratching sound at the front door. As she opened the door, she was brushed aside by Sebastian's charge into the foyer. With his customary canine indifference to human feelings, he shook himself dry, sprinkling her housecoat. Then he pushed up against her, his dark eyes asking for acceptance, for love.

"You're rotten, you really are."

She bent down and hugged his thick, hairy neck. "You stink something awful," she said to the big dog, then straightened up. "Get lost."

When the animal refused to move, she shoved him away rudely, and went back to her clarinet. But her lip was all played out, and she packed up the instrument.

Sitting on the couch, she stared down at Sebastian, who had curled up near the fireplace and was totally indifferent to the tears that clouded her vision.

In 1958 the Asian games were hosted in Tokyo. At the time, there was an estimated 130,000 prostitutes in Tokyo and Yokohama. The Japanese Diet concerned with the embarrassing image of thousands of these women walking the streets ruled their activity as unlawful. Overnight the girls turned into "hostesses", who worked in hundreds of bars and cafés that sprang up out of nowhere.

Recently, my wife and I revisited Tokyo. In a moment of nostalgia, we traveled to Fussa, where I had been stationed at Yokota Air Base in 1958. Instead of bars and cafés with their bright neon signs lighting up the strip on the outside fringe of the base, we discovered restaurants, camera shops, automobile repair shops, and boutiques.

I thought: how sad for all those thousands of young airmen stationed at the Air Base today that they weren't around in 1958 when times may not have been as civilized, but it was a lot more fun.

SNOW ON THE WINDOW

After my year's tour of duty in Korea in 1958, I was reassigned to Yokota Air base in Japan, in the town of Fussa, about an hour outside of Tokyo. Life was simple— an easy five-day week plugging amalgams and pulling teeth, and the rest was fun and games. I enjoyed sumptuous meals at the officers' club, first-run movies at the base theater, and, best of all, young Japanese women, who for ten dollars a night would entertain you handsomely. For a twenty-eight-year-old bachelor, it was heaven at wholesale prices.

The girls worked as "hostesses" in bars located just outside the airbase on a strip about three blocks long. The bars, bright and brassy, were open every day from six to

midnight. Kay's café, its interior decor adorned with hanging lanterns, ancient scrolls on the walls, and good semi-
classical music piped in through a decent hi-fi system, had
an *officers only* reputation. Kay, a woman in her early
thirties, had established this reputation by hiring the best-
looking girls available. She would fire any girl if she
padded the bill. If you made an after-hour arrangement
with one of them, you could count on her to be fair and
unlikely to be diseased.

About four months after being stationed at Yokota, on
a clear, late November evening, I took my customary after-
dinner stroll around the base. Rather than return to my
lonely BOQ (Bachelor Officer's Quarters), I headed for
the strip.

Kay's was relatively quiet. Five or six girls were clus-
tered around a table in a corner drinking tea. Two jet pilots
sat at another table. As I made my way into the room, I
nodded politely to one of them, a first lieutenant, a jet
pilot, who was a patient of mine. He had experienced
dental pain at thirty thousand feet and I'd replaced most of
his fillings, the theory being that dental pain was possible
at high altitudes as a result of the expansion of gases under
improperly packed amalgams.

Seating myself at a secluded booth, I began to browse
through the daily edition of the *Stars and Stripes*. A Glen
Miller standard was being played through the speakers.
One of the hostesses, a girl I had slept with about two
months earlier, sauntered over. She was a pretty thing, her
lustrous, straight black hair falling down her back, her
sturdy, young body revealed to its best advantage in a tight
Chinese dress. She was an addictive gum chewer, and my
best remembrance of our night was that her jaws had never
stopped chomping while I was sweating away.

Looking for a new experience, preferably with someone not addicted to gum, I said I preferred to drink my beer

alone. The girl shrugged off the insult philosophically, and after serving me, retreated to the table where the other girls sat around together. Since it was still early, there was plenty of time for her to find another customer with whom to spend the night. The money she would earn as a percentage of the drinks customers ordered was a fraction of what she could earn after hours. The last customer was the one who counted most.

It wasn't long before Kay invited herself to sit opposite me. "You look sad, Captain," she said.

"I'm lonely."

"So why you tell Janice to go away?" she asked, feigning annoyance.

"Janice is a terrific girl," I said, "but she's a little young. What I crave is a woman with your experience."

"You full of baloney, Captain. Janice has plenty experience."

"Experience, maybe, but not much sensitivity. Not like you.

"What you mean sensitivity?"

"Someone who appreciates nature, someone who appreciates beauty."

"All Japanese girls appreciate beauty."

"Of course, but there are some who appreciate it more than others."

I'd been hanging out at Kay's Cafe almost twice a week since my tour of duty began four months ago. As a rule, relationships with Americans was strictly business with Kay, nevertheless, we had developed a certain rapport that transcended business. If I were to believe her, she had gone to college before the war and claimed she had been awarded a degree in biology, which she quickly discovered was useless during the American occupation. She admitted that for ten years she had worked the bars and streets around the American Air Base at Tachikawa until she had sufficient capital to open her own place in Fussa.

"I need a woman with a little maturity," I said.

When Kay laughed, she displayed gold crowns wrapped around her two front teeth, which amongst Japanese "business women" was considered a mark of success. For a moment, I thought she might be offering herself as the *mature* woman to satisfy my need for *sensitivity*. That would be unprecedented, though one heard rumors that Kay was not beyond spending a night with someone, just for the hell of it. But as it turned out, that wasn't what she had in mind for me.

"I have perfect girl for you," she said, an experienced matchmaker in action.

"Who?" I glanced over at the table of giggling girls, wondering if I had somehow overlooked anyone these past few months.

"She recently come from living in Tokyo. Very sensitive. Just right for Captain."

The woman's name was Hideko. According to Kay, both her parents had been killed in the war. During the occupation, Hideko and Kay had shared a small house together near the Air Base. Hideko, who had been trained to play the samisen, a long necked Japanese lute with three strings that sounded like a cross between a guitar and a harp, specialized in performing at Geisha houses entertaining wealthy Japanese businessmen. After opening her own bar, now and then, Kay would hire Hideko to play at the café. Of late, Hideko had fallen on hard times and had asked Kay if she could work at her café other than as a musician.

"I speak to her tomorrow," said Kay. "Maybe she meet you tomorrow night. You come at ten o'clock."

While serving in Korea waiting for my transfer to Japan, I had read books like Ruth Benedict's *The*

Chrysanthemum and The Sword, and James Michener's *Sayonara*. In these books, I had read about the tea ceremony, Japanese theater, Kabuki and Noh, the art of flower arrangement, Ikebana, the philosophy of Zen, Japanese music.

Up to now, my cultural experiences had been conversations in a butchered, pidgin English with the girls working at Kay's café. For Kays' girls, the road to Satori lay not in the teachings of The Buddha, but in listening to American rock music. Elvis Presley was as much revered as the Emperor.

I was delighted to accept Kay's offer to meet Hideko.

The next night I arrived at Kay's promptly at ten, wearing a civilian suit instead of the usual military dress. I had barely stepped inside the door when Kay approached me, accompanied by a woman, perhaps ten years older than myself, her face all lipstick and powder, and wearing a sequined Chinese dress, one size too small, though the woman was thin as a rail. After introductions, Kay left us to discover each other.

With one of the other Kay girls, I would normally engage in an English-Japanese chit-chat, pretty much the same no matter which girl you spoke to. "You likee Japan?" "When you go back to stateside?" "Maybe you takee me to Hong Kong sometime, *ne*?" "You no worry, I give you *taksun* good time tonight."

The protocol was first to buy a few drinks to allow the house to make a few yen while the parties nailed down a financial arrangement for later. Around midnight the bar would close and you'd go off to the girl's house for the night.

With Hideko I soon discovered there was to be no small talk. Without a moment's hesitation, she said, "We spend the night together, Captain, *ne*?" She asked the question with about the same degree of emotion as if she were asking me if I wanted to share a plate of french fries with her. So much for Zen.

"*Ne?*" she repeated, when I didn't answer her immediately.

"I don't know."

"We make price now, then we can talk, not worry about later."

"How much do you want?" I asked out of curiosity.

"Five thousand."

The going rate to spend the night with one of Kay's girls was in the three thousand yen range. At three hundred and sixty yen to the dollar, an additional two thousand yen amounted to another five dollars and change. Not much, still, it seemed a bit high-handed, especially when there was a question whether the services to be rendered were necessarily going to be of a superior nature.

"Four thousand," I said, bargaining almost as a reflex, even though I wasn't really interested in the product.

"Four thousand, five hundred," she said, then leaned back against her chair and winked. As far as she was concerned, we had a deal.

We ordered the usual drinks: beer for me, whiskey that was really tea for Hideko. Though her English was superior to the other girls' who worked at Kays, she discussed herself in only the most general of ways, and didn't express much interest in me, until she found out that I was a dentist. I realized the reason the first time she smiled. She shot her hand over her mouth, though not fast enough for my practiced eye. Her front teeth were all blackened by decay.

During the course of the evening, this aging prostitute with her rotten teeth and urgent need to please me proved rather pathetic. She seemed so absolutely devoid of any sense of self-esteem. Reluctantly, I decided to stick to her bargain and went home with her after the bar closed. It was, as we say in Yiddish, a *mitzvah*, an act of kindness. Maybe God would love me a little better.

Hideko shared a small house with another woman, whom I glimpsed briefly while removing my shoes at the entry vestibule, the *genkan*. We passed through sliding doors into a tiny room, four and a half *tatami* mats in size, small even by Japanese standards. A child was sleeping on a *futon*, a mattress not much more than a thick blanket. Gently, Hideko picked up the sleeping boy and carried him into another room, which wasn't much larger than a closet, closing the sliding door to afford us a modicum of privacy. Then without a word she undressed and slipped under the blankets on the *futon*.

Other than a few obligatory grunts and a lot of rooting for me to come fast, Hideko was lifeless. Thank God she had the decency not to try and kiss me.

After we were finished, I immediately began to dress. She asked me where I was going.

"Back to the base, " I said.

"You no stay the night?" She appeared offended, which surprised me. Girls never cared if you decided not to stay the night.

I made a lame excuse, something about early morning duty, but I could see she didn't believe me. She sat up in bed, not bothering to cover her small breasts. The room was dark. I couldn't be sure, but I think she was crying.

"I have to go," I insisted. "We can meet again at Kay's. Okay?"

"I'm too old, *ne*?" She let out a soft moan. "Maybe you like me a little?"

"I like you a lot, really I do."

"Then why you go back to base?"

"Really, you're very nice, Hideko. I mean it." She gazed silently at me as I continued to dress, and I felt like I had just kicked a dog too old to move out of the way.

"Maybe you help me?" she said in the same mournful tone as when she had asked me if I liked her.

I thought about the little boy in the other room and reached into my pocket to give her the extra five hundred yen she had originally asked for.

"You fix my teeth?"

"What's that?"

"I go to Japanese dentist, but he hurts so much, and he is *totemo takei* (too expensive). Please, you fix my teeth, Captain-san."

"I don't know, Hideko. I'm not allowed to work on someone outside the base."

"I get my teeth fixed, maybe I do better business. Please, Captain. How you like never to smile?"

"I don't see how I can arrange it."

"You say you like me."

I thought of those blackened anteriors hidden behind Hideko's rather nicely curved lips, and said hesitantly, "I'll see what I can do."

"You promise."

"All right." I was dead tired and wanted only to get away from this sad woman and return to the BOQ.

"You fix teeth tomorrow," she commanded me.

I finished dressing and started for the door. "Tomorrow is impossible," I said. "First, I'm going to have to figure out how to manage it." By now, I was ready to promise anything for a decent night's sleep.

"You tell Kay, *ne?*"

Then she did the unexpected. She jumped out of bed and ran over to me. Before I could get away, she had her hands on my shoulders and planted an affectionate kiss on my cheek, like a sister saying goodbye to a brother going off to war.

For the next two weeks, I thought over whether I was required to keep my promise to Hideko. The promise had been obtained under duress. Therefore, it didn't count. Kay's wasn't the only bar in town, though the idea of serving out the remaining eight months of my tour without being able to enjoy Kay's friendly, cheerful atmosphere was a serious downer. When I thought of Hideko living with those disgusting, anterior teeth, I made a decision.

On a weekend when Colonel Stutz, our base dental commander, and his sidekick, Major Jello (real name Jellosky), were off on one of their semi-annual TDY (temporary duty) shopping trips to Hong Kong, I volunteered to cover all dental emergencies at the clinic. After I made the necessary arrangements, I went over to Kay's and left a message for Hideko. Kay assured me that she would personally give it to her.

The weather was gray and threatening on that damp Sunday morning in early December when, at the risk being of being court-martialed, I signed in Hideko at the front gate as my guest. Dressed in tan slacks and a white blouse, and devoid of all makeup, Hideko looked like any one of the many Japanese women employed on the base at the BX, the commissary, the clinics and the schools.

She greeted me with a certain indifference, as if my fixing her teeth were not a favor that she needed to be grateful for, but an obligation she expected me to honor.

We entered the clinic from a side door, and went to an operatory at the end of the hallway where there was no windows, eliminating the possibility that we might be observed from outside the building. In the morning, I had gathered together all the materials and instruments I would need for the task at hand and laid them out on the tray and the countertop. I could have used an assistant, but decided to work by myself, reducing the risk of being caught treating a Japanese.

I took my time, deciding that I would complete one side at a time. After anesthetizing Hideko, I carefully drilled out all the decay, grateful that the nerves in the teeth were well recessed within the dentin. If I exposed a nerve, I would have had to either extract the offended tooth or do a root canal. Either alternative would have been disastrous, given the circumstances.

I placed good bases within each cavity, and then one by one began to fill them with silicate cement, experimenting with all the available shades at my disposal, much like an artist mixing different colors on a palette, to achieve a perfect blend with the natural coloration of the teeth. After the material hardened, I smoothed down the margins of each filling with my polishing stones and sand paper discs, creating a continuous, even surface between the margins of the cavity material and the enamel of the teeth.

Altogether, I filled ten cavities on six teeth, a process that took me four and a half hours. Except for a need to relieve her bladder, Hideko remained almost motionless in the chair, resting now and then only to relax the muscles of her jaw. When the job was finished, I produced a hand mirror and held it in front of her face.

"Smile," I commanded.

"I smile later," she said. "My son wait for me."

"Please," I begged.

As she smiled, she shot her hand in front of her mouth. The habit of a lifetime had ruined what should have been one of the great moments in my life. I wanted to wrench her hand away from her mouth, but I was too exhausted to express even minor disapproval, and quickly removed the apron around her and led her out of the clinic.

We reached the main gate under a veil of silence. I suppose that after sitting in a dental chair for half a day and still feeling the effects of three shots of Novocaine, no one would feel much like talking. As we parted, my pride had to be satisfied with a perfunctory bow and the usual

"*Arigato gozaimashita,* thank you very much," the absolute minimum in the Japanese mode of expressing appreciation.

"Think nothing of it," I mumbled, and then returned to my quarters, flopped down on my bed, and prayed that I would never have the misfortune of being forced to waste another minute of my tour of duty with Hideko.

On New Year's Eve, the Base Commander's party at the Officers' Club was an alcoholic's Garden of Eden. After two hours, you thought you were sloshing around inside a distillery where they had turned on a giant laughing machine. Attendance by base officers was mandatory, but after two hours of joviality and back slapping, I could stand it no longer and quietly slipped out of the club through a side door. Unwilling to spend New Year's Eve alone in the cheerless confines of the BOQ, I left the base.

My first inclination had been to go to a place other than Kay's, not wishing to risk running into Hideko, whom I hadn't seen since fixing her teeth three weeks ago. But the other cafés, jammed with celebrating airmen and noncommissioned officers, were even more raucous than the Officer's Club.

I opened the door to Kay's, taking a careful look around before entering. A few junior officers were sitting with the usual Kay girls, but for the most part the place was relatively quiet. The required attendance at the Base Commander's New Year's Eve fete had ruined what should have been the biggest night of the year for Kay, who was sitting alone at the bar, staring morosely at a picture of Marlon Brando in an Air Force uniform that was hanging on the wall above the bar. Hideko was nowhere in sight.

I sat down at an empty booth. One of the girls—she introduced herself as Sonja—served me a beer, and then took a seat at my table with a drink of her own. She looked to be in her early twenties, perhaps a little older than most of the other girls. Though not exactly pretty, she possessed a cheerful, amiable manner. Since I had never spent a night with her before, I thought, why not—it was New Year's Eve, and at this late hour (it was almost eleven), I didn't think I'd be able to find anyone better.

Then I saw her! Angling out of the bathroom, Hideko slithered toward me like some feral creature of the night, her brand new white teeth displayed in a smile as broad as the Grand Coulee Dam.

"Captain-san!" she exclaimed. "Finally, you come to see Hideko."

Needing no invitation, she flopped down in the seat next to Sonja, almost pushing the startled girl onto the floor, and, in a guttural, girl-to-girl message, told Sonja to get packing.

To her credit, Sonja wasn't about to be upended from what looked to be a profitable evening by Hideko's bullying tactics. The girl exploded with a tirade of her own expletives, and for a moment I thought things might get physical between them. However, Kay, hearing the commotion, came running over, and after discovering what was going on dismissed Sonja, leaving me defenseless with a jubilant, triumphant Hideko.

"Every night I look for you," said Hideko. "Where you been? You butterfly on Hideko?"

The word "butterfly" was a commonly used verb amongst the girls to denote infidelity, and it appeared, at least from Hideko's point of view, that I now belonged exclusively to her. I had read somewhere that in certain primitive cultures if you saved somebody's life, you became obliged to take care of that person until she died. Did that also apply to saving one's teeth?

"We spend tonight together, *ne?*"

I was too dumbfounded to respond. I began to look around, hoping for a miracle. Sonja had already found herself another officer, and Kay, again seated at the bar, began to nod toward me, clearly elated with the way things had worked out between Hideko and me.

At eleven-thirty Hideko nudged my arm. "We go now," she said.

"Go where?" Instantly, I had a nightmare vision of another loveless copulation in that tiny, unheated house. "Do we have to? It's so nice and quiet here."

She laughed. At least she no longer covered her mouth, and I was finally able to get a first hand look at my craftsmanship. "You crazy," she said. "In a few minutes bar closes. Everybody go home and celebrate New Year's. Come. *Ikimasho, Captain-san.*"

Though Hideko's house was only a few short blocks from Kay's, the walk seemed interminable. Hideko asked me to wait for her by the gate, that she would only be a few minutes, and then she went inside the house. Even as I write this memoir, I cannot explain to myself why I didn't run as hard as I could back to the base, why I waited obediently for her to return.

About twenty minutes later, Hideko reappeared. To my amazement, she was dressed in a beautiful silk kimono, pure white and adorned by hand painted roses and chrysanthemums. Her long black hair was swept up elegantly, and for a moment I thought she might have stepped out of an Utamaro woodblock. Under her arm she carried a large black case.

A light snow began to fall, and I draped my overcoat around her, and we headed back toward the strip where she hailed a cab. We must have driven thirty minutes before we came to a small Japanese inn. While I waited outside, Hideko talked with the innkeeper, an old man with whom she seemed familiar. After she had finished making all the arrangements, the old man ushered us inside to a private room.

The floor was made of new tatami mats, and in the corner was a small recession in the wall, the *Tokonoma*, decorated by a calligraphy scroll, a floral arrangement, and a Japanese doll of a Geisha enclosed in a glass case. In the middle of the floor was a low wooden table with two cushions on either side. The innkeeper beckoned us to sit at the table, and then disappeared. Moments later, a middle-aged woman served us tea and cookies, and then gracefully removed herself through the sliding panels.

"Don't I have to pay somebody?" I asked.

"Not necessary," she said. "Eat sweet cookies. They are special for New Year's."

While I was eating and drinking, Hideko removed her samisen from its case, and played for me, producing a soft, lyrical sound, silk gliding across polished glass. Then she began to sing, *"Hotaru-no hikari, mado-no yuki--."* Her voice, though a bit on the thin side, was deliciously sweet.

When she was finished singing, I asked her what the lyrics meant.

"I see firefly, I see snow on the window/ The days go by with my reading/ Years go by/ I start the day this morning/ It is over, I depart."

She sang several other songs before putting the instrument back into its case.

We undressed and put on cotton kimonos, and she led me through sliding doors to a tiled room with a sunken bathtub heated by gas. There she scrubbed me clean with warm water from a small wooden bucket, and then asked me to go into a steaming bath. Squatting next to me, she wiped my brow with a cold towel all the time humming softly. After awhile, my pores seemed to open up, and I felt marvelously at ease with my body, a sense of calmness coming upon me that was almost magical.

After the bath she dried and powdered me as if I were an infant. Back in our room, the table had been removed and replaced by a large, thick *futon*. I lay down and she massaged my body, her strong fingers running up and down my ribs as if she were still strumming the samisen. Afterwards, she lay down next to me and we wrapped our arms about each other. The final miracle was her passion.

Later we rested in the dark and I asked her "Why?"

"On New Year's you must be with someone you love," she said.

"But you don't even know me."

She kissed me on the cheek. "I remember tonight forever."

Several days later my father had a heart attack and I was given an emergency leave. It was touch and go for a while and I didn't return to Japan for almost a month.

The day after I flew back to the air base, I went over to Kay's and asked for Hideko. Kay told me that she no longer lived in Fussa, that she had gone to live in Morioka Prefecture. Her aunt had died from stomach cancer, and her uncle had requested that she help him raise his three sons. Kay handed me a letter written in English.

"Dear Captain-san,

I wait for you, but you don't come. I have to go now. You say that I don't know you. But you are wrong, Captain-san. I know you and I am always grateful to you. I never forget you. Maybe sometime, you please to try and remember me a little. . . Hideko

I never went back to the strip. In one night, Hideko had given me all of the Japan that I would ever want to know. The rest would have been superfluous.

Richard R. Karlen

On March 10, 1945, three hundred and thirty-four American B-29s dropped thousands of incendiary bombs on Tokyo. Sixteen square miles of the city were incinerated. An estimated 130,000 civilians were killed.

Post war documents indicate that the American High Command had come to the conclusion that inflicting massive civilian casualties on the Japanese would destroy national morale and shorten the war. The Japanese did, in fact, surrender after atomic bombs were dropped on Hiroshima and Nagasaki some five months later, which resulted in the deaths of more than two hundred and fifty thousand civilians.

To this day the debate continues whether any nation is justified in killing thousands of civilians as a means of ending armed conflicts. Since no reasonable person believes that war is a rational process for settling disputes, the debate seems like a big waste of time.

AN APPLE FOR KIYOSHI

March 10, 2003

My arm brushes up against an egg sitting on the kitchen counter, and before I am able to catch it, the egg, like Humpty Dumpty, takes a great fall. Jiro, our brown and white mongrel, is awakened from his morning nap and rushes into the kitchen to lap up the egg yolk that has spilled out of the fractured egg shell onto my recently scoured white linoleum floor.

"Out, out!" I holler at the disobedient dog.

Though I have been living in the States for almost forty-two years, this custom of allowing dogs to live with people in a house is one that no Japanese woman can ever feel comfortable with.

I am on my hands and knees cleaning up the mess when my granddaughter, Kim, enters the room. She sits down at the table and observes me.

"Can I help?" she asks half-heartedly.

"Dogs live better in this country than most people in the rest of the world," I say. "In Japan during the war, people died for an egg. Here, in America, a dog slops up an egg yolk and nobody thinks anything of it."

"That isn't Jiro's fault." Kim is always a bit annoyed when I carry on about how much I dislike having a dog live in the house.

I look toward the kitchen entrance. Jiro stretches out by the door, watching my every move, hoping he'll have the chance to finish cleaning up the remains of the delicious egg. The child is right. Why carry on? Jiro is just an animal doing what animals do.

I finish cleaning up the eggshell and its contents and sit down at the table opposite Kim.

"Why are you crying, Grandma?" Kim asks me.

I touched my cheeks. "Imagine that," I say. "Hand me a tissue, please."

The child offers me a paper napkin from the counter behind her. "Today is March 10th," I tell her. "You won't read about it in school, Kim, but on March 10th, 1945, exactly fifty-eight years ago, the Americans bombed Tokyo and thousands of people were burned to death. I was nine years old, not much younger than you."

"And that's why you're crying?"

"You remind me of my mother, you know. You've got the same wide, inquisitive eyes, the good, solid bone structure. I wonder if you have her courage, too."

"I'm sorry that so many Japanese were killed, Grandma," Kim says.

Richard R. Karlen

"We were in a war with America, Kim. A lot of people were killed—some were American, some were Japanese. Nobody was counting."

The blockbusters made the greatest noise, but it was the incendiaries, the M47 bombs, that did the real damage. Six hours after hundreds of American planes had bombed Tokyo, the fires seemed to intensify, swept along by the high winds. A wall of bright orange flames leapt into the sky and great billows of black smoke spewed into the atmosphere to shut out the moon and stars and form a giant dark cloud that hovered over the city like a malignant blanket.

We had been walking all night, along with hundreds, maybe thousands of other people toward the great Sumida River. Uriko, my six-month-old sister, was tied to my back with a cotton sash. My four-year-old brother, Kiyoshi, walked behind me. My mother went ahead, an enormous bundle strapped to her slender back, bending her almost in half. Inside the bundle were all those household and personal possessions we were able to pack before the fires had forced us to flee from our homes.

As we neared the river that divided Chiba Prefecture from Tokyo Prefecture, Mother stopped and turned. She urged me on: "Hurry, Tomiko, we must find a place on the river bank. If the fire continues to spread, we may even have to go into the river."

"Where's grandfather?" I asked.

I remember being so tired that at that moment dying didn't seem like such a terrible idea. All I wanted was to lie down and rest.

"He's fighting the fires with the other men," Mother said. "We have to take care of ourselves. Now please hurry." She grabbed my arm and began to pull me along on the narrow path that led to the river. "Just a little farther and we can rest." Then she looked over my shoulder. "What happened to Kiyoshi?"

185

An Apple For Kiyoshi

I turned around—no Kiyoshi. I thought he was behind me. Though we had stopped only for a moment to look for him, a tidal wave of people shoved us aside as they hurried toward the riverbank. Bad manners, yes, but easy to understand when you consider that thousands of homes had burnt to the ground and the surviving families, no different than ourselves, wanted to get to the river to save themselves.

"You were supposed to be watching him," Mother said. "I can't do everything, Tomiko. You must help more." I started to cry, until she yanked on my arm again. "Never mind, let's keep going. Once we're at the river, we'll find him. He can't be far."

Sure enough, Kiyoshi had beaten us to the river bank, where we found him on his knees drinking the water. Mother ran up to him and dragged him away from the water's edge. "Get away from the river," she said angrily. I thought she was going to box his ears. The poor little beggar looked so forlorn, so dejected. He hated more than anything to be scolded by Mother.

We spent the night on the crowded riverbank, wedged between several other families. Mother took a small *futon* from her bundle and spread it on the ground for Kiyoshi and me to sleep on. Mother slept on the ground, her arm draped across our bundle, while Uriko nestled inside her kimono, suckling a breast.

In the morning, Mother was sitting up, looking around for Grandfather. Some of the men had returned and were searching for their families. Behind us the smoke was still rising into the sky from the few, small scattered fires that had survived the night. The strong winds that had intensified and spread the fire last night had died down.

I was very thirsty and asked Mother for a drink.

"You'll have to wait," she said. "Soon, Grandfather will find us and we'll go back to our house. Maybe we'll be lucky and our house didn't burn completely and we'll be able to drink water from our well. For now, we must be careful not to drink the river water."

The day passed slowly. Huge logs cut down in the mountains drifted by us toward the sawmills farther downstream. Barges crossed back and forth across the river, bringing medical supplies and food to help the sick and injured. Finally, soldiers arrived on trucks to help clean up and assist the police in patrolling the area. Last night, all I could think about was resting; today, I wanted to get up and move, go somewhere, do something, anything.

Late in the afternoon, Mr. Takeo, an old friend of Grandfather's, wandered by looking for his family. He told us that he had been with Grandfather, but they had become separated. He didn't know where he was. "I'm sure he's all right," he said, and then added regrettably, "However, I'm sorry to tell you that your house has burnt down with the others."

I started to cry. "Tears will not bring back our house, Tomi-chan," Mother said to me. "You must have courage."

I remembered the slogan posted in the classrooms at the school, *"Katsumade wa hoshigaranai"* ("We shall not want until we win.") But the words seemed empty of meaning. Remembering them did little to cheer me up.

Mother decided that we would remain by the river one more night and wait for Grandfather. She gave us each a biscuit and a little cooked rice left over from yesterday's supper. Kiyoshi said he wasn't hungry and mother let me have his share. Ordinarily, Kiyoshi was always hungry. After I had finished eating, I became ashamed when I discovered that Mother also ate nothing.

When Grandfather didn't come in the morning, we set off toward our house. Once again, Mother strapped Uriko to my back. This time Mother, in spite of her own heavy burden, held Kiyoshi's hand.

In the area closest to our house, the fires had died out, though ashes still smoldered in many places. Burnt bodies were everywhere. The district looked like a wilderness, with nothing left but charred wood and hot iron pipes. The lingering stench of cooked flesh was at times unbearable.

An Apple For Kiyoshi

We finally arrived at our house, and just as Mr. Takeo had told us, we found it to be nothing more than a pile of ashes. Even Mother cried.

Finally she stood up. "We must go. There's nothing here for us." She picked up her bundle. "Stop crying, Tomi-san. One day the war will end and Father will come home and build us another house."

When would that be? At the time, my father was stationed in Burma, thousands of miles away. Who could predict when the war would be over? In the meantime, how would we live?

We came across Mr. Nakamura, another neighbor, who was dressing the burns of a young boy. The boy's legs were charred and smelled like burnt pigeon feathers. The boy gasped for air, like there was something stuck in his throat. His eyes were red and swollen. Part of his scalp was singed and bald. I turned away from him in disgust.

Mr. Nakamura told us that Grandfather had tried to help put out the fires and rescue people trapped in their homes, and then, without warning, had collapsed. "He was too old for such an exertion," Mr. Nakamura said. "No one could stop him from trying to help. He had true *bushido*, the heart and soul of a samurai."

"Where is he now?" Mother asked.

"It happened a couple of streets over." Mr. Nakamura pointed toward a spiraling string of smoke. "I don't know where they took him. I'm terribly sorry." Then he continued to minister to the young boy, talking to him softly, urging him to be brave.

Mother bowed and thanked Mr. Nakamura.

"Come," she said to me. "We must keep looking for Grandfather."

We wandered up and down streets talking to people, asking them about Grandfather. We recognized a few old neighbors who were searching amongst the ruins of their houses for objects of value that might not have been destroyed. Firemen and policemen patrolled the streets.

Corpses were everywhere. I vomited at the sight of one dead woman. Her eyes were open and peeled back under her eyelids, the skin around her neck had sloughed off, her nose looked like a dried up fig, the rest of her, skin, flesh and clothes, was all charred black.

A policeman asked us what we were doing in this area. "Everyone is to report to the high school," the policeman said.

Mother bowed politely. "We are looking for my father-in-law," she said.

The policeman, a squat, husky man, spread his legs apart and placed his hands on his hips. "We must clear the streets, or we'll never be able to clean up. Take your children and go off to the school. You'll be provided with food and water there."

Policemen were to be respected at all times. We had all heard of stories where a policeman would attack a person and beat him for almost no reason at all. When Mother said to the policeman, "Please, sir, just a little more time," I found myself tugging at her sleeve, trying to pull her away.

The policeman grunted. He took a menacing step toward us. Mother turned and said to me, "All right, Tomiko, we'll go." Then she bowed once again to the man and we headed off in the direction of the high school.

Miraculously, the building had escaped serious damage. Hundreds of people were crowded into the courtyard, but we managed to find a space next to a half charred fence on the school's perimeter and rested.

Mother said to me, "Don't worry, Tomiko, we'll be all right. I've several kimonos in my bag, which we can sell if necessary. In the meantime, we've still got a few potatoes and biscuits. In the school they'll give us rice and water."

Two days ago we had been a family: Mother, sister, brother, grandfather. We had lived in a fine house built by my great-grandfather. We had a small garden of roses and chrysanthemums, and two fine cherry trees, which my grandfather had meticulously cultivated. Now there was nothing but ashes and tree stumps. Grandfather was missing. Father was fighting in a foreign land. It seemed to me as if the whole city had been destroyed. What would happen to us when there was no more food and nothing left to sell?

Once again, Kiyoshi refused the half a potato Mother offered him. He complained that his head hurt, and that he couldn't swallow his saliva, his throat was so sore. Mother felt his head, and then said to me anxiously, "You must go into the schoolhouse, Tomiko, and see if you can find a doctor. Kiyoshi is burning up with fever."

A large crowd blocked the entrance to the school. A young man wearing an army uniform with five buttons and the mark of the cherry blossom on each button was standing on a box in front of the people. The young man cried out that he would soon join the army and avenge his friends, his family, and his country. Everyone cheered. A friend was holding a large flag of the Rising Sun, which others were trying to sign. Then all began to sing:

"Katue te kuru zoto to/Isamashiku/ Kunio deta kara wa/ Katsuma de wa shinanai."("I made a promise that I will fight bravely and will not return without victory.")

Today I think of all those fools singing and cheering and waving a flag. Didn't they realize that Tokyo had been incinerated, that thousands of people had been killed, that thousands more were going to die before the war would end? And what were they going to do—these boys who weren't old enough to shave? Die? For what? For whom? General Tojo? The Emperor?

Inside the building, I told a lady, who was bandaging an old man, about Kiyoshi. After she finished with the old man, she came with me at once. After examining Kiyoshi, she said to Mother, "We must take this child to the hospital, right now. He could be quite contagious. Wait here, please."

The woman went back into the school, and then returned and waited with us. About fifteen minutes later two police-men arrived. One was riding a bicycle pulling a small flat-boarded trailer used to haul small objects too cumbersome to carry. They lifted Kiyoshi onto the trailer and tied a rope around his body. Kiyoshi cried and tried to stretch his arms toward Mother. "We don't want him falling off the trailer," one of the policeman said to Mother. Then he told her where they were taking Kiyoshi and left.

We walked for hours when we heard the air raid sirens. Along with other pedestrians and bicyclists, we jumped off the side of the road into a large ditch, and buried our heads in our hands. We could hear the distant drone of the planes as they approached, and then the drone turned into a deafening roar and I thought my eardrums would burst. I looked into the sky. Eclipsing the sun were hundreds of planes. The Americans had returned.

One of the planes peeled out of formation and came diving toward us. Mother grabbed my shoulders and pushed Uriko and me under our bundle. There was a horrible ripping sound, like the world was being chewed up by some monstrous reaper and then just as quickly as the plane had come, it was gone, zooming back up into the sky to rejoin the others. The planes passed over Tokyo and continued flying west. After a few minutes, we could hear distant popping sounds, like corks being pulled out of bottles. This time they were bombing Yokohama.

The all-clear siren sounded and once again we were on our way to the hospital. In the middle of the road a man lay under his bicycle, his head immersed in a pool of his own blood. Nobody wanted to go near him as if he might be contaminated. They say war makes people brave, but I saw the opposite. Everyone thought only about their own welfare, how they could best survive.

Only Mother went to the wounded man. She put down her bundle and pulled the bicycle off him. When she tried to drag him off the road, he cried out in pain and she let him go. "Forgive me," she said to the wounded man.

Finally, others came to help. "There's nothing anyone can do for him," she said.

Once again she strapped the bundle to her back, then grabbed my arm and pulled me along. "We've got to get to the hospital before the planes return."

I didn't think I could walk any farther, and Mother took Uriko from me, cradling the infant in her arms as she walked. We went another kilometer before I slid to my knees. "I can't walk any more, Mother." My eyes watered from shame. "I'm sorry."

Mother was more frustrated than angry, but I could see that she, too, was grateful for the rest. We found a small patch of grass under a tree a few meters off the road. Mother nursed Uriko while I tried to sleep.

It had just turned dark when several soldiers passed by. One of them gave Mother and myself two small rice balls and drinks from his canteen of water. Mother stood up and bowed twice, as if she were a beggar. The soldiers stared at her for a long time, and I knew it was because, even though Mother's long black hair was all tangled, and her kimono was filthy and rumpled, she was still a beautiful woman. I was furious the way these men with their leering gazes dishonored her. They were soldiers with no rank, while Mother was the wife of a Captain in the Imperial Army.

Nevertheless, we ate their rice balls greedily. After Uriko had fallen asleep, Mother squeezed a few drops of her milk for me in a small wooden cup. The milk was warm and too sweet. I didn't like it, but Mother insisted I drink the liquid.

In the morning we started out again for the hospital. Houses still smoldered from the fires. People wandered about aimlessly. It was like we were living in a nightmare. When would it end, I remember asking myself? When would our lives once again make sense?

The hospital waiting room was overcrowded and we were lucky to find a small space against the wall. Mother told me to sit down on our bundle and hold Uriko, while she went to find out what happened to Kiyoshi.

A dirty-faced boy, smaller than myself, jammed against me. Lice crawled in his hair and I tried to push him away, terrified that the lice might jump onto me. There was a dark bruise on his forehead and the skin on the tip of his nose was peeling.

"You smell," I said to the boy.

"So do you."

"Pretty soon we'll be going back to our house and then I'll be able to take a bath," I said.

"Our house burnt down," he said. "Can we go with you? We wouldn't be much trouble."

"Why should we bother with you?"

Mother returned and I was grateful to get away from the filthy boy. I don't know why I lied to him. He was so pathetic. Children think only of themselves. They say and do things because it makes them feel superior. They are the most selfish of all creatures. To this day I wish I could apologize to that little boy with the lice in his hair for being so rude to him. I hope he survived the war, as I did, and is today a happy person, and, if he remembers that moment in the hospital, I pray he will forgive me.

Once we were on the road again, Mother explained that Kiyoshi had diphtheria, a disease that gives you a sore throat and a high fever. He was put in an isolation ward where no one was allowed to enter, except the nurses and doctors, and even they had to put on masks and gowns to protect themselves. He was going to need proper treatment and rest, and above all good food. Mother seemed quite nervous when she told me this and I wondered if she were telling me all she knew.

I cried when I discovered that Mother had sold her ring to the hospital director for a promise that Kiyoshi would be well cared for. The ring was Mother's most precious piece of jewelry, a beautiful natural pearl inlaid in gold, which had belonged to my great-grandmother and one day would have been mine. I thought Father would be quite angry if he knew she had sold it, but I was too afraid to say anything since I knew that Mother was probably as upset as I was.

We spent the night inside the ruins of a small tobacco shop that had been abandoned. Though the roof had been destroyed, a part of the floor had survived the fires. We rolled out our *futon*, and I quickly fell asleep.

In the morning Mother nursed Uriko and shared a potato with me. Then she said we were going to the country to buy food for Kiyoshi.

At the train station the platform bulged with people hoping to escape to the countryside. Eventually, we boarded the train to Tachikawa. I don't think one more person could have squeezed into the car. At Tachikawa, we waited another hour, and then took the train to Nishifu. Stepping off the train, I breathed the country air gratefully, and thought I'd rather walk back to Tokyo than again be crushed for hours standing on those trains.

We wandered the narrow, country road looking for a farm where we could buy food. In the distance, beyond the endless expanse of the green and brown rice paddies, was *Fuji-san*, its snow capped peak rising above the clouds with a singular clarity. Here in the country for the moment I could forget the scorched earth, the foul smoke-filled air, the ruined buildings that we had left behind in Tokyo.

Mother must have been reading my thoughts, for she said, "After Kiyoshi gets well, we'll write Aunt Yumi in Nigata. We'll ask her if we can live with her family until the war is over and Father returns."

At the first three farms we came to, the farmers refused to sell us anything. Food was scarce, they said, even here. The government required them to save the bulk of their produce to feed the brave soldiers and sailors who were fighting to save our country.

The sun was dropping below the horizon when we passed through the gate of one particularly large farm. A mother and her grown daughter greeted us coolly, but after

Mother told them that Father was a Captain in the army, and before the war had been the vice-president of the Kunitachi branch of the Fuji Bank, they invited us into the guest room.

They served us tea and a sweet potato, and we talked about the war and yesterday's bombing of Tokyo. What else was there to talk about?

"Terrible, terrible. The Americans are savage beasts," the woman said as if she were reading from one of the pamphlets that the government periodically distributed to the people. "If we lose the war, they will come and eat our children."

She then showed us a picture of her four sons. One had died fighting in the Philippines, another was stationed in Chosen (Korea). The other two were discharged from the army and lived at home to work the farm after her husband had died from cancer.

Mother politely waited an appropriate time before she explained how sick Kiyoshi was and offered to buy food from the woman. She removed a roll of yen from her bag.

The woman shook her head. "I'm very sorry to hear about your son," she said. "But in these troubled times, I must look out for my own family. I ask you honestly, what good is money? It is hardly worth the paper it's printed on." She stared at Mother's bulging sack. "However, perhaps we can make a trade."

Mother drew from her bag a kimono, an embroidered pink garment made of the finest Chinese silk. The woman examined it carefully, holding it up to the light, checking the quality of the fabric. Then she said, "It's a little old, don't you think?"

The kimono was one of Mother's best. Father had commissioned Mrs. Oi, one of the best seamstresses in our district, to make the kimono. Mr. Kawasaki, a distinguished local artist, embroidered white and red chrysanthemums into the fabric. The woman continued to appraise the kimono, then said to her daughter, a girl of about eighteen or nineteen who had pimples all over her face. "What do you think, Hiro-chan?"

"When cousin Yaeko was married she had a chest full of beautiful kimonos," the girl said in a high-pitched voice that made me want to put my hands over my ears.

The woman said to Mother, "The government watches us closely. We would be taking a great risk selling food to you."

Without a word, Mother pulled out of her bag her pale blue kimono, also made by Mrs. Oi. The white and yellow embroidery by Mr. Kawasaki pictured Lake Hakone with Fuji in the background. It was exceptional in its detail. Like the pearl ring, I had dreamt that one day I would own it.

"I have nothing else of value," Mother said.

The girl's eyes lit up at the sight of this kimono, and without hesitation, her mother accepted it. "It's not exactly what I'd like for my daughter, but it will do," she said.

She led us through the house into the backyard to a large storage bin, where she measured three kilos of rice, a kilo of soybean, and six ears of corn. Then we followed her to another part of the yard, where she descended a ladder into an enormous hole, moments later to emerge with several sweet potatoes and six eggs. We discarded old clothes to make room for the food in our bag. Then Mother bowed and thanked the woman and her daughter for their kindness.

On the way back to the railway station, Mother was especially silent. She had traded her most expensive kimono for a small amount of food to a stupid woman and her stupid daughter. I could imagine how humiliated she must have felt.

I said to her: "It will be all right, Mother? Kiyoshi will get better. We'll find Grandfather. Father will come home and build us a new house." Simple-minded, meaningless, childish thoughts. To this day, I'm ashamed that I could not have thought of something more intelligent to say, any small word that might have helped to ease the pain I knew she was experiencing.

Unfortunately, the worst was yet to be discovered. Mother had been concealing from me news about Grandfather. She stopped walking and put an arm around me.

"Grandfather is dead, Tomi-chan," she said. "One of the doctor's at the hospital told me that he had a heart attack and died."

I started to cry. She rubbed her check against the top of my head, a rare gesture of physical affection that even now, as I remember the moment, warms my blood.

"Pray, Tomi-chan," she said, "that Grandfather's soul will find peace in Heaven."

The train was delayed at every station on the ride back to Tachikawa. At Fussa, three policemen boarded the train. One of them blew a whistle and shouted, "This is an inspection. Everyone will show us what they are carrying."

A husky man sitting behind us threw his bag through an open window leading out onto the platform. In an instant, he was out the window, but he wasn't fast enough, and one of the policemen clubbed him. I had never seen a man hit by a policeman's club before. There was this awful crunch and without a sound the man doubled up and rolled to the ground.

Several other people ran to the far end of the car and hopped onto the platform and raced away. Policemen stationed outside of the train chased them as well. I dreaded to think what was going to happen to them, too, when they got caught.

The policemen inside the train began their inspection. People emptied their pockets and opened their bags and suitcases. When a policeman approached us, Mother stood up and bowed very low. "We have nothing, sir," she said. "Only a little food."

The policeman tore at the strings of our sack to open it wider. An egg fell out, smashing to the floor, its yolk spilling into a small yellow and white puddle. He reached inside our bundle.

"You have over five kilos of rice," the policeman said to Mother.

"Not that much," Mother insisted.

"The law provides that no one is allowed more than one kilo on his person." The policeman poked around in the bag with his club. He quickly discovered the sweet potatoes and the eggs and corn, and then demanded that Mother empty the sleeves of her kimono where mother kept her yen.

"I'll be generous with you," he said. He put the rice back into the sack and the money in his pocket. "I'm going to confiscate this sack and your money as punishment for your crime. Be glad I'm letting you off so easy."

Mother bowed very low, and then said, "If you take our money and our food, how will we live. My son, Kiyoshi, is in the hospital. I beg you to leave us a small portion of the food for him."

The policeman was a tall man with gray hair and a smooth, boyish face. He had mean, narrow eyes. "I've been hearing the same story all day," he said. "We're in a war, woman. Thousands of men are dying for our country every day. Don't expect me to have any pity for black marketers."

He picked up our bag and handed it to another police-man. Then he lifted his club and I remembered the man who was lying on the platform, unconscious and bleeding. I pushed myself in front of Mother and bowed very low.

"Please, sir," I said.

The policeman stared at me as if I were an insignificant worm, but then, to my relief, he turned and continued his inspection.

Mother grabbed me by the shoulder. "Why did you do that, Tomiko? He might have hurt you."

"I was afraid, Mother."

"Don't ever do something like that again. Never. Do you hear me?"

When the policeman was at the far end of the car, a woman sitting near us whispered to Mother. "They keep everything for themselves, the dirty thieves."

In Tokyo, we returned to the deserted tobacco store. Without our *futon,* the wooden floor was very hard. Still, it was better than lying outside on the damp earth. My stomach growled as I thought about the sweet potato I had eaten at the farm.

During the night, Mother awakened me. "Tomiko," she said. "I'm going out for a while. Don't be afraid. Stay here and watch Uriko."

"Where are you going?" I asked.

"Never mind. I won't be gone long."

Without Mother lying next to me, I wasn't able to sleep. I began to fantasize and found myself searching through the broken roof for a glimpse of a bright crescent moon that moved in and out of the clouds like a child playing hide-n-go-seek. I wanted to leap into the sky, grab hold of that elusive moon, bounce it around like a rubber ball. Having no concept of time, it seemed that Mother had been gone for hours before I heard footsteps.

My heart beat hard and fast. Had Mother returned? Suppose it was the police? I was terrified. They would want to know what I was doing in a stranger's house. I crept to the edge of the wall, and saw two soldiers and two women. The soldiers were carrying bottles of sake and all four of them were laughing loudly. One of the men tried to slip a hand under the folds of one of the woman's kimono. She slapped away his hand, and they both began to laugh even harder.

The sun had just crept over the horizon when Mother returned. When she saw I wasn't sleeping, she said angrily, "Why aren't you sleeping?"

"I tried to sleep, but I couldn't."

I was afraid she was going to scold me and remember thinking that it wasn't fair to get mad at someone, even a child, because she couldn't sleep.

"Never mind." To my relief, Mother smiled. "See what I've got here." She opened up a little bag and showed me an orange, a sweet potato and maybe half a kilo of good, white rice.

"Where did you get it?" I asked in amazement.

An Apple For Kiyoshi

"I met some friends. Eat the potato and the orange. Later, I'll go to the market and trade the rice for fruit and eggs, and then we'll go to the hospital and give it to Kioyshi."

I ate the food while Mother nursed Uriko. Then we lay down together and slept, until Uriko awakened us, all wet and soiled. Mother ripped strips of material from the cotton flannel garment she wore under her kimono and cleaned her up. She wouldn't let me go with her to the market. I think she didn't want me to watch her dealing with the black marketers.

After she came back, we returned to the hospital. Mother had arranged with the hospital director to allow her to enter the hospital through a back door into the hallway next to the isolation ward where Kiyoshi was being kept. She gave the food to the nurse in charge. We weren't allowed to see Kiyoshi since he was still in quarantine.

For the next seven nights, Mother would wait until dark, and then leave Uriko and myself and disappear. In the morning she'd return with rice or raw fish. Once she even brought a small bag of sugar, which was worth a small fortune on the black market. During the day she'd trade for potatoes, eggs, apples and oranges. She'd feed me and then take the rest of the food to the hospital for Kiyoshi. I don't know what Mother ate herself since she never touched any of the food that she traded for.

Though the nurses informed us that Kiyoshi was getting better, we still had not been allowed to see him. On the eighth day of Kiyoshi's illness, Mother asked when she would be allowed to visit him.

"Diphtheria is a very contagious disease," the nurse said. "You'd be taking a chance. Perhaps tomorrow or the next day."

Outside the hospital Mother kept hesitating, wanting to turn back, I think, and demand to see Kiyoshi. But I suppose she decided that it would be pointless to question the rules of a hospital and we continued to walk back toward our burnt-out tobacco store. We were almost there when Mother discovered an apple that had dropped into the sleeve of her kimono.

"We have to go back, Tomi-san," she said.

"But I'm so tired, Mother."

"Kiyoshi needs all the food we can bring him. Do you want him to die?"

It was hard to believe that Mother really thought that Kiyoshi might die if he didn't get to eat the apple that had fallen into her sleeve. Nevertheless, we turned and headed back to the hospital.

Once we were at the hospital, an attendant pointed to a back door. "They're in there," she said, referring to the doctor and the nurse on duty.

Mother stood next to the door. "*Gomen kudasai*" ("Excuse me"), she said repeatedly, while bowing to the closed door.

"What is it?" called out a woman's voice.

Mother waited almost a minute, and then, when no one opened the door for us, she boldly walked into the room. I couldn't believe her rudeness and was afraid that the doctor and nurse would be angry with her. But Mother wasn't about to leave the hospital without delivering her apple to Kiyoshi.

Squatting around a small table, a nurse and a doctor were eating the same fruit and rice that Mother had brought earlier. The nurse stood up, her face red with anger. "No one is allowed in this room without permission," she said to Mother.

Mother held out the apple. "I forgot this," she said.

"All right. Leave it, then go."

The apple slipped from Mother's hand and fell onto the floor. Mother dropped to her knees to retrieve it. Holding the apple in her outstretched hand, she stared at the nurse, and then bowed, her face almost touching the floor.

"Give me the apple and go," the nurse said.

The nurse stepped forward and tried to take the apple from Mother's hand, but Mother wouldn't give it up, holding on to the piece of fruit tenaciously.

"What's the matter with you?" the nurse asked straightening up.

Mother remained frozen, refusing to speak, her lips held together as if they had been glued. The doctor put down his chopsticks and stood up. "Are you insane?" he said to Mother. When she failed to respond, he added, "What good will such a posture do you? Please leave the room. We have rules and regulations, and, like everyone else, you must obey them."

Mother refused to move. Tears rolled down her cheeks.

The doctor shouted, "You can't stay here!" He threw up his arms in disgust. "Call the police," he said to the nurse.

The nurse, a short, round woman with kind eyes, said to Mother, "Do you think a few extra apples and eggs are going to make your boy well? We receive almost no salary and eat hardly more than a bowl of rice and a few vegetables a day. Are we to be blamed if we seek a little nourishment for ourselves? If we should get sick, who will care for the others?"

Uriko awakened on Mother's back and finding herself in an awkward position began to cry. The doctor said, "Can you make that baby stop crying?" Mother bowed even lower.

"That's enough already," the doctor said. He removed his glasses and rubbed his eyes. "All right, all right. The food you bring here will be saved for your son. Now please get up and leave."

"I must feed him myself," Mother said.

"It's against the rules."

Mother remained rigid, still clutching the apple in her outstretched hand while Uriko continued to bawl. The old doctor looked as if he were about to explode, his face all puffed up and crimson.

The doctor coughed violently. "All right, enough" he shouted. "Feed him yourself."

"If you would please, your excellency, I want to give him this apple right now," Mother said.

"Yes, yes." The doctor turned to the nurse. "Give her a mask and a gown and see that she gives it to him. Just get her out of here."

Two weeks later, after Kiyoshi was discharged from the hospital, Mother visited Mr. Kabayama, a former employee of father's at the bank and persuaded him to rent us a room in the back of his house until we could make a better arrangement. Then she wrote to Aunt Yumi in Nigata, who wrote back that she would be happy to let us live with her until father returned from the war.

We were at the train station when I realized that Mother wasn't coming with us. Not a day in my life had passed that I had not lived with Mother.

"But what will Uriko do without your milk?" I asked.

"In the country there's plenty of cow's milk. You will teach Uriko to drink from a special bottle. Don't worry, your aunt will know what to do and help you."

"Why can't you come with us?"

"Mr. Kabayama knows someone who will give me a job. I'll send money to Aunt Yumi. We don't want to be beggars, *ne?* Take good care of your brother and sister, Tomi-chan. You will have to be their Mother as well as their sister."

She wrote us a letter every week, and, as she had promised, sent money to Aunt Yumi. In her letters she said she was lonely and missed us. Soon we would be together again.

Five months later, in August, the Americans dropped atomic bombs on Hiroshima and Nagasaki, and Emperor Hirohito went on the radio and said that we have "to endure the unendurable, and suffer what is insufferable."

The war was over.

We received word that father had been captured by the British and was being held as a prisoner in Malaya. We were all very grateful that he had not been wounded and would be coming home soon.

An Apple For Kiyoshi

A week before he was expected to return, Mother killed herself by jumping in front of a train at Tachikawa station. She left no suicide note, and no one could explain why she had done it.

Kim props up her head with her hands, a favorite gesture when she is confused. "She jumped in front of a train? Ugh!"

I wonder if I have left something out of the story, some important detail I might have forgotten. In fifty-eight years one can forget a lot. Fifty-eight years from now, what will Kim remember of my story? Probably only the part about Mother killing herself. The rest will be a blur and will make no sense.

Last year Kyoshi died from lung cancer. Uriko was only an infant when Mother died. When I am dead, who will remember her at all? Who will care?

Richard R. Karlen

In war choices are often life and death decisions. Soldiers, who may act coolly and with intelligence under the stress of battle, cannot always be counted upon to be reliable in the aftermath. The nightmare of war bludgeons sensitivities. Nervous systems become permanently shattered.

We say that these men are suffering from "post traumatic stress disorders," which sounds a lot better than saying that they are shell-shocked or just plain crazy.

THE TELEGRAM

1952

SOUTH KOREA

I am helping the stretcher-bearers roll the body onto the examining table when Sergeant Ramsey, the dispensary NCOIC, enters the makeshift quonset.

"Telegram, Leibowitz," Ramsey says.

I suspect that the telegram is a practical joke from one of my smart-ass friends from San Francisco and stuff it into my chest pocket to read later. Right now there is business at hand.

I strip the wounded man's shirt from his body, being careful to avoid the hole in his abdominal wall, and then I listen for a heartbeat.

"He stepped on a mine," says one of the field medics who brought him in.

"Where's the doc?" the other medic asks Ramsey.

Ramsey tells him that a mortar shell had shredded the doc's leg yesterday, and he had been shipped out. Another one is on his way, but he won't be here before this afternoon. In the meantime, Corporal Leibowitz, the ex-medical student, is holding down the fort. He nods in my direction.

The Telegram

With the peristaltic movements of a giant amoeba, the contents of the soldier's peritoneal cavity begin to ooze onto the examining table. I stuff them back into the body and tape over the hole. After applying a tourniquet around the upper arm, I insert a needle into a vein in the forearm and start an intravenous drip. Then I give him shots of penicillin, tetanus, and morphine. With nothing more to do, I step aside and take a breath.

"You'd better read the telegram," says Ramsey. "It's your ticket back to the States."

I hold the telegram up to the light. "Jesus," I whisper. Then I carefully fold it and slip it back into my pocket.

"I've cut your orders," Ramsey said. "If you hustle, you can be back in New Jersey in forty-eight hours. You can ride this soldier to the air base."

I go to my tent, do a quick pack into my duffle bag and return to the dispensary where the ambulance is waiting for me. Ramsey is giving last-minute instructions to the driver as I slip into the back of the vehicle.

Ramsey is a wiry, tough, black man from Detroit with a nasty scar on the right side of his face and keloids on both his forearms, the result of pulling an unconscious lieutenant from a burning tank during the Battle of the Bulge in 1944. He has been my NCOIC since I have been stationed in Korea. Before closing the ambulance doors, he tells me not to take any chances.

"I'm sorry, Jack," he says. He hands me my orders and a couple of months pay stuffed in an envelope.

"I'll be back in two weeks," I say.

"Come back when you feel like it. We'll manage. You've earned a break." He closes the doors.

I've been riding an hour before I begin to unwind, to realize that I'll be leaving Korea. After nine months of field duty, it doesn't seem possible that the getting out would come about with such unexpected swiftness, and that I was still in one piece.

The semi-conscious soldier groans. I lean over and have trouble getting a decent pulse. The man is wheezing badly, and I wonder if he'll survive the ride back to the air base.

I pull out the telegram and reread it. The telegram doesn't say what Mom is dying of. I am so conditioned to violent death, that, for the moment, I cannot comprehend what a fifty-six year old woman with a history of nothing worse than mild hypertension could die from. I even wonder if my family might be employing some sort of desperate ploy on the U.S. Army to get their wayward son back home and out of danger. My father is just the sort of wise guy to pull something like that.

As the ambulance bounces over the bombed-out dirt road, the soldier coughs violently, his chest heaving as he utters deep guttural sounds.

"Hold on," I whisper.

His breathing shortens; there are final gasps. I put an ear to his chest, listen for a ventricular fibrillation, for the last heartbeat, and then I pull the needle from his vein and the tubing from the bottle of saline. The soldier looks to be no more than twenty. I wonder about his family, his father mother, sisters, brothers. Soon, someone in the family will also be receiving a telegram.

It's turning dark when the ambulance arrives at the hospital. After the medics remove the body, I go over to the air terminal, where I show my orders to the airman behind the ATCO counter. He says I'll have to wait two hours for the next plane to Japan. From there he doesn't think I'll have any trouble hitching a ride back to the States.

The waiting room is jammed, and I settle in a corner, flopping down next to my B-bag. Wherever I am, I have this odd sense that I've been there before, which goes along with this feeling that my entire twenty-seven years of life have been a series of movements without any particular direction and for no particular purpose. I try for a little nap.

"Can I talk to you a moment?"

The Telegram

I look up and see an airman with one stripe on his sleeve standing in front of me. He introduces himself as Thomas Jagen.

"I understand you've got emergency orders," Jagen says.

"That's right."

"Your orders just bumped me." Jagen squats down to my eye level. "I've got a forty-eight hour pass, and I've been waiting here for almost twenty-four hours. With your orders you can bump a general. With mine, if I don't make this flight, I'll never get back in time."

"To bad."

I figure Jagen to be nineteen or twenty, about the same age as the dead soldier I had just dropped off. He has this fair, Nordic complexion, the type that burns and never tans. Tall and stringy, he looks like he could use a square meal.

"I'll give you twenty-five bucks," Jagen says.

"No."

"Make it fifty."

"I don't want your money." The guy is starting to get on my nerves.

Jagen is persistent. "I'll be going back to the States in a few months, and it'll be too late." He stands up and stretches his legs. He looks as if he's ready to burst into tears. "I want to get married," he says. "My Japanese girl friend is going to have a baby. Maybe she's even had it already. Chances are, if I don't get to see her now and make arrangements, I may never see her again."

"You expect me to believe this crazy story?"

"It's the truth! I swear it." He crosses himself, and then, just to be sure that he's got God on his side, he does it again.

I stare up into the young man's watery blue eyes. Two weeks ago, I had observed another man's eyes dangling like gelatin from their sockets, the vitreous humor dripping down the cheekbones, pooling with blood to form pink rivulets. Steel shrapnel had torn a hole through the base of the man's skull. He had lived for two hours, crying out in Spanish for his grandmother.

I stand up. "I'll see what I can do."

We go to the counter where I ask the ATCO clerk to give Jagen back his seat and bump someone else.

The man looks from me to Jagen, then back to me. "No can do," he says.

"Then put me on the next plane."

"Look," says the clerk as he touches his head. "No brain, just an Air Force manual."

I elbow my way in closer. "Give him a break," I whisper. "His girl friend's going to have a baby, but she's not doing well."

Discretely, I reach into my back pocket, and produce a letter written in Japanese, and show it to the clerk. "Here, see the letterhead—'*Nigata Byoin*'. That means Nigata Hospital. It's a special hospital for pregnant women with TB."

The clerk peruses the letter perfunctorily. By a miracle, I think I have made a dent into his rules-and-regulations brain, for he says to me, "You might have to wait ten hours for another plane."

I show him the telegram. "My mother's dying. Bump a field grade. You'll go to Heaven."

The ATCO clerk studies my telegram carefully. He looks at me curiously, and then nods. He checks over the manifest and crosses out a name. It would appear that even ATCO clerks have mothers.

JAPAN

Jagen and I sit next to each other on the C-47 flying east across the Sea of Japan toward Honshu, the main island of the Japanese archipelago. Jagen tells me that he is from the South Side of Chicago. His father, brothers, friends, all the *Polaks* work in the steel mills as cinder snappers, but he'd be damned if he was going to spend his life shoveling coal into a furnace. Right after he graduated high school, he joined the Air Force.

The Telegram

My grandfather left Warsaw just before the Nazis invaded Poland and would talk endlessly about Polish anti-Semitism. I knew there was no changing the mind of an old Jew who had eaten as much shit in his life as he had, but there were times when I didn't want to hear any more. I wondered how he'd react to Jagen, a Polish kid from Chicago, who wanted only to love and take care of a woman and her child.

Mom never hated the gentiles. ("They've got their own problems. Who are we to judge?") She was a little over-weight, the extra layer of flesh, soft and comforting for a sick child's head to rest on. Was she really dying, I wondered? When your mother dies, can you ever expect your life to be the same again? People can love you for lots of reasons. But only a mother will love you even if you're rotten.

Jagen asks about the letter that I had showed the ATCO clerk. I explain that it was from a Japanese medical student, with whom I had been friends for over two years when I had been stationed in Japan. I had taught him English; he had taught me Japanese.

"Can you really speak Japanese?" Jagen asked.

"You get tired of playing ping-pong every night. Studying a language can be fun."

I wasn't showing off. Languages were my thing. I could speak perfect Yiddish and German. I could even speak a little Spanish, Russian, Polish and Korean.

I corresponded with Jiro often. Yesterday I had received a letter from him, which I had put aside to read when I had a chance. This was the letter I had pulled out of my back pocket when we were talking to the ATCO clerk.

"You sure pulled the wool over that jerk," Jagen says. He smiles. "You think it's possible for a dumb kid like me to be a father? For months I've been dreaming about Yoshi and the baby. Now I'm going to see them."

Jagen is not a bad fellow. A little green around the edges, but you could see there is a lot of good stuff in him. I, myself, have been a fuck-up all my life. Even when I am

210

desperate to do the right thing, I make the wrong decision. For example: two weeks ago, a second lieutenant with a bad chest wound had been brought in. The surgeon was in the field and unavailable. It was up to Ramsey to decide whether to risk calling in the helicopter. He passed the responsibility on to me. I thought the man had a chance with emergency surgery, and advised Ramsey to radio for the helicopter to pick him up and fly him to the hospital at Ascom. The helicopter was destroyed by ground fire before reaching us, its two-man crew killed in the crash. The second lieutenant died fifteen minutes after the aircraft had been shot down.

Wherever I go, I acquire this reputation for being cool and detached, the sort of person who accepts life as it comes without protest. Even after I had been thrown out of medical school, I never complained. I had been caught red-handed trying to give answers to a classmate on a final exam. The guy I had tried to help was a Palestinian whose family had been driven out of their home by the Israelis in 1948.

The Palestinian claimed that he had never asked me for any help and was put on probation. It was a bold-faced lie, but where was the sense in both of us being kicked out of school by my contradicting him?

I took off for the west coast, bummed around, did odd jobs, stayed one step ahead of the draft. But Selective Service has their ways of catching up to you, and I decided to enlist in the army rather than go to jail for draft evasion. Once I discovered that lying and cheating in the military was pretty much standard behavior, I knew I had made the right decision.

After basic, with my med school background, the army sent me to a training school to be a medic. Once finished, I was cut orders for duty in Japan. That was in 1950. It took two years before some genius at the Pentagon figured out that I might be useful in Korea.

The Telegram

After the plane lands at Tachikawa Air Base, I go directly to the ATCO desk and present my orders. I am manifested on the next plane for California, which is scheduled to take off in three hours. Jagen, who doesn't seem to want to let me out of his sight, asks me to come with him and see Yoshi. "Maybe the baby's been born. We'll have a drink on it," he says.

"Where's her house?"

"Ten minutes from here. You'll be back in plenty of time."

There had to be a better way to spend one's time than hanging around an air force terminal for three hours. "Sure, why not," I say.

After nine months in Korea, you forget the smell and sounds of the outside world. As I walk with Jagen, I am reminded that the Japanese possess cars and buses and have paved roads, that they work at jobs like selling shoes and managing banks, that their children walk to school unafraid of air strikes or artillery shelling, and wear neatly pressed black uniforms with school bags strapped to their backs.

Jagen leads me down winding narrow streets off a main thoroughfare lined with restaurants and bars. Houses of wood and paper are hidden behind tall bamboo fences. Between the houses and fences are tiny gardens, miniature reflections of nature. We stop in front of a house a little larger than the others that we have passed.

"You like it?" Jagen asks me. "It costs me twenty a month," he is quick to add with pride.

We walk through the gate and slide open the front door. Jagen pokes his head inside. "Yoshi," he calls out.

From within comes the wail of a baby. Jagen laughs and rushes into a small, dim foyer where he removes his shoes, and then opens another sliding door before stepping inside the house. I am right behind him.

A young Japanese woman is sitting on a cushion nursing an infant, maybe six or seven weeks old. As soon as she sees us, she wraps her arms protectively around him.

"Where's Yoshi?" Jagen asks, his eyes fixed on the baby. The woman bows, but doesn't answer. Jagen repeats the question several times, until I intervene and say to her, "*Yoshi-san wa, doko ni imasuka?*"

"*Yoshi-san wa koko ni imasen,*" the woman replies. She pulls her shirt over the other breast.

"Who are you? Where's Yoshi?" Jagen says, becoming more agitated. "Is that my baby?"

The woman tightens her grip on the infant, and slides back against the wall. Jagen hesitates. I step forward and lay a hand on his arm. "Take it easy," I say to him. "Yoshi's not here."

Then I squat in front of the woman and tell her not to be afraid, that we're not here to make trouble. I ask her about the baby.

"He is Yoshi's," she says. "My baby died three weeks ago. Yoshi asked me to nurse her baby and she went back to work at the bar."

"What did she say? What did she say?" Jagen asks excitedly.

"Hold it," I say to him. I turn to the girl and ask: "What's your name?"

"Yaeko."

Yaeko-san, this man is the father of Yoshi's baby." I nod toward Jagen. "Every month he's been sending Yoshi money."

She becomes alarmed. "Yoshi never told me anything about the father." She has become more defensive. Something is wrong here.

"Where's Yoshi now?" I ask.

"She works in Nishi-Tachikawa. The Yankee Doodle, I think." She hesitates, and then says with determination, "Yoshi promised me that I could keep the baby if I paid her twenty thousand yen. Yoshi doesn't want him. She doesn't have any milk. I take care of him. I keep him alive." The baby falls off the nipple and starts to whimper. Yaeko rocks him gently while humming to him. Within moments he stops crying, secure in her arms.

"What's going on here?" Jagen demands to know.

I tell him that I think it would be best if we get out of here and leave the woman and the baby alone. Jagen's pale skin flushes. He clenches a bony fist. "What about Yoshi? And my baby?" he asks.

I bow to Yaeko and grab Jagen by the arm. "I'll explain it outside."

On the street I repeat to Jagen everything Yaeko has told me.

"How much is twenty thousand yen?" Jagen asks me.

"About fifty-five dollars."

"I need to talk to Yoshi," he says with conviction.

"I don't think that's such a good idea."

"Can you come with me?" Jagen asks. "Help me make her understand that I want to marry her and take her and the baby back to Chicago."

I glanced at my watch. "I've got a plane to catch."

"You've still got plenty of time. Yoshi doesn't understand English that well. I'll pay you."

"I told you once before—I don't want your money." I turn and walk toward the main road leading back to the air base. Jagen runs after me.

"I'm begging you," he says. He tugs at my arm. "I don't have any time. I have to go back tomorrow."

I look into those cold, blue, alien eyes, and I see another dead soldier. Four years ago I was kicked out of medical school trying to help some dumb, pathetic bastard get through Physiology. I imagine that if I were analyzed, a psychologist would say that I am one of those personalities that never learns from his mistakes. It's like a part of my brain is made out of cement.

"What the hell," I say. "But we'll have to hurry."

In front of the Yankee Doodle, a Japanese dwarf, dressed in a Samurai costume, is brandishing a huge paper sword. As we step out of the taxi, the dwarf greets us with a comic bow. Inside the bar the lights are out. A stripper is going through a few residual grinds and bumps before tossing whimsically her flimsy top onto a wing of the small stage. Almost flat-chested, the girl seems embarrassed before racing off the platform. American airmen clap without a lot of enthusiasm, and the lights go on.

Jagen whispers, "They're all colored in here."

I push him to the bar and order two beers. "Look around," I say. "Do you see her?"

He spots Yoshi on the far side of the room drinking with an Air Force tech sergeant. "What do we do?" he asks.

"Stay here," I say. "I'll talk to her."

I sidle my way past the bar and head toward Yoshi and the sergeant, feeling the stares of the Negro airmen like so many deadly stabs. Standing in front of the sergeant, I say, "I want your permission to give this girl an important message."

The sergeant shrugs. "What's it all about, fella?"

"Her girl friend sent me. Her baby's sick. The doctor thinks he might have diphtheria or pneumonia—or even meningitis."

The sergeant almost spits up his drink. "God, man, that's terrible!" He looks at Yoshi, then back at me. "Meningitis! My baby cousin died from that." His hand is trembling around the bottle of beer. "Where's the baby now?" he asks.

"They took him to the hospital."

Yoshi wants to know what's happening. Her English isn't bad given the usual bar girl standards. She wants to know who I am? What baby is sick?

I tell her in Japanese that Thomas Jagen is sitting at the bar, but she shouldn't look toward him. He wants to see her. I explain to her that I've lied to the sergeant about her baby because I was afraid that Jagen might cause trouble. Would she meet him at the tearoom across the street?

Yoshi is a miracle. On cue, tears begin to form in her eyes. She lays a hand in the sergeant's palm. "I go see baby-san," she says to him. "*Daijobu?* Okay? Later I be back. We have big time together. You see, *ne*?" She is so good that one could almost believe we had rehearsed the scene.

As we are leaving, a three-piece combo has taken over the stage and begins to play *How High The Moon*. The saxophone and trumpet players, a pair of emaciated young Japanese men, blow with fierce facial expressions, substituting loudness for style. Above the din, Yoshi says to me in Japanese that Thomas Jagen is crazy. She told him the last time he was in Japan that she didn't want to be his girlfriend anymore.

We slip through a side door and cross the street to the tearoom. Then I return to the Yankee Doodle and stand at the entrance. Jagen is waiting for me at the bar. I motion to him, and, without a word, lead him to the tearoom where Yoshi is sitting in the corner of the room, her back to the door. Jagen tries to kiss her, but she turns her face and leaves him a powdered cheek.

"Sit down," I say to him. "Try and talk this out like civilized human beings."

But Jagen is too young and too excited to be civilized. Before him sits the woman he loves, the mother of his son, a person he has been dreaming about for the past year while daily risking his life. He says ardently, "Yoshi, I want to marry you. Right away."

Yoshi checks him out with cold, dispassionate eyes. "No," she says. "I no marry you. I tell you last time you here. Whattsa matter, you?"

Jagen appears confused. "Don't you understand? I want to take you and our baby back to the States."

The girl continues to shake her head and says, "You crazy."

I don't like the way the owner of the tearoom begins to stare at us. I decide to interject an opinion before Jagen explodes and we all wind up in the stockade tonight. "Grow up, Tom," I say. "She isn't interested. Don't ask why. That's the way it is with these girls."

He is too dejected to respond, and I turn to Yoshi and say to her in Japanese, "Why don't you spend a night with him? He'll be gone by tomorrow and you'll be rid of him. He's been sending you money for months. You owe him that much."

Yoshi doesn't know about fairness. She pushes forward to the edge of her chair and shakes a fist at Jagen. "Leave me alone. I go back to Yankee Doodle."

As she begins to rise, Jagen reaches across the table and grasps her arm hard. His violent manner freezes her. This type of confrontation is never good for a woman in her business.

"Yoshi, it's me, Tom," he says frantically.

"Take it easy," I beg him. "Let her go back to the bar before she starts shouting."

"Wait a minute," he says. "I've got a few goddamn rights. That baby is mine and I want him!"

"Baby mine, not yours!" Yoshi shoots back at him. She tries to wrench free from his grip, but Jagen holds on.

"I'm his father. I'll adopt him," Jagen says. "I'll take him back to the States, give him to my sister. She and my brother-in-law would raise him like their own." He is enraptured by his own idea and lets go of Yoshi's arm.

"Me payee you hundred dollars for baby-san." Jagen says in pigeon English. He raises an index finger. "You give me baby-san. I give you one hundred dollars." He enunciates each word as if he is talking to a deaf person who reads lips. Then he adds, in the worst accent I have ever heard, "*Taksun Okane*," which means 'a lot of money.'

Yoshi's expression brightens. She flops back in the chair. "Two hundred dollar," she says without hesitation.

She's in the wrong profession. The woman ought to be selling used cars for Ace Auto on Route 22 in Springfield, New Jersey.

"Two hundred! I don't have that much."

"Two hundred dollar," Yoshi repeats. Like any good salesperson, she knows when she's got her customer hooked.

The Telegram

Jagen nods in agreement. "Okay, I'll write my sister. I'll give you a hundred now, and I'll send you the other hundred in a few weeks. In the meantime, I'll take the baby to the Catholic mission. They'll take care of him until I can arrange for him to be sent back to the States." He asks me to translate his plan so there'd be no misunderstandings.

I stand up. "No need. She understands perfectly. I've got a plane to catch."

It is more luck than intelligence that gets me back to Yoshi's house through the maze of narrow roads. Upon entering the house, Yaeko is kneeling in front of a small table, a steaming rice bowl in hand. The baby is sleeping in a basket in the corner.

"You've got to leave right away," I say. Then I tell her about the meeting at the teahouse. "They'll be coming soon for the baby."

She lays the bowl down, clasps her hands together, and begins to rock back and forth, all the time whispering some crazy Buddhist chant.

"Stop that." I shake her by her shoulders until she looks up at me. "Take the baby and go." I am looking into a ruined face.

The reality of her situation begins to dawn on her. Finally, she says, "Where? I have no money. No friends."

"What about your family?"

"My mother lives in the south. I haven't spoken to her in a year."

I think of those two conspirators back at the tearoom in Nishi-Tachikawa bargaining on a child's fate, and I make another one of my great decisions in life, which is sure to turn out disastrously, if one were to judge by the outcome of previous choices I have made over the years.

"We're wasting time," I say. "Get your belongings together. I'll help you."

Within minutes she gathers together a large bundle. I've got the bundle and the baby basket; she cradles the baby in her arms. At the main road, we hail a taxi. I give the driver a hotel address in Ogikubo, a district just outside the central core of Tokyo, forty minutes from Tachikawa.

While we are traveling, I explain to Yaeko that the owner of the hotel is the father of a friend, a medical student studying in Nigata. "Takeda-san will help us," I say.

I am gratified to see once again the strong, square face of Mr. Takeda, Jiro's father, and to remember the many good hours I had spent enjoying the hospitality of the Takeda family.

It is with little pride that I lie to Mr. Takeda about Yaeko. "Her husband, one of my best friends, was killed in the war," I say. "She and the baby have no money, and I want to help her go back to her family."

"How can I help?" Mr. Takeda asks without hesitation.

"She has been evicted by her landlord. Though I offered to pay the rent, the landlord said he had already rented the house to another family." I feel like a monstrous piece of shit lying to Takeda, who is one of your all time straight shooters, but to tell him the truth would involve him in an action that would probably be considered by the police as a crime of kidnapping.

"It will be an honor to have you and your friend as my guests until you can make proper arrangements."

Later, I learn that Yaeko is from Miyajimaguchi, a small fishing village on the Inland Sea about ten miles from Hiroshima.

"From my house you can look across the water and see the great *tori* rising out of the sea as it guards the Ituskushima Shrine." Yaeko tells me this while we are squatting on tatamis in her room. She is nursing the baby, who seems to rise out of the folds of her kimono as if he is an appendage of her body.

The Telegram

"I've been there," I say, remembering a trip I took around Japan with Jiro, which included the Hiroshima area. "It's very beautiful."

Yaeko smiles, and then she tells me that her mother still lives in Miyajimaguchi with her aunt. "They work as seamstresses," she says. "My father died two years ago from cancer in the blood. The doctor thought that it was because he had gone into Hiroshima too soon after the A-bomb had exploded." She relates this information to me without any special anger. I'm grateful to her that I don't have to explain that not all Americans had agreed about our exploding an atomic bomb on a civilian population.

"Does Yoshi know where you're from?" I ask.

"I lied to her. If a person knows you come from near Hiroshima, she would never live with you."

She goes on to tell me how she had wound up in Tachikawa. After her father died, she began to live with a sergeant stationed at the Iwakuni Marine base. She went with him when he was transferred to Yokohama. Several months later, he was sent to Korea. She was five months pregnant when she discovered that the sergeant had been wounded and had been sent back to the States. She decided to move to Tachikawa, to be around the air base where no one knew her. There she met Yoshi, who was also pregnant.

"What happened to your baby?" I ask.

"I awakened one morning and found him dead. He was only two days old." She begins to cry. "He was such a little thing."

Finally she stops crying, and goes on. "I wrapped him in a blanket and that night Yoshi and I buried him under the bridge by the Tamagawa River. If I had taken him to the funeral home, they would have burned him. I could not bear thinking about his flesh being cooked like an animal's. So I buried him, even though it's against the law."

The baby has fallen off her nipple and is sound asleep. She places him back into his basket.

"Tomorrow we'll decide what to do," I say.

Again I lie to Mr. Takeda, telling him that we are going into Tokyo to buy train tickets for Yaeko to return to her parents up north in Morioko prefecture. He is pleased and wishes us good luck.

With the baby strapped to Yaeko's back, we take the train into Central Tokyo, where we taxi to the City Hall in Minato-ku. We are given an assortment of forms and pamphlets, which explains all about the *Koseki Shohon*, the official family register that is a part of every Japanese household.

Afterwards, we lunch at a sushi house next door to the City Hall. I write down my name, home address, date of birth, and army serial number. Then I give her a hundred dollars, enough for her to live on for two or three months.

While awaiting the train to Hiroshima at Tokyo Station, I remind Yaeko to register on her family's *Koseki Shohon* the birth of the baby in both our names at the Bureau of Registry in Miyajimaguchi. This will make everything official.

"You've got all the information you need," I say to her. I give her my army address in Korea. "Write me if I have to sign any papers."

Yaeko is nervous about lying to a government official.

"No one will care," I say. "They're just a bunch of bureaucrats who love to fill out forms. That's their job."

"What if Yoshi finds out?"

"How? She doesn't know where you live, and even if she manages to track you down, she can't prove the baby is hers. You could claim that it was her baby that died, that it was her baby who is buried down by the river."

"I'm afraid."

"The baby will be properly registered with a father and a mother. If necessary, I would come back and swear that I'm the father. Yoshi wouldn't do anything. She's liable to be arrested for burying her baby illegally. They might even accuse her of murder."

"Why do you do this?" she asks. "I am nothing to you."

"A baby needs a mother who will love him."

The Telegram

Before boarding the train, Yaeko bows very low and thanks me repeatedly. I touch the baby's cheek, but it doesn't appear that I've caught his attention. I want to gitchy-gitchy-goo him, but I'm afraid he might cry. I try a comical face. Nothing works, and then, I swear, without warning the little bugger makes this half-smile like he knows everything.

"Will we ever see you again?" Yaeko asks.

"Who knows?" I say. "Remember, he's my baby, too."

At the Air Force terminal in Tachikawa, I pick up my B-bag and approach the ATCO clerk. He whistles when he checks the manifest. "You're a little late, corporal," he says.

"I was in an automobile accident." I take out an extra copy of orders. "Can you book me now?"

The clerk eyes me suspiciously, then mulls over the orders. A comic book drops off his lap as he stands up. "I ought to report this."

"You know how they drive around here. The taxi went off the road and ran into a telephone pole. I was in the hospital overnight." I show him the telegram. "I can't afford to waste any more time."

The clerk remains skeptical, but I don't worry since reporting me will require him to fill out extra forms, an anathema to any clerk in the US military. "Next plane is in an hour," he says. "If I were you, I'd stick around to your plane leaves. A brick is liable to fall from the sky and make a hole in your head."

I have no sooner found a seat in the waiting room when Jagen passes by. He spots me before I can duck him.

"You're still here?" Jagen gives me an incredulous stare, and I'm not sure whether he is going to be polite or belligerent.

"Plane was cancelled." Below his right eye is a gash, the tissue slightly swollen and purple. "What happened?" I ask.

"I'm leaving the tea room with Yoshi when her colored boy friend walks up and sucker punches me before I know what's happening." He becomes incensed, clenches a fist. "What do you think she does? She runs after *him*. The bastard slaps her and walks away. After a while, we go back to her place. The baby's gone, and so is the girl friend!" He touches the bruise below his eye as if he wishes to remind himself how unfair life can be.

"What could I do?" he whimpers pathetically. "I loved that little baby, my son. I would have sent him to my sister. She would have loved him, too."

I suppose anything's possible. But I couldn't help but wonder if she might have found the mixed child as an embarrassment. It's been only seven years ago that the Japanese were still in the business of killing Americans. Mention Pearl Harbor and most Americans still conjure up an image of a little, yellow, buck-toothed Oriental with maniacal eyes swinging a sword at an American GI.

The public address system announces the next flight to Korea. The terminal becomes alive with men stretching, muscles aching from hours of waiting around. Young airmen and soldiers begin to line up in front of the departure gate, gladdened by the prospect of movement, sick of living without reference to time or motion. In less than five hours the denuded mountains of Korea will cross their visions, and where they are going will hit them with silent thuds.

Jagen picks up his bag. "So long, Leibowitz. Thanks for everything."

I have a dark moment of remorse. All that Jagen has been dreaming about for the past year—his love for the Japanese girl, his being a father—has become an illusion. I think I have done the right thing in helping Yaeko, but with all such decisions, you have to wonder a little if you have the right to play God. I pray Jagen will survive Korea and go back to the States to his family. He is young; he can start all over. Hopefully, time will take care of the rest.

I watch him until he disappears through the gate like a man being swallowed up by a giant fish, and I wait for my own flight to be announced.

223

The Telegram

NEW JERSEY

Actually, I stopped believing in God when I was seven, which was about the same age that I stopped believing in Santa Claus; yet as I view at twenty thousand feet the infinite expanse of clouds that hang over the Pacific like thick, white carpeting, I find myself feeling a certain oneness with the Universe and I think that maybe that's God, too.

I remember Mom telling me that God loves everyone, even if you don't do your homework or if you tease your sister. When I was a child, it was comforting believing that someone would love you, even if you were a liar, though I could never understand why God would want to love liars.

From McGuire Air Force Base, the bus sweeps along the Jersey Turnpike towards Newark at seventy miles an hour. Huge cylindrical petroleum tanks and chemical plants with thick black smoke rising from giant smokestacks abut the Turnpike outside of Linden, and I think of the oil flowing from those tanks that warm the quonsets and run the jeeps along the thirty-eighth parallel. For a moment, I feel like I have deserted my friends, and that I am an intruder in a foreign land.

Goldsmith Avenue is lined with cars parked halfway up the block from the three-story framed house that was my home, and I feel a silent thud in my chest as I know I'm too late. I sit down at the edge of the rust colored brick stoop that guards the house like a fort. I had forgotten about the parkway that split the center of the road, the fireplug in front of the house, the basketball hoop attached to Milty Coleman's garage across the street. I look toward the living room window and can almost hear Mom calling me in for supper.

A Caddy pulls up and parks in front of the fireplug. A middle-aged couple, whom I don't recognize, step from the car, and the man asks me if this is the home of the late Sarah Leibowitz. I point toward the front door. Then I leave the stoop and walk toward Weequahic Park, about three blocks away.

Inside the park I cut through the woods until I come to the highway that splits the park in half. At the wood's edge I sit down under a large maple. The lake rises up in the dwindling light and reminds me of Lake Hakone at sunset. I half-expect to see Fuji painted against the sky in the distance. A squadron of birds soars above, diving in V formation toward a cluster of trees at the far side of the lake.

I think of my mother, whom I will never see again. I think of her waiting for me as she lay dying in the hospital, hoping to kiss me a last time, to say a final goodbye.

Then I think about Ramsey and the other men I left behind in Korea, the ones who are still alive and the ones who will return in body bags. I think about Thomas Jagen, and pray there will be no bullet waiting to put a hole into his already broken heart. And finally, I think of Yaeko and the baby in their home on the Inland Sea, safe from those predators who would separate them and destroy that love between a mother and a child, which is the purest love of all.

"Please, forgive me, Mom," I say.

I reach into my pocket for my cigarettes and feel the telegram. I remove the folded paper and roll it into a ball, and fling it into the darkening sky. It goes just about as far as you can throw a piece of paper before it falls and disappears in the rough underbrush.

We think of alcoholics as deadbeats, human beings who have been overpowered by a drug and end up destroying lives, especially their own. We have this image of the alcoholic as a forlorn, homeless man walking the streets, one who is willing to debase himself to any level for a drink. But the reality is that most alcoholics have wives and children and manage to do a job even as they drink too much. They are what I call, "functional alcoholics."

This type of alcoholic seems particularly to abound in the military. Drinking is rampant. Enlisted men, non-commissioned officers, junior-grade officers, field-grade officers—there are no distinctions when it comes to lapping up the booze.

Anyone, who has ever served in the military, must have wondered, at one time or another, how he would ever survive in battle knowing that his commanding officer was a roaring drunk.

APPOINTMENT AT ASCOM

South Korea, November, 1956

The C-119 landed late in the afternoon. It had been a rotten six-hour flight from Japan and my stomach felt like a lawnmower gone berserk. B-bag in hand, I walked across the airstrip toward the terminal building. I was surprised to discover that the building was still pock-marked from old bombings. Since the Korean truce had been signed three years before, I wondered if the base was expendable and I was being thrown to the wolves.

Once inside the building, I called the dispensary and asked for Lieutenant-Colonel Gerald Tittle, the Dispensary

Commander. Tittle said he'd send an ambulance to pick me up right away. "You're a welcome sonofabitch," he added.

As I waited in front of the terminal for the ambulance, I surveyed a countryside painted in grays and browns, the only vegetation being the harvested rice paddies that stretched beyond the base toward the barren mountains. Other than a lone farmer wadding through the paddies, I could see no visible sign of life. It was eerie—all that emptiness—and, as one accustomed to the clutter and noise of a large city, I had the feeling of total exile.

The ambulance driver threw me a great salute, and then tossed my bag into the back of the vehicle. We drove in silence around the perimeter of the airstrip, and I observed that the buildings were all green quonsets, except for the Officer's Club, a mirage of brick and glass.

Colonel Tittle, a big, round, burly fellow, was waiting in front of the dispensary as I stepped from the ambulance. He eyed me suspiciously, and then smiled broadly. "It's about time they sent me a goddamn dentist," he said, and then grabbed my hand and shook it with the strength of a mule.

He led me through the dispensary waiting room, which, with its wooden benches and pot-bellied kerosene stove, resembled the interior of a western frontier church. Once in his office, he went directly to the bottom drawer of the desk and took out two glasses and a bottle of Johnny Walker.

"By the water cooler is a pitcher. Fill 'er up," he ordered in a flat, graveled, mid-western accent.

I did as he asked, then sat opposite him. He measured the proportions of Scotch to water as if calibrating ingredients in a chem lab. He seemed a bit anxious as he handed me a drink. "Most dentists don't like Scotch. Fat beer men."

I thought his comment a bit off line, considering his own generous physique, especially when compared to my bony, somewhat emaciated one, but couldn't come up with any sort of quick, witty retort and figured I better keep my thoughts to myself.

"We haven't had a dentist in six weeks," he said. Unexpectedly, he leaned forward and peered at me closely. "Are you old enough to take care of eighteen-hundred men? How long have you been a dentist?"

"I graduated dental school five months ago." I didn't think it was the appropriate moment to add that I hadn't been near a live patient since graduation, that I had been just hanging around my house watching TV and eating pretzels and chocolate chip cookies while waiting to start my Air Force enlistment. Beginning to feel uncomfortable by his continuous stare, I asked him if it would be possible to see the dental clinic.

"Later." He poured two more drinks.

The tightness in my stomach gradually disappeared, and I wanted to thank Johnny Walker for being such a friend in need. Following a polite knock on the door, a corpsman entered holding a manila folder.

"Sir, Major Williams outside to see you," the corpsman said.

"Office hours are over. I'm interviewing our new base dentist, Lieutenant Marcus."

"The major is complaining that he's still constipated." The corpsman looked uncertain, and then added in a hushed voice, "He's a little upset, sir. Maybe you ought to see him."

Tittle cracked his knuckles defiantly. "Give him an enema bag." With a devilish smirk on his face, he added, "If that doesn't work, Dr. Marcus can stick a drill up his ass."

The corpsman snapped to attention as if he had been wired together with hard rubber, before hurrying out of the room.

Tittle poured two more drinks. This time he didn't bother watering them. "They're all a bunch of sneaky bastards," he said. "Give 'em an inch and they want the whole damn works." He leaned back in his desk chair. "I'm going to give it to you straight, Marcus." The chair balanced precariously, like a boulder teetering on the edge of a cliff. I held my breath waiting for the crash.

"I'm ready," I said, the Johnny Walker now doing the talking as I mocked his aggressive tone.

To my relief, he suddenly lurched forward, the chair landing back hard on its front legs. He glared at me. "You some sort of wise bastard."

I had this instant sensation that my life was about to be prematurely aborted. What probably saved me was that Colonel Tittle wasn't quite prepared to annihilate the only dentist for eighteen hundred men. He suddenly smiled and made a strange, circular gesture with his index finger. "Why don't you grow a mustache?" he asked me. "Make you look like a man instead of a pansy."

I touched my upper lip. "But I have a mustache," I said.

He squinted as he inched closer toward me. "It's just a bunch of goddamn fuzz." He grew silent, seemingly obsessed by my few carefully nurtured hairs. Then he said: "Pencil it in, or shave the bastard off."

In the three-week basic training for physicians, dentists, and veterinarians at the Air Force base in Alabama, we were instructed that a direct order from a superior officer was a command from God. I decided that my best course of action was to pretend that I didn't hear the colonel and get out of his sight as quickly as possible. Once again I requested permission to see the dental clinic, and without waiting for a response began to slowly back out of the room. Tittle was toasting Dwight Eisenhower and Syngman Rhee when I left.

I asked a passing medic for directions to the dental clinic, which turned out to be in the adjacent quonset. At the clinic, I introduced myself to the non-commisioned officer in charge, the NCOIC, Sergeant Raymond Gallagher.

"Glad we're on the same team, sir," Gallagher said.

Gallagher was a skinny, pasty-faced guy, not much older than myself. He spoke with a Brooklyn poolroom accent, and I felt an immediate camaraderie with him.

My NCOIC was ecstatic as he showed me his clinic. We waltzed across waxed floors from room to room, stopping only when Gallagher wanted to detail some accomplishment of organization he had effected during his tour of duty. After we were finished, Gallagher summed up: "Three fully equipped operatories, a lab, two lounges, two johns, waiting room, dental CO's office." I was thinking about making a beeline for one of the johns, when a dental corpsman joined us.

"Toothache outside," the corpsman said to Gallagher.

"No office hours today," Gallagher retorted in a voice no less imperious than Colonel Tittle's.

"He says he didn't sleep all night." Then the corpsman addressed me. "He's got an awful toothache, sir."

Gallagher was furious. I suspected that only my presence saved the corpsman from whatever an irate sergeant with five stripes on his sleeve might do to an insubordinate corpsmen with only one stripe on his sleeve. I arose to the occasion.

"I don't mind taking a look," I said to Gallagher.

"You don't have to. While we've been waiting for a dentist, we've been shipping our emergencies to the army clinic at Ascom City. One more won't matter."

"But I'm here now, and I think I ought to check this patient," I said.

Gallagher's expression bordered on anguish. Nevertheless, after taking a deep breath, he ordered the corpsman to bring in the man. A curious sensation came over me, not exactly unpleasant, as I realized that for the first time in my life I had a power to do things my own way. There was something to be said about the chain of command.

An acne-faced adolescent staggered into the clinic as if it were his knees not his teeth that were bothering him. "Airman Harold Harvey," he said through half-opened lips.

Gallagher shoved him into the dental chair, and then draped him with a towel before stepping back like an umpire behind home plate. Face to face with my first patient since dental school, I found myself in a state of wild animation. Boldly, I stepped forward, mirror and explorer in hand.

"Where does it hurt?" I asked.

"This side." Harvey rolled an index finger around the upper left quadrant of his mouth.

Sure enough, the upper second bicuspid looked decayed beyond repair. To support my suspicions, I gave the offending tooth a little bang with the back of the mirror. Airman Harvey convulsed as if he had been shocked by an electric prod.

"That's the baby," I said. "Rotten to the core."

Tears in his eyes, Harvey begged me to pull it out.

"First," I said, "we need an x-ray—just to be on the safe side.

Without a word, Gallagher half-dragged Airman Harvey to the x-ray room. After they returned, Gallagher set up a sterilized tray containing a local anesthetic, and sufficient surgical instruments to perform an appendectomy. Then he left to develop the x-ray. Alone with

Harvey, I found myself focusing on a hideous blackhead growing on his cheek.

"Do something for the pain," Harvey begged.

Since I thought my injection technique was flawless, I was slightly disappointed that the patient squirmed as if an army of red ants were crawling all over him. We were both relieved when the Novocaine began to take effect, and Harvey smiled in relief. Then Gallagher returned, a dripping x-ray in hand.

"Swell shot," I said, holding the X-ray up to the light, though to be honest the picture looked like a gigantic blur. I guess you'd have to blame my slightly blurred vision on Colonel Tittle's Johnny Walker. But what did it matter, I know what I had to do.

"Thank you, sir," said Gallagher. It was comforting to have my NCOIC, calm and completely professional, standing at my side.

Gallagher then handed me a bicuspid forceps, and I extracted the tooth with such ease that I couldn't help wondering if the whole operation had been a planned gimmick to give me a little needed confidence.

I dangled the bloody bicuspid in front of Harvey as if it were a small but dangerous animal that I had shot down for his sake, and was showing off for him to admire. "One piece," I said proudly.

Harvey's terrified look dissipated as he realized that the villain, who had been pounding his brain for days, had finally been disposed of, and he was still alive.

"Great," he exclaimed. "I didn't feel a thing." He rolled his tongue around, touching the teeth on either side of the bloody socket, and then, unexpectedly, he removed the gauze I had placed in the area of the extraction, and began to poke his fingers around wildly touching the adjacent teeth.

Gallagher became outraged. "Get your dirty fingers out of your mouth!" he ordered Airman Harvey.

Harvey gasped. "Wait a second." Ignoring Gallagher's protests, he continued to explore his mouth. "It's the wrong one," he cried. "You've pulled the wrong tooth."

Gallagher turned beet red. "What're you talking about, mister?"

Harvey touched the upper left first molar, the tooth immediately adjacent to the extracted one. "It's the other one!" he cried out.

"Ridiculous," I said. Calmly, I pointed out to him the large cavity in the extracted bicuspid. "It's a referred pain," I explained.

Harvey was insistent. "No, this is the one." He continued to tap his finger against the first molar.

"There's a small cavity in that tooth," I conceded. "We can fix it next time."

"I'll make an appointment for you," Gallagher said. He yanked the towel from around Harvey's neck and grabbed him by the arm. "This way to the front desk, Airman Harvey."

Before Harvey could protest further, he was whisked out of the operatory. I could hear Gallagher telling him how grateful he ought to be that the "doc" took care of him after hours, and he should quit the carrying on like a fat pain in the ass.

Before anyone else showed up, I decided to scram. My stomach was feeling rotten again, and my nervous system was beginning to show the effects of the long, arduous day. I suddenly longed for a comfortable bed.

Outside the dispensary, the ambulance driver told me that my room at the hospital Base Officer's Quarters, the BOQ, was next to Colonel Tittle's. The driver had already put my B-bag there. Then he pointed the way for me.

The room was distinguished by its lack of size and an enormous kerosene stove in the middle. There was barely enough room for a small cot and bureau. I kicked off my shoes and gratefully flopped down on the cot. I was beginning to drift off, when Colonel Tittle entered without knocking. He was balancing two empty glasses, a pitcher of water, and an unopened fifth of Johnny Walker Scotch. "A little prep for dinner," he said cheerfully, as he placed his armamentarium on top of the bureau and quickly fixed two drinks.

Most surprisingly, the Scotch, as before, had a palliative effect on my stomach. Tittle asked me what I thought about the dental clinic and I told him about the extraction. He shook his fist angrily.

"The bastards don't let you live. Not even here an hour, and already they've got you sweating your balls off."

His protective attitude was reassuring. As the Scotch rewarmed my insides, there was a simultaneous sense of deeper warmth for a system that protects its own. I made it a point to pour the next two drinks.

It had grown dark outside, and a sharp November wind knocked against the porous, window sill, sending a chill through the room. I asked Tittle how the burner worked. He turned a knob at its base, which controlled the flow of oil running from a pipe attached to a small gasoline tank outside the window. After letting the oil flow a few moments, he lit an old piece of newspaper and tossed it inside the stove through an opening protected by a sliding iron cover. There was a tremendous swish, and he slid the lid back to look inside. Flames bolted through the door, and he was barely able to close the lid without being singed.

"Sonovabitches!" he screamed. The flames beating against the sides of the burner sounded like bullwhips thrashing against cast iron. "Out of here!" Tittle hollered. "This burner's gonna blow."

He began to sprint like a raging bull down the hallway and out of the building. I was right behind him, following him into the dispensary, where he called the fire department.

Within minutes, red-helmeted Orientals with maniacal expressions on their faces stormed into the BOQ. Tittle pointed the way. Before we could stop them, the firemen smashed in my unlocked door with an axe and charged into the room. The stove was already cherry red. Not waiting for the explosion, Tittle and I ran back out of the building and jumped into an ambulance. Tittle threw the vehicle into gear and gunned the motor.

"No sense missing dinner," he said, and we zoomed away.

As we drove down a gutted, dirt road, Tittle explained that the idiot Korean houseboy must have allowed the oil to pool up inside the burner. Suddenly, he slammed on the brakes. "We've got to go back," he said. "Those bastards will steal the Scotch!"

"Unless the building has burnt down already," I said.

The idea that the Scotch was going down with the BOQ seemed to hearten his spirits, and he continued on to the Officer's Club.

The Club, furnished with rattan furniture, tatami mats and Japanese scrolls, was as fashionable inside as the outside veneer suggested. Tittle hurried me to the bar, where I met the Korean bartender, nicknamed Charley Chou by Tittle. Charley was famous for his martinis, and we ordered two.

They mixed surprisingly well with the Scotch, so we ordered two more before sitting down to the Club Dinner Special, a sixteen-ounce T-bone. The Portuguese red wine went better with the steaks than with the deserts, warmed apple pie and chocolate ice cream.

Over coffee, a soggy lump began to work its way straight up from my stomach, treading its way through my esophagus and into my throat. For a moment or two, I felt as if I might choke to death; however, the sensation quickly passed and other than a mild headache, I was no worse the wear. On the other hand, quite remarkably, no amount of food or drink seemed to dampen Tittle's ebullient spirits.

After dinner, we retired to the lounge, a small, comfortable room with posh leather chairs, and semi-classical music purring through hidden speakers. We smoked cigars and sipped Napoleon brandy, letting all the good food and liquor soak its way deep into our systems.

"Do we do this every night?" I asked Tittle, as I sank even deeper into the chair.

"Sometimes there's a decent movie on." Tittle yawned. "Once in a while, ping-pong for the circulation."

My eyelids were shutting down like iron weights when I heard my name paged over a loudspeaker.

"Ignore the bastards," said Tittle, already half-asleep.

Charley Chou entered the room. "Telephone, Lieutenant Marcus."

I glanced at Tittle, who appeared to be concentrating on the glass of brandy in his hand, when a big ash from his cigar fell onto his chest, finding a hollow in the natural concavity formed by his bloated belly. I followed Charley to the telephone. It was Gallagher.

"Airman Harvey's back," he said. "The Novocain wore off, and he says he's got another toothache. He insists that you pulled the wrong tooth and is threatening to write his Congressman and sue the Air Force." Gallagher's voice was a bit on the shaky side, and I wondered if he'd been drinking. I told him to wait with Harvey at the clinic; I'd be right over.

Charley called a taxi and I went to inform Tittle I was leaving. Sounds emanating from the Colonel approximated miniature blasts from a tugboat. His chest heaved great sighs of contentment. As I was brushing away the cigar ashes that threatened to burn a hole through his shirt, he opened his eyes. "The bastards never let you live," he mumbled before lapsing back into sleep.

The motion of the taxi rolling over the bumpy, dirt road immediately caused me to heave up good portions of the Club dinner special that made a rather unfortunate mess in the back seat of the vehicle. In spite of my rank, the Korean driver exploded in a series of expletives that, while untranslatable, clearly indicated his dismay. I wish I could have made a proper apology to him, but at this point in my language studies, all I knew how to say in Korean was *hello, goodbye,* and *thank you very much.*

By the time I arrived at the clinic, I was shaking but the sharp pain in my gut had pretty much subsided. Gallagher was waiting for me at the entrance. He was in a state of extreme agitation. Sergeant Gallagher did not like having his carefully structured world messed around with.

Airman Harold Harvey was already draped in the dental chair, holding the left side of his face in the palm of his hand as if it were about to detach itself from the rest of his body. When he saw me, he braced himself.

"Nothing to worry about," I said in my most re-assuring, professional voice. "We'll have you feeling better in a jiffy."

"I told you it was the other one," he moaned.

There was an unpredictable expression on Harvey's face, and I looked around for Gallagher, who was standing in the doorway, his posture disappointingly indecisive. With mirror and explorer, I checked over Harvey's mouth.

A stream of cold water on the patient's upper left molar elicited an infantile scream, and I decided without further ado to extract the tooth.

An injection of Novocain had an immediate calming effect on Airman Harvey and I forced a laugh and said, "Looks as if they were both infected."

"You should have listened to me," Harvey said. "I told you that you pulled the wrong tooth."

His insubordinate tone aroused a conditioned response from Gallagher, who moved in closer and said to Harvey, "Where's your DDS, mister?" It was a relief having Gallagher's *law and order* bravado back in action.

"Don't worry," I said to the patient. "We'll take out the molar, and you'll be fine. You're lucky to have both of them taken out the same day. It saves a lot of suffering."

Harvey closed his eyes as I approached him with my forceps in hand. As I began applying pressure on the tooth, the forceps slipped and there was a horrendous cracking sound. Harvey bounced up on the chair as if a spring had broken in his back.

"This one's a little tricky," I said.

Gallagher ordered Harvey to stop jumping around like a goddamn fool and let the Doc do his job. I positioned myself like a flat-footed boxer preparing to deliver the haymaker, and grabbed hold of the tooth again. This time when the forceps slipped, Harvey passed out cold.

Gallagher's response was a thing of beauty. Within seconds he grabbed several vials of Spirits of Ammonia out of a drawer, crushed one, and waved it in front of the patient's nose. Almost immediately, Harvey's head jerked forward, his eyes opened wide. Ashen and sweating, Harvey leaned back against the headrest and began crossing his chest like a soldier in a foxhole waiting for an incoming to blow him to smithereens.

Gallagher handed me a different forceps, an oversized cowhorn, and I gave it another try. "Nothing to it," I said to myself, as much as to the patient. Encouraged by the good purchase from the new forceps, I braced myself and wrestled with the tooth, a stubborn, three-rooted bastard entrenched in a casing of solid, cancellous bone. Nothing moved but Harvey's head, which began to rotate as if hinged on a rubber casing.

"Tough baby," I said. Finally, I began to feel weak and called time out.

Harvey said he was going to be sick again, but Gallagher told him not to be such a big sissy. "Nothing to it," I repeated.

I breathed deeply and once again grabbed hold of the tooth. Gallagher gave my back a little pat of encouragement, and I went to work, determined to pull the bastard out of Harvey's mouth. Finally, mercifully, the tooth began to yield. I could feel it beginning to slip out of the socket, and with all my remaining strength, I applied a strong, downward force, which precluded the sudden violent movement of the forceps as the tooth cracked in half. Unfortunately, a lower pre-molar cusp was slightly chipped by the handle of the forceps, but Harvey didn't realize this, having already passed out again.

While Gallagher was busy reviving the stricken airman, I meticulously checked the extracted portion of the tooth. After regaining consciousness, Harvey seemed more relaxed. "Thank God, it's over," he said.

"Not quite," I said, before going off to the bathroom, where, kneeling in front of the toilet, I vomited the rest of the T-bone and portions of the warmed apple pie, a la mode. Sitting up, I thought my stomach had been stripped of its epithelial lining, that it had been reduced to little more than raw protoplasm. Nevertheless, duty called, and after rinsing out my mouth, I returned to my patient.

"There are a couple of small root tips that need to be dealt with," I explained to Airman Harvey as calmly and professionally as I could. "No big deal. We'll have them out in no time flat." Admittedly, a bit of bravado, given that in my two clinical years at dental school, I had never once removed a broken root tip from a bloody socket.

"I thought the tooth was out!" Harvey cried.

Good old Gallagher came to my rescue. "Cut out your whining and open your mouth," he ordered Harvey. "We're all tired and want to get out of here."

I cleansed the socket with gauze before poking around with the root elevators. The roots were tricky little mothers, and I succeeded only in generating a futile scraping sound. My stomach was still killing me. When my knees began to buckle, I tossed the elevators onto the bracket table and announced to Airman Harold Harvey, and to the world, that we were finished.

Harvey's eyes lit up ecstatically. "Done?"

"What difference do a few small root tips make?" I said. Detecting an unfortunate expression of disbelief on the patient's face, I was quick to add, "In a couple of years, they'll naturally exfoliate."

"Exfoliate? What does that mean?" cried Harvey.

"The tips will slowly work their way out of the sockets. Then it'll be like removing splinters."

Harvey began to cry. "They'll get infected! I'll get cancer!"

"Calm him down," I said to Gallagher. "I'm going to bed before my stomach completely dissolves."

Gallagher drew me into a corner and whispered. "Maybe we ought to ship him off tomorrow to the clinic at Ascom, sir."

"Good thinking," I said.

As I was leaving the building, I could hear Harvey screaming "*Cancer!*" I was breathing the night air before I heard Gallagher's retort, but I felt safe remembering that Harvey's one insignificant stripe was no match for Gallagher's five big ones. I continued on into the BOQ where I completed the evening's regurgitations on the bathroom floor.

Staggering to my room, I discovered my B-bag floating on half of the door that the firemen had smashed. I waded through a large puddle of water that had accumulated in the course of watering down the overheated kerosene stove, and collapsed on a dry portion of the bed.

I don't know how long I had been sleeping before being awakened by a loud thumping noise. I opened my eyes to discover Colonel Tittle banging both fists against the wall with the passion of a bongo drummer. His eyes were glazed, and what was left of his gnashed and shredded cigar was stuck between his teeth as if it were a decaying root of a tropical plant growing out of his mouth.

"Where the hell you been?" asked Tittle.

I sat up and threw my feet over the edge of the bed. "What time is it?" I inquired innocently.

"Looky-here—the Scotch!" Tittle laughed like a madman as he sloshed his way toward the bureau. "The bastards didn't take it after all." He held up the bottle as if he were exhibiting a trophy he had just won at a tennis tournament.

"Go to bed, Colonel," I begged him.

Tittle guzzled the Scotch straight from the bottle until he realized he was ankle deep in water, and then retreated to a drier part of the floor closer to the wall. "Hey, whatta ya say we shave off that stupid mustache," he cried gleefully.

I touched the undernourished wisps with the back of my hand. His suggestion seemed inordinately unfair, but under the circumstances, I was more than willing to compromise. "How about tomorrow morning?" I asked.

"Now!" he shouted, and rushed from the room. I jumped to my feet, and ran after him into the hallway where I saw him disappear into his room, only moments later to come tearing out waving a double-edged razor in his hand.

I dashed back into the room, crawled over my bed and ducked behind the stove. Tittle came roaring into my room and went straight for me. We dodged about until he cornered me. Then in desperation I kicked him in the shin—whacko! Field goal—three points! He shimmied back and forth precariously, and then I kicked him in the other shin. This time he tottered and hit the floor like a fallen oak. I hovered over him, not certain exactly what I'd do if he made the wrong move. I bent down and pulled the razor out of his hand. He looked up at me, fat tears in his eyes. "All I wanted to do was shave off that chicken-shit mustache," he moaned.

Water-logged, he weighed a ton, and I thought I'd rupture a disc dragging him back to his room. I didn't have the strength to get him back onto his bed, but he was so out of it he didn't seem to mind curling up on the cold wooden floor. I laid a pillow under his head and covered him with a blanket. After hiding the razor in the bottom of a bureau drawer, I returned to my room. Within moments, miraculously, I once again fell asleep.

It seemed as if I had barely closed my eyes when Tittle was calling me through the broken door. "Five past seven, Marcus." There was a sober ring of authority in his tone. "Out of bed. Let's get going."

I stumbled to my feet and greeted him with a desperate grin. He stood before me, in full uniform, a freshly scrubbed tin soldier ready for combat.

"My God," he said. "Look at this room. It looks like a cyclone hit it. We'll have to move you out until they clean this place up. And you, doctor, are a mess. Office hours at 0800. But first, breakfast, and we have to check you in. Get snapping, Lieutenant."

My senses were slowly coming to grips with this amazing reality. "Can't we sleep another five minutes?" I begged him. He looked at me as if I were deranged, then turned around and marched away.

Later, while we were walking toward the ambulance, I noted he was limping badly. "Strange thing," he said as if he were reading my mind, "both my shins are bruised. I must have taken a fall." He appeared genuinely perplexed.

I took a deep breath. The air in Korea on this crisp autumn morning was as fresh and calm as anywhere else I had ever been on this earth. In the clear morning light, even the barren mountains looked alive. I smiled, and took another deep breath before catching up to Colonel Tittle, who, in spite of his gimpy walk, was one big step ahead of me.

AVAILABLE THROUGH IRONBOUND PRESS

DEVIL'S DANCE
A Novel
By Richard R. Karlen

"If I chance to talk a little wild, forgive me: I had it from my father."

William Shakespeare, *"Henry VIII"*

Harry Stone's life is falling apart. At age forty-four, an English professor, he begins to dress in black and ride motorcycles in the night. After impregnating one of his students, he is forced to resign from the University. Unable to tolerate his strange, sometimes cruel behavior, his wife, Sandy, throws him out of the house. His younger brother Roger, an internist, is puzzled by his actions until he discovers that Harry is suffering from Huntington's Disease, a rare genetic condition which he, himself, is at risk to develop.

Narrated by Roger, Devil's Dance is ultimately the story of brothers locked in a love-hate relationship under the shadow of this deadly illness.

DEVIL'S DANCE may be ordered at all bookstores, or through the internet at www.ironboundpress.net.

DEVIL'S DANCE: ISBN 0-96608831-0-5

AVAILABLE THROUGH IRONBOUND PRESS

LOOKING FOR BERNIE
A Novel
By Richard R. Karlen

"I intend to die in a tavern; let the wine be placed by my dying mouth, so that when the choirs of angels come, they may say, 'God be merciful to this drinker!'"
Walter Mapes, C 1140-1210 *"De Nugis Curialium"*

Bernie Hirsch, a fifty-two year old dentist from Newark, New Jersey, has left his office to go on an alcoholic bender in New York. There, he encounters Dwayne Lincoln, a young African-American from Chicago, and this odd pair travels the streets of lower Manhattan for five days in an odyssey filled with misadventure and mayhem. As Bernie's wife Paula, and his twin children, Danny and Diane, anxiously search the city for him, the novel explores the impact that Bernie's drinking and compulsive gambling have had upon his family.

Set in the year 1956, two years after the Supreme Court decision holding segregation in public schools as unconstitutional, LOOKING FOR BERNIE is also an examination of race relationships in an era in which American society was finally beginning to come to grips with its moral deficiencies.

LOOKING FOR BERNIE may be ordered at all bookstores or through the internet at www.ironboundpress.net

LOOKING FOR BERNIE: ISBN 0-9660831-1-

AVAILABLE THROUGH IRONBOUND PRESS

ANSWER MAN
A Novel
By Richard R. Karlen

"They say, best men are moulded out of faults;
And, for the most, become much more the better
For being a little bad."

Shakespeare, *"Measure for Measure"*

George Grossman has worked for twenty years as an assistant manager of Men's Clothing at a downtown department store in Newark, NJ. He is a quiet, modest man with no special ambitions, other than to provide a decent life for his wife and two sons. The head manager dies of a heart attack, and Grossman's life is turned around dramatically. This quiet man becomes enraged by events that seem to conspire against him, and, ultimately, he fights back against those who would suppress his spirit and self-esteem.

The title of the book is derived from Grossman's obsessive need to acquire knowledge through the reading of almanacs and encyclopedias, a dubious virtue given his benign nature when dealing with a sometimes cruel, unsentimental world.

ANSWER MAN may be ordered at all bookstores, or through the internet at www.ironboundpress.net

ANSWER MAN: ISBN 0-96608831-2-1

AVAILABLE THROUGH IRONBOUND PRESS

MURDER AT THE SEXI
A Novel
By Richard R. Karlen

*"If thou remember'st not the slightest folly
That ever love did make thee run into,
Thou hast not loved."*

Shakespeare, *"As You Like It"*

Six months after the death of his wife, Jonathan Cole, a forty-two year old internist from Scotch Plains, New Jersey, takes a vacation to Spain's Costa del Sol. After landing in Malaga, Cole picks up a hitchhiker, a young Dutch sculptor, and together they travel up the coastal road to the town of Almuñecar. Cole soon finds himself involved in murder, drugs, and romance. It is September, 1973, a time when Spain was still a fascist state under the rule of Francisco Franco and Spanish justice could be arbitrary and cruel.

MURDER AT THE SEXI is a psychological thriller in which a middle-aged, depressed doctor encounters a series of extraordinary circumstances and, in the course of dealing with them, redefines himself as a man.

MURDER AT THE SEXI may be ordered at all bookstores, or through the internet at www.ironboundpress.net

MURDER AT THE SEXI: ISBM 0-9660831-4-8

**TO BE PUBLISHED BY IRONBOUND PRESS IN
THE SPRING OF 2004**

WOLFE'S CHOICE
A Novel
By Richard R. Karlen

*"The paradoxical and tragic situation of man is that his
conscience is weakest when he needs it most."*
Euripides, *"Hippolytus"*

Max Wolfe, a forty-year old internist, runs down and kills a
young schoolteacher. In the course of the next ten years,
Wolfe must deal not only with the consequences of
covering up his crime, but with his conscience as well.

WOLFE'S CHOICE is the story of a successful physician,
whose life and the life of his family has been turned upside-
down because of a single, disastrous moment. He must
make choices and ultimately he chooses the one where
there can be no equivocation or looking back as to what
might have been.

WOLFE'S CHOICE: ISBN 0-966083180

ABOUT THE AUTHOR

Richard R. Karlen, author of SATURDAY LUNCH and other stories, grew up in Newark, NJ, where he practiced dentistry for thirty-five years. He currently lives in Scotch Plains, NJ with his wife, daughter, son and twin grandchildren.

Dr. Karlen's sixth work of fiction, the novel, WOLFE'S CHOICE will be published by Ironbound Press in the Spring of 2004.